PRAISES FOR Carless A. Grays'
FOGGY WINDOWS

This is one of those books you'd better have time for once you've started because you won't want to put it down until you've read the last sentence. You'll laugh, cry, and feel triumphant. A tale of Chelsey's life, torments, conquests, and a celebration of the tenacity and depth of the human spirit. This book soars!

---C. Thomas, Kississmee, FL

Foggy Windows is an engaging novel recommended to readers who enjoy stories of redemption and overcoming [life's obstacles]…I love your writing voice and felt your story.

---A. Menchan, APOOO Book Club

Foggy Windows…evokes emotion and is filled with everything a great work of fiction requires…Oprah needs to read it and place it in her book club list… I think telling a good story with the right timing and content can tell me the lessons I need or want to learn much easier. Your lessons and messages were loud and clear and anyone reading **Foggy Windows** should get them. I sincerely hope you have more novels in you because I'm definitely a fan.

---M. Richard, Long Beach, CA

My congrats to you for a job well done. I can tell that you are a scholar in your writing. You have an extensive vocabulary and sassy style. I like that. Keep up the good work and I look forward to your next novel!

---M. Napoleon, Duncanville, TX

This is by far the best book I've read this year. I cried some, laughed some, got really mad, and was held in suspense; could not put this one down. I loved everything about this book. I'm sure **Foggy Windows** touched a lot of hearts.

---M. Bryant, Houston, TX

I started reading [Foggy Windows] sometime after 10 p.m. It captivated me so, that sometime after 2:30 a.m., I forced myself to put it down to get a few hours of sleep. As I read, I experienced a range of emotions…joy and pride knowing that [my cousin] had written such a delightful piece of work, laughter, sadness, anticipation at the ups and downs of the characters…I realize its fiction; that reaction is just a result of your extraordinary work…I hope your windows are foggy less---now and forever.

---V. Grays, Atlanta, GA

LOVED IT! There were really some laugh-out-loud moments for me…I felt like I knew all the characters personally…very funny and very good.

---T. Gant, Hollywood, FL

I had a chance to read your book while on vacation. Please keep in mind that I am not a reader, however, I could not put the book down…You are a fantastic writer. Foggy Windows brought back a lot of memories for me---some good and some bad…I can't wait to read your next book.

---D. Dunham, Houston, TX

I loved it! If [your next book] is half as good as Foggy Windows, it will be an instant success!

---D. Potts, Houston, TX

Finished!!! For a minute, I thought you were telling my story!!! I really enjoyed reading it…I'm looking forward to the next one!

---K. LeBeaux, Houston, TX

Foggy Windows

a novel by

Carless A. Grays

Bloomington, IN

authorHOUSE®

Milton Keynes, UK

This novel is a work of fiction. Any references to real people, events, establishments, organizations, or locales are intended only to invoke a sense of reality and authenticity. Other names, characters, places, and incidents portrayed herein are either the product of the author's imagination or are used fictitiously.

AuthorHouse™
1663 Liberty Drive, Suite 200
Bloomington, IN 47403
www.authorhouse.com
Phone: 1-800-839-8640

AuthorHouse™ UK Ltd.
500 Avebury Boulevard
Central Milton Keynes, MK9 2BE
www.authorhouse.co.uk
Phone: 08001974150

First published by AuthorHouse 1/4/2008

ISBN: 978-1-4259-7427-5 (e)
ISBN: 978-1-4259-7426-8 (sc)

Library of Congress Control Number: 2006910913

Printed in the United States of America
Bloomington, Indiana

This book is printed on acid-free paper.
Back cover author photograph by Carter-Gaines Images

For my mother, Myrtle Grays,
who made sure I always had someone to love…
and someone to love me back

ACKNOWLEDGEMENTS

This book could not have been written without the longstanding love, steadfast support, and unrelenting humor of my best friend, confidante, co-conspirator, advisor, and sister-in-the-spirit, Michele Dudley Williams. When I visualize the one person who knows *everything* about me...I see you. To my other best friend, Kesa Guest, how would I have survived without you in my life? I once told you that the title "best friend" really doesn't fit because the bond we share is so much deeper than that...that's still true. Pamela Davis-Noland, you are my creative rock and "thank you" doesn't feel adequate for all you've done...I'm so thankful you believed in my *coffee-colored dreams.* Susan Scarlett, you are infinitely amazing...I've never stopped thanking God for blessing me with you. Carrington Lei, I didn't know I could do this...*until I met the mountain.*

To my maternal and paternal siblings, aunts, uncles, cousins, nieces, nephews, and especially my mother and father, I love you all. Adria Carter, they don't come any better than you---stay on *fertile ground*, my sister. Sherry Wright-Gulley, I keep your caring spirit with me at all times...thank you for inspiring me to write again. Christie Grays, Twane Grays,

Ken Grays, John Dudley, Wayne Hughes, Freda Humber, Rodney Dove, Michael Davis, Sharon Cole-Braxton, Joan Green, Faith Nealon, Sharon Washington, George Russell, and Garrett Noland, you all know what you did…and my heart thanks you!

Sharon Harrington, Stephanie Moseley, Gwen Rodgers-Busby, Cheryl Thomas, Sherry Calhoun, Kendra Shelton, Debrah Fields, and Sara Jackson Watson, thank you for years of laughing with me in the sunshine and crying with me in the rain. Micheal Helm, thank you for being such a wonderful part of my world. Ken Taylor, thanks for your enduring friendship and unwavering support---but thanks most of all for sharing your adorable mom with me. Karen LeBeaux, thank you for buying the very first copy of my very first book, sight unseen.

Sharonda Allah, Jeanne Ellenstein, Lauren Scarlett, Mike Robinson, Stacy McIntosh, Susan Chapron, Robert Sanders, Maite Xydis, Ebony Jones, Shirlene McNeil, Priscilla Brown, Donna White, Dazi Lenoir, Virginia Gilbert, Patrick Bourgeois, Mike Johnson, Joyce Adejumo and Mitchie's Gallery in Austin, *all* of the book clubs who have chosen **Foggy Windows**, The Church Without Walls Ushers' Ministry, the Houston Area Urban League Guild, *everyone* at the Houston SSA offices, the Irving Black Arts Council, University of Texas alumni, and *countless* fans, old and new---whether in the remote past or the here-and-now, your support and words of encouragement will never be forgotten!

And above all, I thank my Heavenly Father who carries me when I am too weak to walk…and gives me the strength to soar. Father, I give You all the glory, honor and praise!

Foggy Windows

PROLOGUE

From the moment of my conception, men have found increasingly innovative ways to complicate my life. Now this one had to turn up dead. When I opened the door to the seventeen-hundred-dollar a night penthouse suite with the key he had given to me only forty-eight hours earlier, thick balmy blood had shamelessly oozed its way out of his corpse onto the beige Berber carpet. His eyes were wide open, seemingly oblivious to the three bullets lodged almost symmetrically in his chest. The scene was surreal to say the least. How many times in the last three years had I wished Michael dead? At least a hundred. Maybe two. But I was too afraid to contemplate my existence without him in it. Instinctively, I made the best decision I could at the time. I quietly closed the door behind me and left.

Trying not to look too guilty, I hurried down the long corridor to the elevator. With each step, my heart rate tripled and I became convinced that my own untimely death was only moments away. "Water! I need water!" I blurted out loud, as the elevator doors locked me inside. I wondered how in the name of God it could be that a dying woman wasn't permitted a single glass of water in her final minutes. My mind flashed through a thousand reasons why such a simple last request was being so cruelly denied. *Maybe I shouldn't have become involved with a married man. Maybe I should have forgiven my father for what he did to me. Maybe I should have mailed that stupid chain letter.*

The elevator seemed to stop on every floor as it made its way down to the lobby. A young mother and two impatient boys were waiting on the 22nd floor. A starched businessman, complete with laptop and briefcase, entered on the 18th. An elderly woman and the dutiful porter carrying her luggage shuffled on board on the 15th. Two giggling girls—whose parents apparently had enough money to put the family up in one of the most exclusive hotels in Los Angeles—squeezed in on the 9th. Just seconds before I thought I would lose my mind, the elevator doors opened, spilling all of us out into the bustling lobby. Straight ahead, I saw the revolving door leading to the outside, but its counter-clockwise spinning made my head spin in much the same way. All of a sudden, I became acutely aware that one tiny drink of water might very well save my life, or at the very least, my sanity. I quickly scanned the lobby for a water fountain, but spotted only a chair. It was a friendly looking chair and it seemed to be calling out to me. *Chelsey. Chelsey George. Come, sweetheart, I'll protect you.* The safety of the chair immediately became my next destination. My plan was pretty simple, actually. I'd sit down for a minute, close my eyes, unscramble my thoughts, and if luck was finally on my side, I'd wake up from the horrific nightmare in which I now found myself. Or I'd remember where I'd seen the water fountain. I wasn't asking for a lot. I only needed one little drink. Just enough to wet my lips, soothe my throat, and make me stop listening to words of comfort from furniture.

The limpness of my body fell into the chair like strawberry Jell-O not yet congealed. I was unconsciously thanking God for chairs when a telephone sitting on the small table next to me caught my attention. No sooner had I put the receiver to my ear than a faceless hotel operator said, *"Good afternoon. How may I help you?"* Startled by the unexpected voice, I slammed the receiver down as though it had become too hot to hold. The adrenaline began to mount again. *Shit!* I had to figure something out and I had to figure it out fast. Everybody knows dead bodies begin to stink after a while. Although common sense tried to assure me it was impossible, in my mind, the entire lobby was spinning like it was caught in the eye of a tornado. The spinning lasted for almost one full eternity. When it stopped, it was five years earlier— and I was almost dead.

CHAPTER 1

Now that I had actually done it, I wondered what death would be like. I didn't really want to die. Not really. I just wanted the pain to stop. Twenty-four years was long enough for any one person to inhale the exhilaration of hope and exhale the devastation of despair. I decided that life wasn't fair for those of us who were predominantly innocent. After all, if you took the time to analyze the big picture, you would see that the only crime I had ever really committed was that I had been conceived and had the audacity to be born without the benefit of something as overrated as holy matrimony. Was being born a bastard truly enough evidence to justify a life sentence without parole? Life was incredibly exhausting. *Even if death turns out to be worse,* I thought, *at least it'll be a change of scenery.*

I've never been much on patience. I was even born six weeks before I was supposed to be. Needless to say, I was one sick baby. In fact, I was so sick they told Mama I probably wouldn't make it. But just like she always had, I survived, too. Fortunately—or unfortunately, depending on how you look at it—my only lasting birth defect was that the delicate chambers of my heart were too small to comfortably accommodate the emptiness that kept forcing its way in. It was a familiar feeling, the emptiness was. Unaware that I had given it permission, it made itself right at home in important places like my heart and my stomach and my throat. I had grown just as accustomed to it as I had to the mole on the left side of my mouth that seemed to wink when I smiled.

My only real source of comfort over the years had been my journal. Little black girls in the Deep South didn't typically keep journals, but I had kept one since I was eight years old. My father had given it to me, though he didn't call it that at the time. I wrote in it whenever I felt extremely happy or extremely sad or extremely confused. The particular feeling really didn't matter too much. The only necessity for gaining entry into my journal was that it be extreme. Kind of like Antarctica in the dead of winter or water in a teapot on the verge of boiling over. That tiny, unpretentious journal was one of my most valued possessions and I cherished it long after the pages had been used up and the light illuminating my father's memory had dimmed.

My eyes began to well up as I remembered the powder blue book with the little white princess on the front cover. This time the emptiness had decided to wedge its way into the small, circular space behind my eye sockets where I kept all of my tears safely stored away. I hated when it went there because it felt like somebody was throwing darts in the corridors of my brain and my head always hurt for hours afterwards. It didn't really matter where the emptiness went this time, though, because soon, I wouldn't feel anything at all.

I leaned forward to retrieve the journal from the glass-top coffee table where I had placed it that morning. Today—the one I had carefully chosen to be my last—I wanted to be near the few memories I had left of my father. It was for that very reason that I had dug it out of the old dusty trunk my mother had given to me when I left for college and hoped against hope that somehow I might be comforted by it in my final hours. I had grown quite weary of feeling my father's absence and wanted nothing more than the feeling of his presence to consume me before death did. All in all, I didn't think I was asking too much.

My sweaty hands clung tightly to the gift as I remembered every detail of the day I received it. It used to be slick and shiny like the new patent leather shoes Katie and I always got for Easter, but the passage of time had turned it old, dull, and lifeless. Now, it seemed to be an appropriate metaphor for what I had turned out to be. When my father handed the wrapped package to me, I instinctively responded with a polite 'thank you'. Mama always said that it was proper and decent to thank people when they gave you things. *People don't have to be nice,* she would say. *You ought to let them know you 'preciate their kindness.* Every single phrase my mother ever uttered became permanently embedded in my brain. I didn't know which ones to keep and which ones to throw out, so I kept them all, stacking them up like old magazines.

My father watched as my nimble fingers meticulously unwrapped the package, trying not to tear little drummer boy paper in the middle of July. When I saw it was a book, my eyes sparkled like stars on a perfectly beautiful night. *I loved to read! How did he know that?* My eight-year-old mind quickly decided that it was because fathers just know those things about daughters. Instantly, I thanked him again with a hug, a kiss, and eyes as bright as the August sun at high noon.

With the exuberance of a child on Christmas morning, I opened the book, only to find that there were no words on the pages, just faint blue lines. In the midst of my confusion, I saw the scribbled handwriting on the inside of the front cover and became momentarily distracted. "To my litle princes," I read out loud then, gave my father a third 'thank you' in as many minutes. Neither of us noticed the spelling errors because the outdoor air had suddenly filled with the unmistakable odor of fresh, clean happiness.

But as happy as I was to receive the gift, I still had no idea what I was supposed to do with a book full of empty pages. I only knew how to read books with words in them. *Maybe I'm supposed to glue pictures on the pages,* I thought to myself, trying to unravel the mystery. *But I have to save my glue for school,* I remembered. *I can't just waste it on something like this. Mama wouldn't like that one bit.* Finally, I decided to ask the one person who would know. Looking straight into eyes that reminded me of my own, I asked, "What am I supposed to do with this?" (I was forbidden to call my father 'Daddy', and calling him 'Lester' never felt right, even though that was his name. So, I never called him anything at all.) "I can't read it because there're no words except the ones you wrote in it," I said, turning page after page, still finding each of them blank.

My father laughed heartily. "You ain't s'posed tuh read it, Chelsey," he said, in his down south, third grade dialect. "This here is what they calls a die'ree. It's a book fuh writin' in."

"What am I supposed to write?"

"Whatevah you feel like writin'," he said, with the wisdom of the world's greatest intellectual. Even though he knew I was uncertain about what to do with it, he knew that writing in my new journal would soon become one of my favorite pastimes, and his toothy smile grew as wide as the Mississippi after a rainstorm. "You can write down what you did yestiddy or what you gon' do tumorruh. Mostly, it's fuh writin' down yuh thoughts an' yuh feelins an' all."

"What kind of feelings?"

"All kinds, chile! If'en you feel happy, write that in there. If'en you feel blue, write that in there, too. It's jes' uh good way tuh keep track uh yuh life an' yuh feelins. It ain't hard a'tall."

His smile never faded as he looked down at me, all the while admiring just how much I looked exactly like him. Like he just spit me out, as the old folks would say. My spunkiness came from my mother, but just about everything else about me came from him. My nose. My forehead. My mole. All had his name on them. In fact, I had heard Ms. Irma say more than once that I looked more like him than *him*. He was definitely proud and he wished he knew just how to tell me so. But he never talked to me much. For some reason, it was just too hard for him. It could have been because he never knew what Mama might have told me about him. All he knew was, chances were, it wasn't good. Instead, he said, "You always been a smart young'un, Chelsey, so I jes' knows you gon' write some good stuff in it. You always been good wid words, you know. I guess you got that there from the good Lawd 'cause me an' yuh mama ain't nevah been too good at puttin' words togethah."

I wanted to believe that my father wished he could be there to watch me grow into a young woman and actually witness me discover my essence through my writing. But he had already convinced himself that God Almighty had mapped out another course for him. Mixing preaching with illegitimacy would complicate the situation too much and southern folk didn't take kindly to things like that. He told himself that he had to think about what was best for the town. That would be what God wanted and that's what he had to do. Someday, he told himself, he would explain it all to me and even if Mama still didn't understand, he was certain I would. Something in his mind told him that his little girl would be just fine without him. He ignored the eerie feeling in his gut telling him something else.

No matter how hard I try—and I've tried *hard*—I can't forget the day I received that damned journal. How can I? It was the day my father made the conscious decision to permanently alter the course of my history. I can tell you right now that if anyone at all had bothered to tell me that I would never see him again, I wouldn't have wasted the afternoon going first to the corner store for lemon drops I didn't need, then to Winslow Park to play on rusted old swings that would still be there when he wasn't.

If I had known then, what I know now, my line of questioning that day would have been entirely different. It wouldn't have focused on stupid stuff like writing down thoughts and feelings. Thoughts and feelings that hurt more often than not. On our last day together, I would have asked my father questions that would make a difference in a little girl's life. You know, questions like, why do fathers leave and why do little girls need them to stay, anyway? And, why does loving someone with all your might not automatically make them love you back with all of theirs? And, how *do* you love yourself when not one single person ever told you that was a good thing to do? And I would most definitely have asked how a little girl can make her father want her, cherish her, and love her, all the while not appearing too needy?

As I think about it now, I would also have asked questions that my eight-year-old mind had often thought about but that my eight-year-old logic couldn't even begin to figure out. I'd go right up to him, look him dead in the eyes and dare him to look away, and I'd say, "Daddy,"—yeah, that day, that's what I would have called him—"Daddy, why does happiness last for only brief moments in time while pain lingers on like a bad toothache? And, exactly how *do* you make the hurt stop hurting?" But, the one question I'd definitely ask would be, "Daddy, how do you forgive and, *my God,* what in the world can a little girl do simply to forget?" If only I had it to do all over again, that's exactly how I would spend the last afternoon with my father. But my austere reality was that I couldn't do it all over again and I had long since missed the one opportunity I had to do it right. *If.* It seemed to be the only word in the English language that began and ended with regret.

Blinking back tears, I opened the journal to the first page. *July 15, 1971,* the entry read. *My daddy gave this writing book to me today. He said I should write my feelings* in it. *I'm not sure why, but I feel really, really scared. Like I'm lost deep in a forest and nobody is looking for me. I scream and scream, but only God and maybe the trees can hear me.* I turned a few more pages. *August 12, 1971. I overheard Mama on the phone with Ms. Irma today. She was crying, but tried to pretend she wasn't. I think Mama loves my daddy. Even though I've never heard her say it, I can see it in her eyes and today, I heard it in her tears. But he doesn't love her back. For some reason, she's not good enough to love, either. I guess that's why we have to stick together, Mama and me.* I flipped to the last entry on the last page of the tattered journal. Through painful tears that became so profuse I could hardly see the words on the page, I silently read the entry: *January 5, 1973. Every day, I ask God to bring my daddy back. But something in the pit of my stomach tells me he's not coming back. It hurts a lot, my stomach does. Like somebody is pushing a sharp knife in through my belly button, up through my chest, and clear through the back side of my heart. I don't know what I did to make my daddy want to leave. I don't know what I can do to make him want to come back, either. If I had one wish, just one, I would wish for a way to make him love me. Even if it's just a little bit. All I really need is a little bit, anyway. I hope I get to see him again, but I know I won't because last night, that's what Mama told Ms. Irma. And Mama's right about most everything. Like that time when she said the tooth fairy would leave me a nickel if I put my tooth under my pillow before I went to sleep. Sure enough, the next morning, I looked under my pillow, and there it was, a shiny new nickel. Like I said, Mama's right about most everything and she's probably right about my daddy, too. After all, what reason would he have to come back? I'm only his daughter. That's all I've ever been, my father's daughter…only nobody knows it. Goodbye, Daddy.* Elementary handwriting had signed the entry, *Your loving daughter, Chelsey Christina Payne.*

"Damn!" I said, out loud. Life's circumstances can be so incredibly confusing for little black girls trying to cope with that pervasive *'less than'* feeling that seems to go along with their existence as naturally as bright, blue eyes go with little white girls. When you're eight, and happen to be black, you're convinced that your short, nappy, black ponytail needs to be a long, straight, blond ponytail like the one on the doll you got for your last birthday. You believe that your charcoal-colored skin needs to be at least three shades lighter so you can feel pretty in your red or yellow or even bright orange sundress, if that's what you feel like wearing that day. And you're positively certain that your nose needs to be narrower, your lips thinner, and your butt smaller, like the little girls you see on television and in magazines and on the front of cereal boxes. Being a dark eight comes with a lot of strings attached. Not knowing why your father doesn't love you only complicates an already messed up situation. When I was eight, I remember hoping that nine would be a lot less confusing.

I closed the journal and attempted to return it to the coffee table but somehow miscalculated the distance and it fell to the floor with a thud. I stared at it as though if I blinked, it would explode right there on my nice tan carpet. As I tried to concentrate on the difficult art of breathing, the memories came flooding back with a vengeance. The voices in my head grew louder, seemingly mocking the very day I had been born. I squeezed my eyes tight and covered my ears with both hands to drown out the noise but the voices were still there. *Chelsey, Chelsey, Chelsey…,* I heard a man's voice say as it trailed off to nothing. *Goodbye, sweet princess. Goodbye, goodbye, goodbye.* I let out a deafening scream. "No, Daddy, no! Please don't leave me! Please don't leave me, Daddy! Come back! Daddy, please, come back!" At that very moment, the doors of my memories slammed shut. Silence enveloped the room like death. I collapsed onto the floor in a defenseless mass of anguish, tears pouring from my eyes like running water from a faucet. The journal lay beside me in quiet contemplation…and the little white princess just stared.

* * *

Hour-long minutes passed before I was able to lift the heaviness of myself from the floor and return my body to the chair. Almost immediately, my eyes landed on the only other gift my father had ever given to me. Well, he hadn't *given* it to me. He had actually mailed it to me the year after he left, but it was mine just the same. I remember opening the box the very minute Mr. Nathaniel, the nice mailman with the Sammy Davis, Jr. smile, left it on the front porch. Inside the box was a dainty, gold-plated necklace with an oval locket dangling from it. Inside the locket was a small picture of my father. Now, the picture was so tiny and unfamiliar that had I not already known, I would never have been able to tell to whom the face in the picture actually belonged. I never did figure out why he mailed the locket rather than give it to me in person, especially since Mama had heard back in '72 that he had moved only thirty-some-odd miles down the road.

Sixteen years had passed and here I was trying to visualize what my father looked like now. I wondered if he thought about me as often as I thought about him. Or if he even thought about me at all. *Absence makes the heart grow fonder. Out of sight, out of mind.* In the middle of wondering which cliché suited my father best, I decided that today, it really didn't matter one way or the other.

I fastened the tarnished chain around my neck and settled my head on the back of the chair. Suddenly, it came to me that I was still incredibly alert for someone who had swallowed fourteen, two-hundred milligram sleeping pills nearly two hours earlier. When was eternal sleep going to overtake me? I began to worry that I hadn't taken enough, but remembering that I had taken all I had, I closed my eyes and decided I would simply have to wait and see if tomorrow came. The logic in my mind hoped it would, the pain in my heart hoped it wouldn't, and the weariness in my body, which felt much more comfortable in the reclining position I was now in, didn't know what to hope for.

CHAPTER 2

When the phone refused to stop ringing, I realized my question had been answered. Fourteen pills had not been enough to stop time forever. It had only been enough to make me really, really sleepy. I summoned up all of my strength to focus my vision on the digital clock next to the 19-inch television with my mother's picture on top. It was ten-thirty-four in the morning. I had slept for nearly fifteen hours. At least it was Saturday and I wasn't late for work.

"Hello," I said into the receiver when I finally figured out where the telephone was.

In a muffled voice that sounded strangely familiar, I heard, "Chelsey? Chelsey?" Several seconds passed before I identified the problem—I was speaking into the listening end of the telephone. Using two unsteady hands, I somehow managed to turn the receiver right side up.

"Hello?" I said again, this time into the mouthpiece.

"Baby? Is that you?" It was Mama. She always seemed to call just when I needed to hear her voice. It was as though she had a sixth sense when it came to me and my sister, Katie—sight, sound, smell, touch, taste, and *mama-knows*. I loved that about my trash-talking, take-charge mother. She had an answer for every problem you could possibly have and even if the solution made no sense at all, it made you laugh out loud just hearing it. If something surprised her or caught her off guard, she might say something like, *"Shit fire and save the matches!"* It made no real sense at all, but was funny as hell every time Mama said it. She had always been like that, too. Funny, like Richard Pryor in his hey-day, and take-no-shit like John Shaft in his. That was my mama.

"Yeah, Mama, it's me," I said, yawning. "What's up?"

"You don't sound like yourself. What's the matter, chile?"

"Nothing, Mama," I said, as I cleared my throat and my head to make room for more intelligible speech. "I'm, I'm just tired, that's all. Very, very tired." I made no attempt to suppress a series of yawns.

"Okay, baby," Mama said apprehensively, not quite sure she was ready to accept my explanation and move on to the real reason for her call.

Sensing her hesitation and not wanting to answer any more questions, I forced myself to sound perky. "Really, Mama, I'm fine. Is everything okay at home?"

Thankfully, she decided to drop it. She released a deep breath before saying, "No, baby, it ain't okay. It's your daddy."

Daddy? When did Lester become 'daddy'? Something must really be wrong. "What about him?"

"There was a accident out on ol' Dale Road las' night. This fool teenage boy racin' cars with one of his friends, los' control of his car an' hit your daddy's car head-on. Police say your daddy an' that boy both died right there

13

on that very spot. Only one lived was the one that fool was racin' with an' they say he jes' hangin' on by a wheel an' a prayer ovah at County Gen'ral."

"Lester's dead—" I said, not really sure if I was asking a question or simply making a statement. "When's the funeral?"

"Saturday."

"What time?"

"Two o'clock."

"Where?"

"St. John's Tabernacle." Mama paused. "You gon' come to the fun'ral?"

"I don't know, Mama. I've got this thesis to finish and work and—," I stopped mid-sentence. My excuses sounded lame, even to me. "I'll come if I can."

"You okay, baby?"

"Sure, Mama. I'm fine," I lied. I'll call you back when I know whether or not I'm coming. I'll talk to you later, okay?"

"Okay, baby." Mama didn't hang up. "Chelsey," she said, with all of her mother-love pouring out at once.

"Yes, Mama?"

"It's okay to cry, baby. He *was* your daddy, you know."

"Yeah, I know. Listen, Mama, I've gotta go now."

"Okay. Call me later, you hear?"

"Yes, ma'am, I will." I hung up the telephone, although it seemed to be a much more cumbersome task than it generally was. I stared into space for a length of time only God really knew. I was numb. When it came to Lester—*daddy*—I had spent years feeling confused, then hurt, then angry, then indifferent. Now that he was

14

gone, I didn't know what to feel. What do you feel when you never really knew your father and now you never would? What do you feel when your father dies suddenly, leaving you twice in one lifetime? What do you feel when you don't know what to feel?

I couldn't talk to my mother about it. The subject of Lester had always been taboo when he was alive. Even though death had upgraded him to 'daddy' status, I was sure it wouldn't be any different now that he was dead. I decided to call Nicki. We had shared each other's joys and sorrows since we were both still wet-behind-the-ears freshmen at the University of Oklahoma. She would know exactly what I should do.

Nicki answered after the third ring. The unofficial telephone code of ethics for single women clearly stated that it did not look right to answer a telephone on the first ring and answering on the second one made it appear much too obvious that you purposely didn't answer on the first. The third ring was always the safest bet. "Hello?"

"Nicki, it's me."

"Hey, Me! How's that thesis coming?"

"It's coming along fine. Do you have a few minutes?"

"Damn, Chelsey! You sound like your dog just died. But I happen to know you don't even have a dog. So, what's the matter? Those racist professors getting to you again?"

"Lester was killed in a car accident last night," I said, rather matter-of-factly. "The funeral is Saturday. Do you think I should go?"

"I'm so sorry, Chelsey," Nicki said, apologizing more times than she needed to. "Me and my stupid jokes. Is there anything I can do? Anything at all?"

"No, I'm fine, thanks. So, do you think I should go?"

"Do you want to go?"

"He was my father. I feel obligated to go."

"Then you should consider going. If you go, it won't hurt anything. But if you don't go, you might regret it later."

"Regret what, Nicki?" I asked, not realizing I was angry. "He never regretted abandoning his daughter! What regrets could I possibly have?"

"That you never said goodbye to him," Nicki said, gently.

"He never said hello to me."

"All the more reason to consider going."

* * *

"Mama, I'm coming to the funeral."

"Good, baby. When you gon' git here? Friday?"

"No, it'll be early Saturday morning before I can catch a flight out. I have to do some home visits Friday night."

"Lawd, have mercy, chile, that job gon' work you to death!"

"That's exactly why I'm getting my master's, Mama," I said. "So, I won't have to work in the field forever."

"Well, I for one sho' is gon' be glad when you git through. I know I done tol' you to git your education an' all, but I declare, you needs a rest, baby! Even the good Lawd took a break every now an' agin."

"I'll be glad when I can rest, too, Mama. I'll be glad, too…" My voice trailed off. I knew that the kind of respite I needed wouldn't be accomplished by merely finishing graduate school. "I better get going, Mama. I've got a lot of things to do before Saturday."

"Okay, baby." Mama paused for a second, then added, "I'm glad you decided to come. Your daddy would like that."

CHAPTER 3

St. John's Tabernacle was the largest black church in Wade County and it was packed to capacity by ten after one on the day of my father's funeral. People were seated in the balcony, the foyer, and extra folding chairs strategically placed next to each of eighty-four pews. Some of the teary-eyed mourners had to sit in the choir stand and one or two even tried to find a seat in the pulpit. The church was so full you would have thought Lester himself was going to get up and say a word or two. A lot of people knew, and apparently loved, the man of the hour. I loved him, too, but I was different. I didn't know him.

A full one-third of everyone in the church was related in some way to the deceased: nieces, nephews, aunts, uncles, first, second, and third cousins, in-laws, parents, sons, and one daughter. I was amidst Lester's extended family for the first time in twenty-four years. *Damn!* I thought to myself. *There sure are a lot of ugly people in this family!* I quickly put my hand over my mouth to hide the impropriety of my smile. The ugly relative seated next to me—who probably thought I was a niece, or perhaps, a second cousin—mistook the gesture for grief, offered a tissue, then patted my knee several times to let me know that everything was going to be alright. "Thank you," I said to the stranger, as I used the tissue to dab at tears that weren't even there.

I didn't have to ask Mama to come to the funeral with me. Somehow, it was just understood between us that she would be there. I assumed she came primarily as a source of support for me, but I'd be lying if I said I wasn't wondering if she was also there because she never stopped loving my father. Of course I was too afraid to ask that particular question. She hadn't made one disparaging comment about Lester since he died, true enough, but that affectionate streak could leave just as quickly as it had come if I asked too many of the wrong questions. I didn't always know what the wrong questions were, but I had a pretty good idea. Katie had no desire to come with us. She figured that two Georges at one funeral were enough representation. As Mama and I walked out the front door, she hollered that she might come by the fellowship hall later for a bite to eat. Everybody knew that some of the best food you ever tasted was after a funeral.

At ten after two, the choir rose to sing the first hymn. *If anybody asks yooouuu, where-ere I am go-iiing, where-ere I am go-iiing, sooonnn, I'm going up YON-der, I'm going up YON-der, I'm going up YON-der, to be with my Looorrrrd...* Someone at the back of the church shouted, "My Lawd! My Lawd!" then promptly fainted, as if on cue. *It's going to be one hell of a long day,* I thought. After the hymn, there was a poem read by a niece, a resolution from St. John's Tabernacle read by Sister Turner, the church clerk, kind words from various relatives and friends, a prayer by Rev. Richards, the associate pastor, another hymn, more fainting, more crying, more shouting, and finally the eulogy.

Everyone in town loved to hear Rev. Johnson preach a eulogy. *Remen' Johnson sho' can preach, cain't he, girl?,* the older women would say to one another. *He sho' can. He got the gift. Um-hum. Praise the Lawd.* Some say that a few people in the church didn't know Lester from Joe Blow. They just heard Rev. Johnson was going to preach a eulogy, so they put on their Sunday-best and got to St. John's Tabernacle early so they could get a good seat. It was common knowledge that unless somebody got married too late or died too soon, nothing too exciting ever happened in Wade County anymore.

Rev. Johnson was a tall, dark, educated man in his early fifties, though he didn't look a day over forty. He had an alluring, sophisticated flair about him and he spoke with the eloquence and precision of Dr. King. He wore the best suits tithes and offerings could buy, drove a showroom-quality Cadillac, and slept with only the prettiest women in his congregation. Everybody agreed that next to God's word, Rev. Johnson's word was the gospel. Even if God didn't say it, if Rev. Johnson said he did, then there must be a misprint in the Good Book.

"Good afternoon, my brothers and my sisters," Rev. Johnson began. I was already bored, so I opened the program to scan the obituary. My name wasn't listed among the survivors. I felt a sick sensation in my stomach. If anyone should have made the list, I should have. I had survived more than any of them could even imagine. Rev. Johnson continued. "We've come here today to bid farewell to our beloved brother, Rev. Lester Theodus Payne. Brother Payne was snatched from our midst before any of us wanted him to go, yes he was! But he's in a better place now, brothers and sisters!"

"Yes, Lord, yes, Lord," the congregation said, in agreement.

Rev. Johnson's voice became louder and more forceful, just like it did on Sunday mornings when he got to the good part in his sermon. "Yes, Brother Payne has gone on home to glory to be with our Father in heaven, can I get a witness?" It wasn't a question. It was a command.

"Yes, Lord, yes, Lord," chimed a church full of obedient witnesses.

"Rev. Payne was a good man, a kind man, a gentle man. He was a good and faithful servant to God Almighty, his church family, and his loving wife of twenty-three years, Sister Dorothy Lee."

"Yes, he was. Tell it, Remen', tell it!"

"He was a good preacher, a good husband, a good provider, a good father…"

Rev. Johnson's last words reverberated in my ears like cymbals. *A good father. A Good Father. A GOOD FATHER!* I saw myself step outside of my physical body. In my newly formed existence, I had been asked to perform the eulogy for the great Rev. Lester Payne. I rose from my seat and solemnly approached the pulpit. I cleared my throat to remove the fear, adjusted the microphone, and began delivery of my father's eulogy to a congregation only I could see:

Good afternoon, ladies and gentlemen. You have all come here today to bid farewell to Rev. Lester Theodus Payne. That, too, is why I am here. Many of you have never heard of me because I have been his best kept secret for twenty-four long years. My name is Chelsey Christina George and

Rev. Lester Theodus Payne was my father. Yes, the man for whom you have all gathered to pay homage has a bastard daughter. The congregation listening to my eulogy gasped in disbelief, but I didn't care. It was time they heard the truth. And I had nothing but time.

Your great Rev. Payne—my father—planted the seed of life, but refused to cultivate the soil to ensure that a healthy crop would grow. I did not ask to be here, my brothers and sisters. I came into this world amidst shame and dishonor. As my father's daughter, I have painfully worn that badge of humiliation for nearly a quarter of a century, just as some of you are wearing your precious hats and perfect ties, today.

I took a long pause, trying to remember exactly how to breathe. After several deliberate breaths, I continued. *My brothers and sisters, I stand before you to say that although I always wanted to be, I was never a daddy's girl.* My eyes began to well up with tears, but I forced myself to go on. *The price I have paid for my father's disregard has been devastating. Loneliness. Shame. Confusion. Anger. Self-hatred. More loneliness. I deserved none of it. I felt all of it.*

You see, ladies and gentlemen, I relied on my father to affirm me, to communicate my value to me, to tell me I was loved. That's what fathers are supposed to do. Little girls need that. In his absence, my father boldly communicated that I was of no value at all. His absence told me I was worthless. Over the years, I've cried oceans of tears for him. I've always wondered if he ever cried once for me.

Friends of my father, I am certain you will miss him. I, however, will not. One cannot miss what one has never had. I also know that most of you will forgive my father. You will tell yourselves that he simply made a mistake. Good church folk always find a way of accepting the unacceptable when it's one of their own. But regardless of what some of you might think, I was not a mistake. You see, my heavenly Father made me and if any of you ever bothered to open those Bibles you hold so sacred, you'd find out that he doesn't make mistakes.

In closing, I ask you, "How can you honor a man who would not honor his daughter?" To my father, Lester Payne, I ask quite simply, "How could you do this to me?" Warm, slow tears fell from my eyes, confirming the pain my words had already adequately expressed. *I have often wondered if I will ever truly find peace on this earth. I pray that the peace I have longed for will some day be mine.*

Having finished the eulogy, I returned to my seat. Voices from the other side sang *"Peace Be Still."* The dissociated congregation filed out one by one, until only my dead father and I were left in the sanctuary. I approached the opened casket and fell to my knees, crying out, *"Why didn't you love me, Daddy? Why?"*

At that moment, my father rose from his casket and cradled me in his arms. *"I do love you, my sweet angel. You're my little girl and I was never happier than the day you were born. I'm so very sorry for hurting you."* Suddenly, an unexpected peace enveloped me. For the first time ever, I felt almost whole.

I reentered my physical body just as Rev. Johnson said to the congregation in St. John's Tabernacle, "Let us pray." The congregation dutifully rose to their feet and grasped the hand of each person standing next to them. "Dear Lord," Rev. Johnson began to pray. "We come to you with bowed heads and humble hearts, Lord, asking that you comfort and heal the Payne family during their time of sorrow. They need you now more than ever, Lord God. Help them to understand that you have taken their loved one because his work down here was done. Help them to understand, Lord, that our brother, Lester Payne, can now put on a long white robe in glory and hear you say, "Well, done! Well done, my good and faithful servant!"

As if speaking directly to me, Rev. Johnson continued in a more reverential tone. "And Lord, if there is anyone here today who did not have an opportunity to make peace with our dearly departed brother before he left this place, touch them now, Lord. Touch them, that they may be released from the shackles that bind them, Lord. Free them from their hurt, anger, and pain, Lord God, right now and forever more. And all God's children said, 'Thank you, Lord'."

"Thank you, Lord," echoed the congregation.

"Amen," Rev. Johnson and the congregation said, in unison.

As the choir sang, *If I Had Wings, I'd Fly Away From Here,* six pallbearers dressed in somber black suits and white gloves took their places in front of the sanctuary. When the Bible-toting funeral director gave the appropriate head nod, two obedient pallbearers carefully removed the ornate floral arrangement donning the center of the casket. With military precision, two more raised the lid of the casket, exposing Lester's body for viewing. When an usher standing on the far left side of the sanctuary raised his white-gloved hands, each mourner under his direction stood to march to the front of the church, take one last look at the dead man, express thoughts of sympathy to the family, and exit the church to get in line for the motorcade processional to the cemetery.

The viewing ritual was always hard on family members who would then be obligated to accept warm embraces and words of comfort from every mourner who took his or her turn at viewing the body. *"He look jes' like hisself,"* someone would say to the family. *"Like he jes' sleepin',"* another would add. *"Call me if you need me, you hear, Sister Dorothy Lee?"* Occasionally, a professional mourner would appear more grieved than even the wife or children as she—the *professional* was always a she—viewed the body of the deceased. When that happened, one of the funeral director's observant staff members would gently take the woman by the shoulders, whisper something like, *"He's in a better place, now, Sister,"* and with feigned compassion, forcefully walk her weeping body down the aisle and out of the church. Without question, the final viewing was exhausting for the family, but closed casket funerals were considered impolite in the polite South. Even though wakes had become commonplace and the body typically lay in state day after day for at least a week prior to the funeral, few mourners seemed to have time to go by the funeral parlor to pay their last respects beforehand.

Soon enough, it was time for the people in my section of the church to view the body one last time. Following the lead of the pews behind us, we marched, single-file, to the front of the church to bid farewell to my father. My legs felt as though they were going to collapse beneath me. Hesitant steps alerted Mama that I was seriously contemplating turning around, foregoing the long, tedious journey to the front of the church. It was at that precise moment that she placed her hands on my weary shoulders and whispered, "You got to go roun', baby. You got to go see your daddy for one las' time." Mama's touch seemed to give me strength I didn't know I had and my legs began to move forward with renewed commitment. Before I knew it, I was face-to-face with my father for the first time in sixteen years. The only difference was that unlike when I was eight years old, I knew this would be the last time I would ever see him.

His body was clothed in a crisp, navy blue suit and a very white, very starched shirt. His attire came complete with a coordinating pocket handkerchief and beige boutonniere pinned to his lapel. As I studied my father's face, time seemed to turn back. Except for a few gray hairs and the ever-present mole that had grown larger over the years, he looked exactly the same. One fact suddenly became crystal clear to me—I was glad I had come. Now it would be impossible for me to forget my father. Indeed, it was his face I saw every time I looked in the mirror. Even Sister Dorothy Lee could see that I was, by the strictest of standards, my father's daughter. Not even death could alter that truth.

Without thinking, my right hand reached into the casket to caress my father's face. I leaned forward, thinking that if I looked hard enough, I might be able to notice something about him I had not noticed before, or maybe smell a familiar scent. As I looked at his expressionless face, liquid pain fell from my eyes like fresh, morning dew. "Goodbye, Daddy," I whispered under my breath. As I walked away with the protection of Mama's arms around me, I said what I thought was a silent prayer. "Dear God, please show me how to forgive my father."

Not realizing I had spoken out loud, I was startled when Mama said, "He will, baby, he will," then used one hand to wipe away the pain of her own tears.

As we drove back to the two-bedroom house my mother had managed to purchase when I was eleven, we were both lost in our own private thoughts. Finally, she broke the sereneness in the air. "They sho' did put him away nice, didn't they?"

"Yeah. They sure did," I responded with my mouth, while my thoughts were still somewhere else. Several more minutes passed when I heard somebody ask, "Did you love him, Mama?" It was my voice asking the question, but it didn't feel like it.

Mama had always felt uncomfortable discussing her feelings. Especially her feelings about Lester. The memory of her first true love hurt so much that, generally, she wouldn't even allow herself to think about it. Not for too long, anyway. Responding in the usual fashion, she ignored the question, hoping it would go away, but somehow knowing that today, it would stick around like labor pain.

"Please, Mama. I need to know," I pleaded, as though my very life depended on her answer. "Did you love my father?"

Mama decided to buy herself some time. "Why you need to know that, baby?"

"I don't know," I said, even though I did. At the time, it seemed like the wrong answer was the right one. "I just do, that's all."

Holding back tears and memories just like she had practiced for years, Mama stared straight ahead at the

road in front of her and said, "Yeah, baby. I loved him.
More'n he evah wanted."

"Me too, Mama. Me, too."

CHAPTER 4

I returned home painfully aware that I had voluntarily tried to take my own life only hours before my father's had been involuntarily taken from him. I couldn't help but wonder where my sanity had gone when I convinced myself that dying seemed like a good idea. I was selfish, plain and simple. Even if I didn't love myself, there was no question that I loved my mother, so there's really no other way to describe leaving the one person in the world who—no matter how bad things got—would never leave me. Mama didn't deserve the kind of grief a dead child brings. Her life had been tough enough already, though it hadn't started out that way at all.

By the time she hit puberty, most of Wade County had decided that if Hattie Mae George wasn't the most beautiful girl in the world, she was definitely the most beautiful girl in the Woodlawn Housing project. At the age of fourteen, my mother was already five feet, eight inches tall in stocking feet. Bushy eyebrows, unrelenting eyes, exotic cheekbones, a baby-soft complexion, and a perfect smile guaranteed her absolute dominion over every boy bold enough to look at her twice. Her flawless face was appropriately placed on a long, sleek neck that sat just above two mounds of brown flesh so perfectly sculpted that Michelangelo would have felt less than adequate. Her chiseled legs were longer than the last mile of a monotonous journey and her figure was, well—it just *was*. Boys were captivated by her. Girls envied her. Mama was annoyed by them both.

By the time she was twenty-one, my mother had earned a reputation for speaking her mind, regardless of what happened to be on it at the time. Whether she was cursing you out on Saturday night at the Stardust Café, or praying to the good Lord on Sunday morning at the Solid Rock Missionary Baptist Church—and she did both faithfully—her message was full of fire and conviction. *You black bastard, I'll knock the holy hell outta' you* and *Lord, thank you for the many blessings you done give me,* were equally convincing when coming out of Mama's mouth. Somehow, you just knew she meant every blessed swear.

Mama loved to cook, too. Since she was knee-high to a grasshopper, she had followed her mother around the kitchen, memorizing her every move. Not only did she know the secret ingredient to every one of her mother's recipes, she knew exactly how much of it to use. Like every respectable southern cook, my mother was insulted by the mere mention of measuring cups, spoons, or any other utensil that implied she wasn't an expert in her field. *Season to taste* was the only tool of measurement she needed—and it worked every time. On any given Sunday, our kitchen smelled of oven-baked pot roast with brown gravy and cooked vegetables, country-fried chicken, collard greens with dry salt pork and ham hocks for flavor, the sweetest yams in Wade County, macaroni and cheese made from scratch, hot water cornbread, sweetened iced tea with fresh-squeezed lemon, and no less than five unrelated and usually uninvited dinner guests.

Because Mama was the best cook within a hundred-mile radius, our house was never as empty as her heart had been since her mother died from too much fatback and the like when Mama was only twelve years old. Although he had five other daughters—all grown and out of the house before their mama passed—Grandpa Henry had no idea how to raise a pre-teen female who had already started her period. So he did what he thought was right and held a Gestapo-like reign over her. Some say that's why Mama was unmarried and pregnant with my sister before she was fifteen. Good thing cancer took Grandpa Henry before the next harvest because if he knew Mama was pregnant with me just after her seventeenth birthday, he would have killed her and her good-for-nothing boyfriend, Lester Payne, too.

My father was eight years older than my mother and as smooth as Billy Dee Williams in *Lady Sings the Blues.* He was tall, good-looking, and the color of night. Unabashedly vain, he was meticulous about his appearance, even when no one was looking. Casual, to him, meant only a tie was required and hell would freeze over before you would catch him in a pair of jeans and tennis shoes. Eventually persuaded by his irrefutable charm, Ms. Irma, my mother's slightly older, slightly wiser best friend, brought the fast little country girl and the town-playboy-turned-preacher together.

"So how long you an' Irma been friends, Hattie Mae?"

"We always been friends but we got real close when my mama died back in '58."

"You know I been wantin' tuh meet you fo' uh long time, but ol' Irma wouldn't let me git near you. She ack jes' like uh ol' motha' hen, that Irma."

"She don't mean no harm. She just bein' protective of me an' lil' Katie, that's all. Besides, she say you got a reputation an' that if I ain't real careful, I'm gon' end up like all them other women."

"End up how?" Lester asked, pretending not to know what everybody in town knew.

"Broken-hearted, bitter an' by myself."

"I ain't nevah 'tentionally broke nobody's heart. Is it my fault if'en women gits attached tuh me befoe' I gits attached tuh them?"

"I s'pose it ain't. But everybody know you done gone through most of the single women an' three or four married ones in Wade County, Lester." Both of them laughed, Lester more arrogantly than usual. Hopelessly attracted to him and wanting to know what specific accoutrements she would need to reel him in, Mama asked, "What's it gon' take to make you wanna be attached anyways, Lester?"

"Oh, it's gon' take a real special lady fuh 'dat, Hattie Mae. I been called tuh do the Lawd's work, you know. I needs a spirit-filled woman behin' me fuh that. A preacha's wife got tuh ack like a preacha's wife. I cain't be wid no hell-raiser."

"Humph, I guess you ain't heard," Mama said, with a coy grin all over her face.

"Heard what?"

"I'm one of the bigges' hell-raisers in this here town."

"Well, maybe Ah'm gon' be the one tuh tame the bigges' hell-raiser in this here town," Lester replied, with his own coy grin in place.

"And maybe you gon' be the one that *gets* tamed," Mama said, as she swished away in her thigh-high skirt, leaving Lester behind in a befuddled mass of intrigue. She was on top of the world. She had won the preliminary round with the town's most eligible bachelor.

CHAPTER 5

Mama had known Lester for four months when she missed her period. She waited until she missed the second one before she told him, partly because she kept hoping it would come and partly because she just didn't think her luck could be that bad. Hell, Katie was barely out of diapers. She couldn't possibly be pregnant again.

Almost six months later, just when the bluebonnets were beginning to bloom and the sweet smell of a fast-approaching summer was in the air, I made my obtrusive entrance into the world. Years later, Mama would tell me the story of how sickly I was as a newborn, how my baby skin was so rough and scaly that even Johnson's baby oil didn't help, how I had a 103-degree temperature for three days, how I almost died before I even had a chance to live.

Like Katie's father before him, Lester was black history the moment he learned fatherhood was imminent. He never changed my diaper when I was wet or warmed my bottle when I was hungry or comforted me with gentle rocking when I was fussy. He never held me in his arms or watched me fall asleep or told me he loved me. He died not even knowing that my bachelor's degree was in social work, my birthday in April, and my heart in pain. When I really want to hate him, I make myself remember that the number of days he saw me could be counted using a one-month planner. And you wouldn't even need the whole month. Isn't it crazy how the only person who can make you feel like something, is the exact same person who made you feel like nothing in the first place? That's how I feel sometimes. *Crazy.*

Most people might assume that Mama was the stereotypical unwed mother but they would be dead wrong. She may have been unwed, but there was nothing stereotypical about her. She generally held no less than three domestic jobs at a time in order to provide for me and Katie. And though she barely graduated from high school, she held several Ph.D.'s from the *University of Life*. Not surprisingly, Mama instinctively knew that if she didn't make a difference in her daughters' lives, our lives just might not be different. Her personal philosophy was simple: Put God first, love her children completely, demand that we get an education, beat our little asses when we needed it, and refuse to let anyone fuck with us.

An unsuspecting teacher who tried to break Mama's last rule got a rude awakening in the beginning of my third grade year at Sojourner Truth Elementary. Somehow, Mrs. Franks had missed the '*whatever-you-do-don't-mess-with-Hattie Mae-George's-children*' warning that every teacher in the Wade Independent School District received some time between signing their employment contract and their first day in front of a class.

The school year had just begun and as was typical for classrooms in Wade, Georgia in 1971, the 'smart' students (all white) and the 'slow' students (all black with an occasional Mexican) were separated into two groups within the same classroom. The separate groups of developing minds would receive disproportionate treatment from the *oh-no-I-treat-all-my-students-the-same* teachers. Even the designated 'slow' students knew that was a lie.

Now, while I was no genius, I was no where near slow. Consequently, Mrs. Franks had no choice but to place me in the 'smart' group of children. Nonetheless, to punish me for not being stupid like she felt I should have been, she assigned me to the last seat in the last row of the automatically presumed smart children. Physical degradation was Part A of her plan. Part B—psychological degradation—was more subtle. For the first four days, when Mrs. Franks counted out the homework assignments for each row, she didn't count out enough for the last student in the last row to receive a copy. For four days, Mrs. Franks had trouble counting to eight and handed out enough assignments for exactly seven white children. By the time the homework assignment was received by number six, there was only one copy left to pass back to lucky number seven. Number eight—me—was just shit out of luck, as Mama would say.

Of course, I hated to make scenes like my mother was infamous for making, so for the first three days, I told myself that it was an honest oversight and politely took the long walk to Mrs. Franks' desk at the front of the classroom. But when her trouble with simple mathematics occurred on the fourth day, Mama's strength, pride, and anger kicked in with a vengeance. Jennifer Blaylock— lucky number seven—felt terribly bad that the number of assignments distributed consistently fell short of what our row actually needed. Refusing to look me straight in the eyes for the fourth time, she shamefully turned around, focused her vision on my desktop, and said, "I got the last one, again, Chelsey."

"I know," I replied with dignity, remaining superglued to my chair.

"Aren't you going to ask Mrs. Franks for the assignment?" Jennifer asked, as she somehow found the courage to look at me.

"Nope. I'm not doing that anymore." I had decided to do what any respectable black child would do. I would go home and tell my mama.

To say my mother was furious would be to say the *Titanic* was a cute little boat. Though I had been embarrassed by her instant willingness to blame white people for everything that happened to black people countless times before, I was proud of my loud, obnoxious, *take-no-shit* mother that day. Suffice it to say that on the fifth day—after a not so pleasant conversation with my mother—Mrs. Franks made a remarkable recovery and her ability to count to eight was restored, literally, overnight. Like that time Lazarus got up and walked, it was a bona fide miracle.

It didn't really matter, though, that the math teacher was mathematically literate again because Mama had me removed from her class immediately. She was adamant about not having Mrs. Franks degrade her daughter in school when her little girl already had enough battles to fight being black and female and fatherless and all. Mama fought tirelessly to have Mrs. Franks fired so that she wouldn't be able to strip other little black children of their

self-worth. While that never happened, Mrs. Franks—
who was seventy if she was a day—retired in the spring.
Though she died of heart failure two summers later, she
was the talk of the town for the rest of the decade.

It was funny how the real story got more distorted
with each year that passed and by each person who told
it. *"Girl, Ah heard Hattie Mae wuz so mad dat she beat dat
de're math teacha' 'til she couldn't multiply no mo'. Ah heard
she had tuh git uh job where she didn't haf'ta do nuthin' but
add an' subtrac',"* somebody swore. *"Chile, Ah heard dat
white woman wuz so scaid, she up an' had uh heart attak
jes' so Hattie Mae wouldn't kill 'uh foe she died,"* somebody
else reported. By the late seventies, it was even rumored
that Mama was still so angry that she had Mrs. Franks'
ghost drawing her bath, tending her garden, and doing
odd chores around the house.

CHAPTER 6

I was about seven years old when it first occurred to me that my family was at least one vital member short. You know how it feels when you're playing in the sandbox at the park one day and you build the best sandcastle *ever* and nobody is there to see it? That's what I felt like—every day. It was a shitty feeling to say the least, but I didn't say anything about it for a long time because I knew silence was what both my mother and my sister preferred. Mama, because she, too, felt empty and Katie because talking about it always put Mama in a foul mood for the rest of the week. For years, the elephant just sat in our living room while the three of us walked carefully around it, changed chairs when it blocked the television screen, or left the room when its presence was so large that only it could fit.

By the time I reached the ripe old age of nine, I had decided that remaining silent just wasn't working. At least not for me. I was determined to find out why I, seemingly all alone, carried the burden of fatherlessness. Why was I consumed by it while Katie, who was in the same predicament, didn't seem to care in the least? In the past, talking to my mother about my father had consistently failed to provide sufficient answers to fill the void his absence had created, but with the passage of another year, determination had become the cornerstone of my existence and I couldn't make myself stop the regular inquisitions.

One July afternoon when it was too hot to play outside and I had grown bored with playing with my dolls and cooking on my *Easy Bake Oven*, I tried once again to get to the bottom of things. I desperately needed to know whose fault it was that I did not have a father so that when I explained my situation to my two-parent peers at school, I would be able to put the blame in the proper place and leave it at that. I was certain that if I understood it, I could make them understand it, too. School was going to resume in a little more than a month and I simply could not go through another year of embarrassment. Knowledge was power and I needed it to give me the strength to face the incalculable cruelty of fourth graders.

Before beginning the conversation with Mama, I told myself that if I received satisfactory answers to my questions, I would wait until mid-August before asking her to explain why my heart felt so broken, my soul so empty, and my spirit so angry over something that didn't seem to bother Katie or the other kids in the housing project who didn't have fathers, either. I decided it was best to tackle my concerns a little bit at a time so as not to shut her completely down. In nine long years, my luck hadn't been so great, so I definitely didn't want to push it too far in one short afternoon.

"Mama, can I talk to you?"

"I don't have time for your silly questions today, chile," Mama snarled, as she continued to iron. She was already irritable. Maybe it was the heat this time. Maybe it wasn't. Either way, I needed to proceed with caution.

"Would you tell me about how I was born, Mama? About how I was sick and scaly and almost died and everything?" My plot seemed ingenious to me. I knew my mother loved to tell the story of how her baby girl was deathly ill and how she single-handedly nursed her back to health with a special milk formula, olive oil, and prayer. I patiently listened for the umpteenth time, hoping Mama's mood would lighten as she retold the story of her own motherly heroics. When she was finished and I saw her smiling, I knew it was safe to continue. "Do you still love me that much, Mama?"

"Of course I do, baby. Do you think I work all these jobs for nothin'?" Not waiting for an answer, she kept talking. "I wouldn't put up with them spoiled white folks if I didn't love you. And I been seein' how you been lookin' at that lil' pink bike in Hampton's Department Sto' winda'! Well, those things cost money, baby, an' what do I tell you 'bout money?"

"Money doesn't grow on trees," I recited from the *Hattie Mae George Handbook of Life* that was stored in my head.

"That's right. And that's why I work so hard—because money don't grow on trees an' I love my baby girls." She leaned forward and kissed my corn-rowed head. Her kiss gave me confidence and I forgot I still had to be careful.

"How come you don't ask Lester or Katie's father to help you, Mama? Maybe you wouldn't have to work so much then." I knew better than to call Lester 'daddy', and I had never even heard the name of Katie's sperm donor.

"Because neitha' one of 'em done evah been worth a quarter. If they wanna do somethin' for ya'll, they knows where you live. They's grown men an' I ought not to have to ask 'em to do what they s'posed to do anyways."

"Do you think Lester loves me, Mama?"

"Do you see him roun' here on a reg'lar basis? Has he evah bought you anythin' for your birthday? Has he evah done one damn thing for you, *evah*?"

Even though I was just a kid, I knew what the answer to her questions *should* have been, but for some reason, instead of saying, *No, Mama, he's never done one damned thing for me in my entire life,* I said, "Well, he bought me those boots I wanted." I knew that defending my father—no matter how trivially it was done—was never the right thing to do because that particular edict was clearly spelled out on page twelve of Mama's handbook.

"One damn pair a boots in nine damn years! You think *that* means he loves you? Hell, that ain't love! Nevah have been an' nevah will be!"

"Why doesn't he love me, Mama? Why didn't he want me?" I fought back the tears. Like I always did, I would release them when I was alone because then nobody could accuse me of loving somebody I shouldn't.

"I don't know!" Mama yelled. "Ask him yourself the nex' time he decide to come roun' here—*if* he evah decide to come roun' here again! You know you cain't depen' on his sorry ass."

The conversation had become excruciating, but I had to keep going. School was beginning soon. I disregarded Mama's mood, took a deep breath, and pressed on like any temporarily insane person would do.

"Why didn't you and Lester get married, Mama?"

"Because he didn't think I was good enough to be a preacha's wife," she spat.

"Why didn't he think you were good enough? Everybody says you're pretty."

"Because I speaks my mind, that's why. He wouldn't a been able to make me take his foolishness, so he married that heffa' he with now. He could do whatevah he wanted to with her, but not with me, an' he knew it."

"If you had been nicer, do you think he would have married you, instead of her?"

"Oh, so you think it's my fault that me an' Lester ain't married, huh?"

I was sure it wasn't the heat that was making Mama irritable, now. "I'm not saying that. I'm just saying—" Mama angrily interrupted me.

"Sounds like that's what you sayin' to me! Sounds like you blamin' *me* 'cause *he* ain't here!"

"That's not what I'm saying at all, Mama! I just want to know why you and Lester aren't together. I don't understand why you didn't get married if you liked each other enough to make me!" Mama wasn't the only one irritable, now. "I didn't ask to be born! Why didn't you just let me die when you had the chance? At least then I wouldn't feel so bad all the time! At least then I wouldn't hate everything about me! Why did you do this to me?" My tears disobeyed direct orders and came, anyway.

"I didn't do nothin' to you! Look roun' here! He's the one who ain't here! He's the one who ain't man enough to be a father!"

"And why isn't he here, Mama?" I screamed right back. "Is it because you fuss and fight with him every time you see him? Is it because you're not woman enough? Is it

43

because—" My words were cut off by the sting of Mama's hand across my face. I grabbed my burning cheek, looked at my mother with fear and hurt and anger and pity, then ran to the safety of the small bedroom I shared with Katie, where I could allow my tears to flow freely. Mama held the hand that inflicted the pain, stared at the empty spot where I used to stand, then retreated to her bedroom where she could allow hers to do the same. If tears could have brought my father back, he would have come home that night.

* * *

Because of the answers that never came, deep self-hatred replaced determination as the cornerstone of my existence. But that was one secret I decided to hold inside. I told myself that if anyone knew that I didn't know how to love myself, they would point an accusing finger at illegitimacy and hate me, too. Or even worse, feel sorry for me. Pity was the last thing I needed. That would only increase the pain I had too much of already. I decided that I had to be good at everything and liked by everyone. As a result, I found myself incessantly striving for perfection. Perfection, I told myself, would overshadow the indignity of my birth. If I was the best daughter, sister, friend, *whatever anyone wanted*, no one would care whether I had a father or not. In my mind, it was a win-win situation.

Although I didn't realize it at the time, doing and being what others wanted was where I felt safest because it prevented me from confronting the real issue. As bright as I was, the child, and later the young adult, could not figure out any other way to play the unfair hand I felt I had been dealt. Endlessly giving of myself to others was the card that just kept coming up, no matter how many times I tried to shuffle and re-deal. I gave myself away until there was nothing left. Then I gave some more. No sacrifice was too great if it meant others thought I was a wonderful person. Over the years, I managed to convince relatives, friends, teachers, lovers, and countless, nameless others that I was a confident, well-adjusted young woman. Only my mother and I knew I was living a lie. And since neither of us was talking, my secret was safe. Before I turned the bedside lamp off that night, I wrote in my journal: *If everybody thinks I'm so wonderful, why does it still hurt so much?*

CHAPTER 7

Poverty was a customary way of life for the residents of the Woodlawn Housing Project. Quite frankly, I despised the custom. The run-down apartments. The rats and roaches. The single mothers. The absent fathers. The accepting children. My sister's ambivalence. My mother's mistakes. My father's disregard. The sperm donor's disinterest. My mother. My father. My sister. Myself. I despised it all. I reserved a special contempt for the rats, roaches, and other vermin that roamed as freely as we did because they were indisputable evidence of our inferior status. Along with the development of an irrational repulsion to filth and disorder, I developed a phobia for all creeping, crawling, or furry creatures. I carried these idiosyncrasies with me into adulthood, along with the rest of my baggage. No one ever understood why a dusty chest of drawers, a singing cricket, or a cuddly hamster could all make me break out in hives.

Attempting to rid myself of the squalor seemingly inherent in poverty, I became obsessed with cleanliness and order. Mama didn't have the time or energy to concentrate on cleanliness in her own house because she was always cleaning someone else's so we would have food on the table at mealtime and toys under the silver pom-pom Christmas tree we put up year after year. Katie was essentially a non-entity because she was generally indifferent to anything that really mattered. And since our damned maid never did show up for work, it was up to me to change our unenviable circumstances. Like a complete fanatic, I sprayed roach killer, set out rat poison, swept rugs, mopped floors, washed dishes, dusted furniture, scrubbed bathroom tile, and sorted dirty clothes for the Laundromat. But, no matter how hard I cleaned, the stench of poverty lingered, relentlessly. I woke up with it, carried it on my back all day long, went to sleep with it, had nightmares about it, then woke up and began the routine all over again. I blamed it mostly on my father. If he was a part of my life, I told myself, things would be a whole lot different. But he wasn't and they weren't and I cursed him on all the days of the week that ended in the letter 'y'.

Fantasy became my primary mode of escape. The stories I told my little white dolls inevitably included a princess—always named Chelsey—and a prince, whose name changed from fantasy to fantasy:

Once upon a time, there was a princess named Chelsey who lived in a sparkling clean castle with a moat and servants and store-bought dresses. One dreadful day, a wicked witch with a big wart right on the tip of her nose kidnapped the princess from her kingdom and took her to live among the peasants in the housing project. As soon as Chelsey's father, the powerful and mighty king, discovered his daughter was missing, he gathered up an army of soldiers and went straight to the housing project to rescue her because there was nothing in the world that he loved more than his little girl and nothing

47

in the world that he hated more than wicked witches with warts on their noses. The strong, fearless king killed the witch, rescued his little girl, and immediately ordered the soldiers to tear down the housing project. He then built a prosperous city in its place, where the people lived in cleanliness and godliness and happiness. Soon thereafter, Princess Chelsey married a very handsome and very charming prince named Jamal. Prince Jamal vowed to protect Princess Chelsey from all hurt, harm, and danger, to never, ever judge her, and to love her forever and ever and ever and—

"What 'cha doing, princess? Daydreaming again?" Quickly realizing that the oversized head poking its way through my bedroom door belonged to Eddie, Mama's boyfriend of the last eight months, and not to Jamal, my prince of the last eight minutes, I snapped out of my fantasy.

Captain Edward Malone was stationed on the army base in Greenville, Georgia situated less than twenty miles north of Wade. More than half of his forty-two years in the world had been spent serving his country, first in Junior ROTC in high school, then in the United States Army. His father, Franklin Malone, was a highly decorated, retired army colonel and Eddie wanted nothing more than to follow in his footsteps.

Most people agreed that God or nature or *something* had been unbelievably good to Eddie. Every sighted woman in the entire state of Georgia swore on her great-great-grandmama's grave that the definition for '*good-looking*' was listed under the *E's* and if you looked in any dictionary, right where the definition should be printed would be Eddie Malone's picture, instead—bold, black, and beautiful, just like he was in person.

Eddie was the embodiment of tall, dark, and handsome, only he wasn't really all that dark. More of a honey brown complexion, actually. But the tall and handsome parts were dead on. He was six-four and a half, with broad shoulders, muscular arms, and tight buttocks. Army regulations required that he keep his face clean-shaven, however, on some weekends, he felt rebellious and allowed facial hair to sprout wherever it felt comfortable. His rough and rugged weekend look was even more appealing to women. Many of them had made love to Eddie in their fantasies, while in reality, they were being penetrated by hardworking husbands and boyfriends who naturally assumed the screams of ecstasy that pierced their ears were for them.

Rumor had it that Eddie had once been engaged to a woman so flawless that if she died, angels would flatly refuse to allow her into heaven, fearing she would expose their own blemishes. As the story goes, one day Eddie dropped by her house unannounced, only to find the very thing that came right *after* the very last thing he ever expected. As it turned out, his flawless betrothed was just as freaky as she was flawless because there she was, in bed kissing another man—who was screwing another woman. Sexual exploits aside, she was just as surprised to see Eddie as he was to see her. After the two extra people found their clothes and made a quick exit, she told Eddie she was sorry and that she loved him more than anything in the world and that he just had to believe her when she said that was the first time anything like that had ever happened. She had hoped he would interpret the *first time* part of her story as the first time she had ever cheated, rather than the first time she had ever gotten caught. Her hopes for forgiveness were dashed when Eddie walked over to the bed and removed the engagement ring from her left hand. Amidst more than the standard amount of crying, begging, and pleading, Eddie made it clear to her that once she had done her little friends, she had done away with any chance she had of becoming Mrs. Edward Malone.

Though he remained calm and composed throughout the entire twenty-minute incident, Eddie was devastated by her betrayal. He had loved her with the might of ten men and thought she had loved him just as deeply. In the seemingly endless days that followed, he often wondered what had gone wrong. He was unwilling to accept the twisted opinion of his best friend, Joe, who insisted that black women don't want good men. Unless the man is a dog, Joe had told him, sisters aren't interested. Though Joe's theory was the most ridiculous thing Eddie had ever heard—excepting his ex-fiance's *first time* defense—the thought did cross his mind that maybe, just maybe, Joe was on to something.

After the devastating incident, Eddie retreated into a self-imposed exile. His daily agenda consisted of two items: going to work at 7:30 in the morning and going back home at 6:00 o'clock at night. He made stops at the drycleaner or grocery store only when absolutely necessary. It was a warmer than usual Saturday night in April when he decided he needed to stop moping around the house and put himself back into circulation. His job had been his mistress for two and a half months and he craved something less frigid to hold on to. That was exactly how he found himself at the Officer's Club on base that night.

When he saw a shapely young woman standing alone by the bar in a slinky black dress that appeared to have been tailored to her exact proportions, he decided he had picked the perfect night to stop mourning a love gone bad. Before approaching her, he nervously pulled his pants up at the waist as though they would fall down if he didn't. Straightening his tie gave him confidence, so he took a minute to do that, too.

It was only by chance that Mama had also ended up at the Officer's Club that night. Since Katie and I were spending the night with friends, she had decided to take full advantage of a quiet night at home alone. She had a million and one things to do, not the least of which was finishing our Easter dresses before next Sunday morning. Just as she was sewing the last two buttons on Katie's dress, the telephone rang.

"Hey, Hattie Mae, it's me. Girl, I'm tired of sittin' at home. Let's go see what's happenin' at the Stardust tonight."

"You got to go without me this time, Irma. I'm stayin' in so's I can finish up the girls' Easter dresses."

"Hattie Mae, you got a whole 'nother week to get them dresses finished," Ms. Irma said. "Come on, let's go. I needs to have me some fun an' it sho' ain't nothin' goin' on at this here house."

Ms. Irma pleaded until Mama's resistance was worn down. "Jesus, Irma!" she said. "I'll go if you just stop with your whinin'. You givin' me a headache."

"Great!" Ms. Irma responded, victoriously. "I'll pick you up in forty-five minutes." Laughing, she added, "An' make sure you look good 'cause I cain't handle all those men by myself!"

"Have I ever disappointed you?" Mama boasted.

"Now that's what I like to hear!" Ms. Irma said, before hanging up.

Mama sighed loud enough for her dead daddy to hear then hung up the telephone. Since she hadn't planned on going out, she had no idea what she was going to wear. She thought about the red dress, then remembered she didn't like the way it fit anymore. She liked the way she looked in the navy blue dress, but it was dirty. And she had worn the green skirt with the beige blouse the last time she went to the Stardust. Times were hard, but she wasn't going to have people thinking she only had one nice outfit.

In the midst of eliminating one selection after another from her closet, she happened across the little black dress. Even though she had gained two or three pounds since finding it on sale at Hampton's, she knew it still fit just right in all of her *just right* places. When she finally decided what to wear, she realized she had less than twenty minutes to get ready, so she tossed the dress on the bed, dug out her only decent pair of black shoes from the bottom of the closet, and retrieved some panties, a lace bra, and a pair of black stockings from the antique dresser that used to belong to her mother.

Undergarments in hand, she dashed to the tiny bathroom down the hallway to begin a bath that would be so short she would have to limit herself to washing only the really important parts. If other parts happened to get wet, it would simply be a bonus. She found herself laughing out loud as she negotiated the terms of her bath with herself. She had no idea what to do with her hair, but was hopeful she would figure that out, too, in the few minutes she had remaining.

By the time she heard the sound of Ms. Irma's horn honking, Mama had been dressed for a full minute and a half. She took one last look at herself in the mirror and feeling completely satisfied with what she saw, grabbed her purse and keys and rushed out the front door. As they drove to the Stardust, they exchanged sincere compliments, each one assuring the other that she would have all the men at her mercy within minutes of their arrival.

"Damn!" Ms. Irma said, as they drove into the all but barren parking lot. "This place couldn't be deader if it was a cemetery."

"Ain't that the truth," Mama said, clearly disappointed. She had gone to all the trouble of getting dressed for nothing. If she had stayed home, she would have been finished with Katie's dress and almost finished with mine by now.

Refusing to be defeated, Ms. Irma said, "Let's go to the Officers Club. It's always somethin' happenin' there."

Frustrated, Mama replied, "We ain't officers an' we don't know none, so how you think we gon' get in there?"

"Chile, chile, chile," Ms. Irma said, shaking her head back and forth as she backed the car out of the parking lot. "Ain't I taught you *nothin'* in all these years? Pretty women don't have trouble gettin' in nowhere!"

Mama looked at Ms. Irma as though she had just lost her mind. Ms. Irma glanced back with a devilish look in her eyes. "Well, we might as well try it," Mama said, suddenly overcome with laughter. "Hell, I sho' didn't get all dolled up to look at your ass all night long!"

"And as good as you look tonight, girl, I don't wanna look at you all night long, either," Ms. Irma said, laughing just as loudly.

As Ms. Irma had predicted, a reasonable portion of external beauty was the only credential they needed not only to gain entry onto the army base, but to gain entry into the Officers Club as well. Almost immediately, Ms. Irma was pulled onto the dance floor by one of her old boyfriends. On her way to the bar, Mama turned down two offers to dance. She had never been to the Officers Club before and she wanted to look around and take it all in for a little while. When she got to the bar, she ordered a glass of water with lemon, no ice. She didn't drink alcohol and found it to be poor judgment to waste good money buying one Coke for the same price at which she could get a six-pack at the grocery store. While daintily sipping her water like it was a gin martini, she heard a deep voice coming from behind. "Would you like to dance, beautiful lady?"

Like most women, Mama appreciated sincere compliments. To her, they felt a little like sunshine on a rainy day. Insincere compliments, on the other hand, felt like dime store jewelry. Whenever she received one, her general rule was to instantly seek out a sufficient method of punishment for the perpetrator. Since the voice from behind could see neither the beauty on her face, nor that in her heart, she found herself more than a little perturbed. She turned around, primed and ready to reject the voice and the man attached to it, but when she saw the million-dollar man with the billion-dollar smile that sparkled like the rhinestone earrings she wore, her disposition shifted from ice cold to red hot. *Humph*, she thought to herself. *Punishing a guy for a compliment? What a stupid rule.* "I'd love to," she heard herself say.

Moving seductively to the sound of Marvin Gaye's vocals, Mama decided that her admirer was definitely an older man. She could tell by the way he carried himself. She had to be careful not to grin too much because the last thing she needed was for him to think she was an immature twenty-nine. Breaking the news that she had two little girls at home would be a big enough hurdle for him to jump.

The dance floor was crowded, but they managed to secure a corner of it for themselves and danced to three fast songs in a row. Mama was captivated by his smooth moves on the floor. So smooth, in fact, that she found herself wondering what other talents he might have. After the third fast song, the DJ put on a slow record and still more couples made their way to the floor.

"May I have one more?" he asked.

With the sincerest voice in her repertoire, Mama replied, "I'm a little tired right now. Maybe later." She had another rule she decided not to break—never slow dance with a man until you know his middle name. Slow dancing was like sex. Extremely personal. You just couldn't do it with anybody. Just like its name suggested, a girl had to take it slow and, at that point, she didn't even know her dance partner's first name, yet.

"Sounds fair. Well, can I buy you a drink?"

He smiled his award-winning smile again and Mama had to lock her knees to keep from falling. "Yes, thank you," she said, hoping her voice had not cracked too much.

Returning to the bar together, Mama ordered a Coke—because it wasn't poor judgment to waste someone else's money—and Eddied ordered a mixed drink. "So, what's your name, lovely lady?"

"Hattie Mae George. What's yours?"

"Edward Malone. But everybody calls me Eddie."

Mama and Eddie had been talking at the bar for almost thirty minutes when Ms. Irma resurfaced. After Eddie promised he would drive Mama home and Mama promised she would call Ms. Irma when she arrived safely, Ms. Irma left with Big Money, her old flame who had monopolized her time since she first walked through the door. Mama could no more figure out why Ms. Irma was so crazy about Big Money than why everybody called him Big Money in the first place. From what she had seen, he never had more than ten or twenty dollars in his pocket that he didn't already owe to somebody else. She always thought a more appropriate name for Big Money would be *No Money* or maybe, *Just A Little Money,* so a girl couldn't be misled by an image created in the corners of Big Money's own mind.

Mama and Eddie shut the Officers Club down that night. They covered every topic from me and Katie and absent fathers to broken engagements and broken hearts. Each felt as though they had known the other for at least two lifetimes.

"What's your middle name, Eddie," Mama asked, as they approached her front door.

"I don't have one. Why?"

"No reason," Mama said, with a polite smile. "No reason a'tall."

CHAPTER 8

Within thirty minutes of meeting Mama, Eddie was captivated. Within thirty days, he had become an almost permanent fixture at our house. Within three months, he had fallen head over heels in love with her. The best part about it was that he adored me and Katie just as much. To him, we were the icing on the best damned cake he had ever tasted.

Personally, I was crazy about Eddie. I liked him a thousand times more than any of the other boyfriends that had been unceremoniously paraded in and out of my life. He took time to talk to me and listen to me and take me to the corner store for *Now-And-Laters, Blow Pops,* and my all-time favorite, lemon drops. Sometimes, he even told me he loved me, just like I had heard Rochelle's father say to her one day when he dropped her off at school.

Seeing Eddie in the doorway of the small room I shared with Katie, I catapulted off the bed and landed in his unprepared, but nonetheless strong arms.

"Eddie! What're you doing here?" I giggled, as I hugged his neck and tried to hold on to keep from falling.

"You mean you're not happy to see me?" he said, with a grin almost as wide as mine.

"Don't be silly! I'm always happy to see you! But it's Tuesday and Mama won't be home from the Peterson's for at least another two hours."

"Oh, that's right,' Eddie said, with genuine disappointment. "I forgot what day it was." He leaned forward and all of a sudden, my feet were back on the floor. Then, in his best chastising voice, he said, "How come you girls are in this house with the door unlocked? Your mother wouldn't like that one bit if she knew."

"That's Katie's fault," I tattled. "I guess she forgot to lock the door when she left for Jessica's house. They're working on a class project together."

"Okay, you little tattle-tale, but next time she leaves, you go make sure the door is locked. I love you too much for anything to happen to you." He leaned down and hugged me and my beaming eyes. "When's Katie coming home, anyway?" he asked.

"Last night, she told Mama she wouldn't be home until around six-thirty."

"Well, looks like it's just you and me, kiddo. Wanna go get some lemon drops?"

"Yes!" I screamed, at the same time running to the closet to get my pink flip-flops. Hurriedly putting them on my feet and grabbing my door key from the top of the rickety dresser, I proudly announced, "I'm ready. Let's go!"

I loved the times I spent alone with Eddie. Going to the store for candy was one of my favorites. Like dozens of times before, we found ourselves walking hand in hand down the quiet streets of Wade, looking like a

Norman Rockwell painting that had somehow been set into motion. It was exactly the kind of life I had planned for myself, only at some indeterminable fork in the road before I was born, I had made a wrong turn somewhere and wound up right in the middle of an existence clearly meant for someone a lot less deserving.

Without question, I couldn't have loved Eddie more if I tried. His presence filled almost all of the abnormally large hole in my heart. Even so, being with him was like a double-edged sword. Sometimes, its sharp edges provided fierce protection from my memories, disallowing the painful ones to penetrate my consciousness and disturb my momentary equilibrium. At other times, however, being with him seemed to pierce the very center of my being, releasing the pain that had stained my life in a way no one seemed to be able to understand. Being with him was both exhilarating and excruciating, sometimes all in the same day.

Mama had grown to trust Eddie more deeply than she had any other man, not counting Grandpa Henry. She frequently confided in him about significant aspects of her life, not the least of which was me and Katie. *Katie does jes' fine without her daddy bein' roun',* Mama had told him. *But Chelsey, well, all I can say is she completely diff'rent. She jes' love her daddy. My love don't seem to be enough for that one, no sir. She want her daddy's love. He ain't spent more'n twenty minutes with her in her whole life, but that's who she want.*

Eddie sensed my inner turmoil long before Mama had felt safe enough to disclose the full details to him. Without a word from her, he knew I would spend life's precious moments mourning something I never had if no one tried to stop me. More than once, he had prayed that God would show him a way to relieve me of the burdens placed upon me in part by life, but mostly by me. Though I certainly didn't realize it at the time, our walks were more than mere candy expeditions for me. They provided me with the one thing I wanted most from a man but had never experienced until he came into my world. It was the exact kind of father-daughter connection I had craved every since I could remember.

On this particular day, just as we had on countless others, we set out on the short journey to the store by going the long way around, unnecessarily passing Ms. Eula's beauty shop that she ran out of the back of her house and Mr. Jack's Chicken Shack whose claim to fame was that Richard Pryor's gardener's mother's friend once bought a three-piece and fries there. We routinely turned the five-minute walk into fifteen.

"So, how old are you now, Chelsey?" Eddie asked, as we rounded the corner on Jefferson Street.

"Don't you remember, Eddie? My birthday party was just a few months ago."

"Let me see," Eddie said as he closed one eye and arched the opposite eyebrow to help him to remember. "Twenty-four?" he kidded.

"No, silly!" I said, laughing and punching him in his side with a tiny fist that did absolutely no damage. "You know I'm only twelve."

"Twelve!" Eddie exclaimed. "My, you're a big girl now, aren't you?"

"That's right. I'm old enough to babysit Ms. Ethel's kids. I made seven dollars when I kept them last Saturday night," I boasted.

"Then I should let *you* buy the candy, today, Ms. Money Bags." We both laughed heartily, as I secretly planned to buy enough candy that would last at least until Saturday if I spaced it out just right.

Once we got to the store, it took less than two minutes for one excited little girl to fill the countertop with three boxes of lemon drops, two packages of apple *Now-And-Laters,* two candy necklaces—one for me and one for Katie—three cherry *Blow Pops*, and two of every flavor of *Jolly Rancher* candies in the store. "Thank you," I said, when Ms. Iola, the store attendant, slid the bag of candy across the counter to me. Clinging tightly to my newest acquisition, I looked up some two-hundred feet to my idol and said, "Thanks for the candy, Eddie. Want a *Jolly Rancher*?"

"No thanks, sweetheart," he replied with a smile. Waving goodbye to Ms. Iola as we walked out the door, Eddie said, "See you next time, Iola. Give that grandbaby a great big hug for me."

We took the short route on the way back, so we were home in a matter of minutes. As I was unlocking the front door, Eddie asked, "Hey, princess, do you think your mother's going to feel like cooking tonight?"

"No way!" I said.

"I don't think so either. What d'ya say we take her out to dinner?"

The question was a no-brainer for me because like store-bought dresses, I loved store-bought dinners. "Yeah, let's do it!" I squealed.

"Okay, it's a done deal. I've got to run by the office to review a file for a briefing tomorrow morning, but I should be back by the time Hattie Mae and Katie get home. Then we can all go out for four big, juicy steaks. Now, you get on in the house." As Eddie headed to his car, he turned back and yelled, "And lock that door!"

Smiling with every tooth in my head, I went inside and locked the door behind me. Pulling back the sheer curtains Mama had made, I watched Eddie through the window until he was out of sight. When he was gone, I ran to my bedroom and dug out my journal from the secret hiding place in my sock drawer. It wasn't as nice as the journal my father had bought for me, but it was what my babysitting money could afford and it suited my needs just as well as the original one had. *One of these days,* I wrote, *Eddie's going to ask Mama to marry him. When that day comes, Mama will have a husband, me and Katie will have a daddy...and the sun won't ever stop shining.*

* * *

Exactly thirty-two minutes later, there was a knock at the front door. Since it was too soon for Eddie to be back, I ran down the hallway to the living room, yelling, "Who is it?"

"It's me, Chelsey," I heard Eddie say. "Open up."

Opening the door, I saw that he had a briefcase in one hand and a half-empty bottle of soda in the other. "Mama and Katie still aren't home, yet," I said.

"I didn't think they'd be," he said, as he came through the door, pushing it closed with the bottom of his foot. "I decided I could just do my work from here while we wait for them to get home. That alright with you, Ms. George?"

I loved it when Eddie called me Ms. George. It made me feel all grown up. "That's fine with me, Captain Malone," I replied, with a quick salute and a long giggle.

Eddie sat on the worn, brown sofa opposite the side with the loose spring. After neatly spreading out several pieces of paper and a large, green ledger on the wooden coffee table, he removed a calculator and a pencil from his briefcase and began adding numbers from the papers and writing the results in the ledger. I sat Indian-style on the floor as I watched him work. The game I had been playing with my dolls had suddenly become insignificant. I preferred to watch Eddie, instead. Those silly dolls weren't going anywhere.

Watching him take care of business, I became transfixed. *He's good at taking care of things,* I thought. Nearly half an hour passed before he put down the pencil and stretched his arms. "Are you done working?" I asked, hoping that he was. I wanted to talk to him about something important before Mama and Katie got home.

"Umph-um," Eddie grunted, in the middle of his stretch. "I'm just taking a little break."

"Oh."

Even though he had been working, Eddie had noticed that I was uncustomarily quiet. At first he thought I was simply trying to be quiet while he worked, which I suppose I was, sort of, but since I rarely spoke just one word at a time, it immediately became apparent to him that there was much more to it than that. After several minutes of silence, he said, "So, what's on your mind, princess? Talk to me."

"Well," I began slowly, "I was wondering if I could ask you a question?"

"Only if it's an easy one," Eddie joked, trying to lighten whatever load I had bogged myself down with at that particular moment.

"It's hard for me, but I know it won't be hard for you," I assured him, forcing myself to smile. I usually wasn't nervous when I talked to Eddie, but this time I was. It was an important question.

"Okay, go ahead. What's your question?"

"Do you like the way I look?"

"Do I like the way you *cook*?" Eddie teased.

"No, Eddie! I said *look*. Do you like the way I *look*?"

"Oh!" Eddie said, with mock surprise. "Do I like the way you look?"

"Yeah. Do you, well, do you think I'm pretty?" There. I had said it.

The expression in my eyes and the wrinkle in the middle of my forehead were dead giveaways. Eddie knew it was a serious question that needed a serious answer. "Why do you want to know?" he asked, trying to begin at the root of my problem.

"I don't know. I was just wondering, that's all." Suddenly embarrassed, I said, "Oh, never mind. It's a silly question, anyway."

Eddie got up from the sofa and sat himself next to me on the floor. I was *as serious as a heart attack*, as southern country folk were often heard saying, and he wanted to make sure he was eye-to-eye with my vulnerability. More importantly, he wanted to make sure that I not only *heard* his answer, but that I *felt* it, too. "Hmmm…do I like the way you look? Chelsey Christina George, I think you're one of the prettiest little girls on God's green earth," his love said to me. "Everything about you is unique and precious and wonderful and those are facts *nobody* would disagree with. Your cute little button nose, your bright little eyes, your innocent little smile—they're all beautiful. And all of those things rolled up together make you even more beautiful. When you look in the mirror, don't you see it? Don't you see how pretty you are?"

"Not really," I said, slowly. I had never seen myself as pretty. Not like I saw Mama and Katie. They were the pretty ones. Katie looked like Mama and Mama looked like pictures I had seen of her mother. Me, well, I just looked like Lester. And there was nothing pretty about a girl who looked like a boy. My throat tightened as I tried to control emotion I didn't want Eddie to see. I didn't want him to think I was some wimpy little crybaby. He might not want to be my father if he thought I'd cry at the drop of a hat.

"Why not? Why don't you think you're pretty?"

"I don't know." I paused, then added, "I was just thinking that if I was pretty, I'd have a father."

"You *do* have a father, sweetheart."

"Yeah, I know I *have* one. I know everybody *has* one. But I don't understand why mine left. I've been trying and trying, Eddie, but I just don't understand why my father didn't want me." The cracking in my voice was evidence that it was becoming increasingly difficult to conceal the pain that was now a big knot in my throat. "I was just thinking that maybe he would have stayed if I was prettier. Maybe he wanted a pretty little girl and all he got was me—so he left."

"I promise you, sweetheart, that's not why he left," Eddie said, tenderly brushing the side of my cheek with the back of his hand. "How you look had nothing at all to do with it."

"Then why did he leave, Eddie? Why didn't he want me to be his little girl?" My eyes filled with tears as the sharp edges of the double-edged sword accidentally pierced my soul again.

"I suppose he was scared, Chelsey. He was just scared and he didn't know what else to do."

"Scared of what, Eddie?" I asked, pleading for understanding.

"Probably scared that he wouldn't know how to be a good father to you, sweetheart. Scared that he would have messed things up even more if he had stayed. You see, Chelsey, you're one of the best daughters any father could possibly hope for. I know it and your father knew it, too. I'd bet everything that in his heart of hearts, he really wanted to stay."

"Then why didn't he?" I said, crying softly. "Why didn't he?"

"He made a mistake, Chelsey. He made the biggest mistake of his life." *And of yours, too,* Eddie thought to himself, as he rocked my weeping body back and forth in his arms.

That night, the pages of my journal got wet as I wrote: *He left because he was scared—I'm scared because he left.*

CHAPTER 9

Mama stood in front of the bathroom mirror trying to decide whether she should wear her hair up or down for the special evening Eddie had promised. He had called earlier in the day to tell her he had something he wanted to talk to her about. Something really important, he had said. He asked if she would do him the honor of allowing him to take her out for a romantic dinner. When she agreed, he asked if she would wear the same dress she wore the night they met. The excitement in his voice made her feel excited, too.

"I don't mind wearin' that dress, baby, but tell me what's goin' on. What you got up your sleeve, Eddie Malone?"

"None of your business, Hattie Mae George," Eddie playfully responded. "I'll pick you up at nineteen-hundred hours." He started to hang up the telephone then remembered one more thing. "Hattie Mae," he said quickly, hoping she had not yet hung up.

"Yeah, baby?"

"I love you."

"I love you, too, Captain." Mama hung up the telephone, but lost in her own thoughts, never removed her hand from the receiver. The last year with Eddie had been the happiest year of her life. He was madly in love with her and she couldn't seem to breathe without him. And he loved me and Katie as though we were born of his own blood. That part really didn't count, though, because Mama would never have been with anybody who didn't. Any man who didn't like her baby girls was dismissed with a quickness. She just didn't have time for foolishness like that.

Katie and I loved Eddie, too. Not only did he talk with us and play with us and help us with our homework, he offered fatherly advice, never missed a special occasion like birthdays or Christmas or an "A" on a spelling test, and he told us he loved us almost as often as he told our mother.

Mama couldn't stop wondering what Eddie was planning. He was always full of surprises, but this one felt different from the others. *Was tonight the night?* "If that man asks me to marry him," she inadvertently announced out loud, "I'm gon' say 'yes' so fast it'll make his head spin!"

* * *

At precisely seven o'clock that evening, there was a purposeful knock at the front door. Eddie was nothing if not prompt. He got that first from his father then the army reinforced it. When I heard the knocking, I bolted for the front door, yelling, "I got it! I got it!" There was no real reason to run to the door so fast because Katie was on the phone and wouldn't have gotten off if the house had been on fire and Mama wanted to make a grand entrance for the beginning of whatever night this would turn out to be. That left me exclusively in charge of door answering.

The moment I opened the door, I literally jumped into Eddie's arms. As he had long since grown accustomed to being greeted with such exuberance, his entire body automatically braced itself whenever he heard the sound of two little feet. "Hey!" he said, entering the house with me dangling from his neck. "What did I tell you about opening the door before you find out who's standing on the other side?" he scolded.

"Oops! I'm sorry, Eddie. But I already knew it was you. Mama said you were coming to pick her up at seven, so I knew it had to be you."

"Well, little Miss-Know-It-All, it might not have been me at all." He began tickling my ribcage until I fell to the floor in front of him, succumbing to uncontrollable laughter. "It could have been the boogie man standing out there, you know! And he doesn't love you nearly as much as I do!"

"Okay, okay, okay!" I giggled, trying to escape the torture of his tickling fingers.

"Now, what are you going to say the next time somebody knocks on the door?"

"Who is it? Who is it?" I said, through giggles.

"That's right! Now, do you think that gorgeous mother of yours will be as happy to see me as you are?"

"I *know* she will!"

"Then what are you waiting for? Go tell her that her king is here to pick up his queen."

I picked myself up from the floor and hurried down the hallway to Mama's bedroom. "Eddie's here, Mama,"

I said, as I entered the room. "He said to tell you that the king is here to pick up his queen."

"Oh did he, now? Well, the queen isn't so sure she's ready. How does she look, baby?" Mama did a pirouette, waving her arms above her head as she turned.

"Beautiful, Mama! You look beautiful!" I meant every word. I thought my mother was the prettiest mother in the entire world. At least once a day and twice on Sundays, I wished I had one or two of her genes, instead of all the ones belonging to my father.

"Thank you, baby," Mama said, as she grabbed her handbag from the foot of the bed, kissed me on the forehead, and headed for the living room.

Dashing ahead of her, I made it there first. In an announcer's voice, I said, "King Eddie, I present to you the beautiful Queen Hattie Mae!"

When Eddie saw Mama, his eyes glazed over like a star-struck teenager at a rock concert. To him, she was beautiful all the time, but sometimes she was just stunning. Tonight was one of those times. "Heaven *must* be missing an angel," he said, as he took Mama by the hand and twirled her around. "Hattie Mae George, you take my breath away."

"Why thank you, Captain Malone. You ain't so bad lookin' yourself. Now, shouldn't we be goin'?"

"Affirmative!" Opening the front door with one hand and making a swaying motion in the air with the other, he said, "Your carriage awaits you, my love." Mama kissed me again, made me promise to be a good girl and mind Katie, then sashayed through the door to begin her Cinderella evening.

Anywhere you want to go in Wade is less than fifteen minutes away from anywhere you happen to be, so it wasn't long before they found themselves seated at a cozy table in Mama's favorite restaurant. "Order whatever you want, baby. The sky's the limit tonight," Eddie said, as the waitress presented a menu first to Mama, then to him.

"The sky's the limit," Mama repeated. "What pile of money did you fall into?"

"Can't a man treat his lady to a nice dinner if he wants to?"

"Depends on who that man is. Is he good as you?" Mama said.

"Better."

"Then, yes," she said, trying very hard not to smile and blow her vixen cover.

They spent the next hour dining on garden salads with bleu cheese dressing, well-done T-bone steaks, baked potatoes piled high with all the fixings, and hot garlic bread. Seconds after swallowing the last bite, their plates were scooped away by an almost overly attentive waitress. When Mama excused herself to the ladies' room as Eddie knew she would after dinner, he had the opening he had been waiting for. When she returned several minutes later, he put his plan into motion.

"Tonight's a special night," he said, as he held both of her hands in his across the table. "Would you have a drink with me, sweetheart?"

"You know I'd do anythin' for you, baby. But you still ain't told me what's so special 'bout tonight."

"I'll tell you, but let's have a glass of champagne first, okay?"

Mama's heart was racing. "Okay."

Eddie motioned for the same attentive waitress to come to the table. "Ma'am, would you kindly bring out two glasses of your best champagne, please?"

"Certainly, sir." The waitress returned with two glasses of champagne balanced on a sterling silver serving tray. She placed one glass before Mama and the other before Eddie. Within seconds a string quartet appeared from nowhere and began serenading them with soft music.

"Hattie Mae George, I love you," Eddie said, as he picked up his glass for a toast. "To us."

Mama picked up her glass. "To us," she repeated. When she brought the glass to her lips, that's when she saw it. Something shiny and sparkly was in the bottom of her glass. "Oh my God! Oh my God! Oh my God!" she kept saying, trying unsuccessfully to remove the ring from the bubbling liquid.

"Wait a minute, baby," Eddie said, more than pleased with himself. "Let me help you." His long slender fingers removed the ring from the bottom of the glass and dried it off on the napkin in his lap. With the string quartet still playing and all eyes in the restaurant on their table, Eddie kneeled down on one knee. Taking her left hand in his, he said, "Hattie Mae George, I want you in my life for the rest of my life. I want you. I need you. I love you. Will you marry me?"

Tears of joy had begun pouring from Mama's eyes since she first saw the ring in the bottom of the glass so although Eddie was only inches from her, she could see neither his loving eyes, nor his nervous smile. "I love you, too," Mama said. "Yes, I'll marry you, baby!" Eddie placed the ring on her finger and hugged her as though he was never going to let go. Even though the night belonged exclusively to them, they willingly shared it with the applauding patrons in the restaurant.

Needless to say, I was ecstatic when I heard the news. *Thank you, God,* I wrote in my journal. *Thank you for giving me my very own daddy!*

CHAPTER 10

Only a month and a half had gone by when Eddie telephoned from his office with the latest development. "Baby, I got my new orders, today!"

"What orders?"

"You know I told you my tour in Georgia would be up pretty soon. They're reassigning us to another base."

"Where, Eddie?"

"Ft. Bragg."

"Where's that?"

"North Carolina. I have to report for duty in sixty days, so we've got to speed up those wedding plans, baby." The phone was silent. "Baby? Hattie Mae, are you there?"

"I'm here, Eddie."

"Did you hear what I said?"

"Yeah, I heard you. We movin' to North Carolina."

* * *

Mama felt like the bottom of her world had fallen out. She knew that as a military wife, sooner or later, she would have to move wherever Eddie was assigned. But she had hoped it would be later, rather than sooner, if only to give them a chance to settle into their new life as man, wife, and family first. Everything had changed in a two-minute telephone conversation.

Mama had a lot to think about. Katie wasn't very expressive about her feelings, but she did seem to blossom when Eddie was around. My feelings, on the other hand, oozed out of me like hot lava from Mt. Etna. It was no secret that I wanted Eddie in our family. I couldn't have loved him more if it was his DNA running through my veins. Mama loved him, too, and she couldn't deny that she had fantasized about becoming Mrs. Edward Malone at least a thousand different times. She also couldn't deny, however, that in her world, men were unreliable. She had been disappointed more times than she cared to remember and she had no intention of getting her little girls—especially me, the already fragile one—excited about a man who might be here today and gone tomorrow. No matter how wonderful a man might appear to be, she believed that you just couldn't count on love lasting until the end of time. Hell, it might not even last until the end of the week, depending on the particular man in question.

In Mama's estimate, she had more than sufficient evidence to justify total lack of faith in the phenomenon known as the American male. She couldn't just pack up our lives and go traipsing off into the unknown on something as tentative as love and marriage. What if in a week or a month or even a year, Eddie changed his mind? What if he decided at some point that a wife and instant family were too much for him to handle after all? The three of us would be all alone in a place where we wouldn't know a soul except the man who changed his mind. What would we do then?

I had already been torn apart by one daddy gone. Mama wasn't sure if I could survive losing another one. After much soul-searching, she decided that the risk was just too great. She didn't have one heart to protect. She had three. It was over. She looked down at the small diamond on her finger. As much as she loved Eddie, she had to tell him she could not marry him. All things considered, that was going to be the easy part. Consumed by emotion, Mama began to twirl the ring on her finger… already mourning the loss of a life she never had.

* * *

"Baby, I don't understand this. I love you. The only problem there could be is if you don't love me. Is that it?" Eddie was sitting on our sofa with his hands clasped together and his elbows resting on his knees.

"Don't be ridiculous, Eddie. You know I love you. I've loved you since the day I met you."

"And you know I love Katie and Chelsey, too, don't you?"

"Yeah, I know that too, but this ain't 'bout love, Eddie. It's 'bout doin' what's best for me an' my girls. Ft. Bragg is your destiny, not ours." Mama paused before making a final plea. "You know, baby, you could jes' get out of the army an' then we wouldn't have to go nowhere. You can get a job right here in Wade an' we can all be together jes' like we planned."

"Do you know what you're asking me to do, Hattie Mae?" Eddie didn't wait for an answer. "You're asking me to give up everything I've worked for all these years because you're too scared to trust me and believe that I'll always take care of you and those two little girls." Eddie stood up and headed for the front door. "You can give up on your dreams if you want to, Hattie Mae. But don't ask me to give up on mine."

"I cain't help bein' scared, Eddie," Mama said, with tears in her eyes. "I cain't help it."

"Stop living in the past, Hattie Mae. You're not the only one who's scared. I've been hurt, too, but I've never allowed the past to keep me from loving you with my whole heart. And even though that very same heart is breaking right now because I know I'll always love you, I'm going to be okay. Do you know why?" Mama looked at him with all the love she had, but said nothing. Even if she could have found the strength to speak, she wouldn't have known what to say. The emotion in Eddie's eyes was visible, but his voice remained strong and firm. "I'm going to be okay," he said, "because I still believe in the power of *real* love and I won't let you, or anyone else, take that away from me. If my heart has to be broken a million more times, then that's just what it'll be. It's a risk I'm willing to take because, someday, real love is exactly what I'm going to have. I thought I had it with you, but I guess I was wrong."

"You do have that with me, Eddie. Lovin' you is all I've evah done."

"Well, Hattie Mae, loving someone—*really* loving someone—means that if you ever find yourself at the very edge of a cliff and you look down and see nothing below but danger and destruction, you believe one of two things will happen. Either you believe you'll fall to your death if you take one more step—or you believe that if you take that step, you'll be taught to fly." Eddie opened the front door. "Tell the girls I love them and that I'm sorry I couldn't say goodbye." He stepped out onto the porch, then turned back to my mother and said, "I believe I can fly, Hattie Mae. Call me when you believe you can, too. That's when you'll know you love me with *your* whole heart." In the very next instant, he was gone.

The weight of Mama's body fell against the door. "I can't fly, Eddie," she said out loud, "but I'll always love you—with my whole heart."

* * *

I never understood how I could go to sleep one night on the verge of having a daddy of my own, yet wake up the next morning without one. *We had diff'rent long-range plans.* That's all Mama had said about it. As usual, I interrogated myself endlessly trying to figure out what had made Eddie leave. Did he not love us like he always said he did? Had Mama done something wrong? Or Katie? Or worse yet, was it me? I asked myself those questions repeatedly, but they always led to the same dead end.

Just like Lester, Eddie was gone. I wondered how fathers—even substitute ones—could just disappear when kids who were depending on them were sound asleep. Wasn't there someone, *anyone*, who could tell them what their betrayal does to the kids they leave behind? The handwriting was finally on the wall—it just wasn't safe for a little girl to let her guard down. Not even for a few hours of much needed sleep. If I had been awake, I would have been able to convince Eddie to stay. I'm not quite sure how I would have done it, but I know I would have. In fact, I would have promised anything. Not almost anything. *Anything.* Up to and including selling my soul to the devil. God would have understood why I did it. He would have known just how important it was...and that I really had no other choice.

CHAPTER 11

Life can be a real bitch whether you expect it to be or not. The first two men I had dared to love had left me high and dry before I was thirteen. No explanation. Just gone without a trace. If that's not messed up, I don't know what is. I grew to despise feelings because the ones I had were suffocating, at best.

Significant life events came and went for me. Menstruation at thirteen. High school at fourteen. Loss of virginity at fifteen. Cheerleader at sixteen. Junior class secretary at seventeen. Graduation at eighteen. But no matter how many wonderful experiences I had, nothing lifted my depression or my self-esteem. Camouflaging anguish remained my specialty. In expert fashion, I had learned to cope with perpetual sadness interspersed with momentary joy. I knew of no other way to exist.

As I grew older and more resentful, Mama and I became like vinegar and oil—we just didn't mix. I despised her unplanned pregnancies, the string of men who mistreated her, her refusal to face legitimate questions about the past, her unwarranted and very public displays of anger, and her complete disinterest in the cleanliness of the place we called home. Along that same vein, Mama detested my state of never-ending irritability at home, my fake persona in public, my refusal to let go of the past, my hatred for anyone she dated, my lack of appreciation for her hard work, and my ridiculous obsession with cleanliness. Fighting became a daily ritual for us.

"Mama, can I use the car to go over to Heather's house for a cheerleader meeting? I should be back around six-thirty."

"How come your uppity lil' cheerleader friends cain't meet over here, sometimes? You shame of me an' your sister or somethin'?"

"Please don't start with me, Mama. The only thing I'm ashamed of is this house. I never know if it's still going to be clean when I get home from school, so I never offer to have meetings here."

"Oh, so my house ain't clean enough for you an' your fake-ass friends, huh?"

"No, it's not clean enough, Mama!" I said, with the usual irritation. "Is it asking too much for you to take your shoes to your room instead of letting them pile up at the front door? It looks like a shoe sale in the living room every day, for Christ's sake!"

"If you so concerned 'bout my shoes, move 'em your damn self! I work too hard to haf'ta worry 'bout where I can take my shoes off in my own damn house!" We were both yelling, but we were so used to it, we didn't even notice. "I don't want your prissy friends meetin' at my house, anyways. You treat them better than you treat me."

"Maybe that's because they treat me better than you do, Mama."

"Well, I'm sorry if you ain't got the life you wanted, Chelsey George!" Mama screamed, through angry tears. "I do the best I can with no help from anybody an' you don't 'preciate none of it!"

I hated the guilt my mother regularly placed on me but I had long stopped being moved by her tears and her *I-do-the-best-I-can* speeches. The truth of it all was that I was extremely grateful for her strength, perseverance, and the never-ending sacrifices she made for me and Katie. Working two and, oftentimes, three jobs at a time to make ends meet. Giving me and Katie excessive presents on birthdays and at Christmas. Buying extra shoes for us when she didn't even have a decent winter coat. Making sure we had sufficient school supplies. Somehow finding the time to attend almost all of our parent/teacher meetings at school. Borrowing money to meet deadlines to pay for cheerleader uniforms and band instruments. Taking us to *Six Flags Over Georgia* at least once every summer. I appreciated all of those things but the depth of my own inner turmoil refused to allow me to express even the simplest of gratitude to her. Whenever she started crying, feeling sorry for herself, and pouring on the guilt, I lashed back. "Well, you know what, Mama? You brought this on yourself! I didn't ask to be born and I wish I never was!" Then, I was gone. I was already late for my cheerleader meeting.

I hated the way my mother treated me. More than that, I hated the way I treated her. But I didn't know how to stop the vicious cycle. All I knew was that I had to stop crying before I rang Heather's doorbell.

CHAPTER 12

The perpetual friction between me, the wounded child, and my mother, the wounded adult, continued until the summer after I graduated from high school and left Wade, Georgia to attend the University of Oklahoma, some 700 miles away. I was a first generation college student and it was all because of my mother. She had so firmly planted in my mind that college was not so much a road I could *choose* to travel, as the road I *had* to travel, that I now had a full, four-year scholarship to one of the most revered colleges in the country.

The University of Oklahoma was no joke. It was huge. Like a city within a city. I was convinced that the main administration building was at least five times larger than any of the buildings in downtown Wade. I was even more convinced that Jensen Hall, my home away from home for the next four years not counting summers, could accommodate three or four large family reunions at the same time. Like all the buildings on campus, Jensen Hall was named for some unknown white guy who had given a zillion or so dollars to the university in exchange for display of his name and likeness in as much prominence as his money could buy. A grandiose picture of Mr.

Harry Alexander Whitfield Jensen was conveniently placed in the main lobby where grateful students could dutifully pay homage without disrupting their day too much. Smaller 20X24 portraits of the dead man were placed in the dormitory's dining hall, recreation area, and miniature lobby on each of its nineteen floors. When I opened the door to my dorm room, I fully expected to find an 8X10 picture of Jensen on my desk or at least a few wallet-sized photos I could carry in my purse or give to close friends. To my surprise, all I found was an information packet, a generic welcome letter signed by the president of the university, and a personalized welcome letter signed by both the dorm director and resident assistant for my floor. I decided to learn the names of all those important white people some other time. Right now, I had more pressing matters to attend to, like unpacking my belongings and claiming the best twin bed before my roommate arrived.

Just as I was putting my last pair of socks in the chest of drawers situated nearest to the bed I had chosen, the door opened. Not counting the housekeeper I spoke to in the hallway, it was the first black face I had seen since I said goodbye to Mama and Katie at the bus station back home. Seeing my new roommate, my mind said, *I love this university!* The friendly smile I had learned to instinctively paste on my face for non-family members was real this time, and it was met with an even friendlier one from the girl who entered the room. It was obvious that both of us were thrilled to see the hue of the other.

"Hi, I'm your roommate, Chelsey George. Need some help with your bags?"

"No, but thanks anyway," she said, as she put a small brown, leather suitcase and matching overnight bag on the floor. "My dad's bringing the rest of my things up in a minute." Suddenly realizing she had not yet introduced herself, she extended a petite hand. "I'm sorry, Chelsey! Where're my manners? My name's Nicole Mitchell, but everybody calls me Nicki. Pleased to meet you."

"Same here," I said, as we shook hands.

Entering the room seconds later were Nicki's father, carrying a nineteen-inch color television set, followed by her mother carrying a large suitcase that matched the two pieces of luggage that were already in the room, followed by a set of four-year-old, identically dressed, identical twin boys, carrying a toy truck a piece. Her father found a place for the television on top of the chest of drawers nearest to the bed that had clearly not been claimed already, while her mother simply put her suitcase on the floor right where she stood.

"Chelsey, these are my parents, Mr. and Mrs. Mitchell." Pointing to me, she said, "Mom, Dad, this is my roommate, Chelsey George."

"Pleased to meet you," both parents said together, as though they were one person in two bodies.

"Same here. And who are those little cuties?" I said, looking at the twins who were busily exploring every inch of the room with toy trucks clinched tightly in their fists.

"Oh, those are just my annoying little brothers, Joshua and Jonathan. Come here, boys," Nicki lovingly commanded of the twins, who clearly didn't annoy her in the least. Instantaneously, they stopped looking in drawers and under beds and ran to their adoring big sister.

"This is Joshua and this is Jonathan," Nicki said, pointing first to the twin holding on to her right leg, then to the one holding on to the left.

"Oh, my! How in the world will I ever be able to tell you apart?" I said, as I stooped down to meet their bubbling, brown eyes.

"I'm the oldest and the tallest," Jonathan said, with absolute authority.

Given that the order of their birth wasn't tattooed on their foreheads and Jonathan's taller-ness could not be seen with the naked eye, I simply smiled and continued to wonder how I would be able to tell them apart. "Oh, yes. *Now*, I can see the difference," I fibbed, as I stood up, took a few steps backward, and eyeballed the twins up and down while holding my chin with my thumb and index finger.

While the boys returned to exploring, Nicki investigated the closet space and Mr. Mitchell checked the locks on the door and windows to make sure they were in good working condition. Mrs. Mitchell completed the motherly tasks of making sure the mattress was comfortable enough and there was sufficient lighting in the connecting bath that her daughter and I would share with the two girls who would reside in the room next door. I found myself staring at the activity of all the Mitchells. *So, this is what a real family is like.* My thoughts were interrupted when the twin I guessed was Jonathan rolled a tiny dump truck across my foot. I playfully scooped him up in my arms, proclaiming, "Hey, Jonathan, that'll be five dollars for running over my foot!"

"I'm Joshua," he giggled, as I tossed him in the air.

Immediately noticing he was missing out on some fun, the real Jonathan commenced running over my foot with his tiny truck, yelling, "Me, next! Me, next! I ran over your foot, too!"

I played with the energetic twins until Mr. Mitchell finally announced, "It's time to go, boys." Each departing Mitchell exchanged hugs and *I love you's* with the one they were leaving behind, waved goodbye to me, and disappeared as quickly as they had appeared.

"You've got a really nice family, Nicki," I said, as she closed the door behind them.

"Thanks. I think so, too. I'm going to miss them so much—especially those two little munchkins."

"I bet you are. They just couldn't be more adorable." Changing the subject, I said, "Hey, wanna go down to dinner together?"

"Sure. Do you think the food's any good?"

"I doubt it. But we've got to eat it sooner or later."

* * *

Over dinner, I learned that Nicki was eighteen years old. Her father, a cardiologist, and her mother, a pediatrician, met, fell hopelessly in love, and married while in their second year of residency at Johns Hopkins. Unable to get pregnant after eight years of marriage, they adopted Nicki and moved to Tulsa when she was just eleven months old. Twelve years, nine months later, the twins were an unexpected surprise to her parents, who were a stone's throw away from fifty. Their big sister proudly christened them *Joshua Nicholas Mitchell* and *Jonathan Nicholas Mitchell.*

Nicki was a social work major with hopes of obtaining a master's degree. Like me, she had received full scholarships to several major universities. Unlike me, however, she had chosen the University of Oklahoma because she *wanted* to be close to home and family. While we originally thought we had been paired together simply because we were both black, we soon discovered that our responses on the freshman questionnaires we had completed along with the rest of the orientation paperwork were remarkably similar. We were both honors graduates who had participated in multiple extracurricular activities in high school. We both planned to pursue master's degrees and careers in social work. We both loved to read novels, write poetry, and listen to all types of music ranging from gospel to soul to rock and roll. And, although we both could appreciate a good, side-splitting comedy, our all-time favorite movie was *Imitation of Life,* especially the part where Mahalia Jackson sang at the funeral and Sara Jane ran through the crowd to hug the horse-drawn carriage that carried her mother's casket. As we talked and ate cheeseburgers and French fries under the watchful eye of Mr. Jensen, we knew we would be friends for life.

CHAPTER 13

Neither Nicki nor I had ever lived away from home and we relished the newly acquired freedom to live our lives exactly as eighteen-year-old girls deemed appropriate. Although we were conscientious about keeping up with our studies, we weren't bookworms by any stretch of the imagination. Between the two of us, we made more than enough time for fun.

Nicki seemed to fall in and out of love with a different *he's-so-perfect-I-love-him-so-much* boy every semester. Now that I think about it, I really can't remember a time when she *didn't* have some semblance of a boyfriend around. The problem was that she bored easily. When she decided a boy's time was up, she wrote a *Dear John* letter to him or simply stopped taking his phone calls. One way or the other, he eventually got the message. For the time she loved him, though, she loved him infinitely, doting on him as much as a first-time mother dotes on a new baby. Although one was understandably hurt and confused, none of them complained when the roller coaster ride ended sooner than they had anticipated because Nicki had made the adventure so exciting along the way.

As for me, I trusted no one whose penis happened to be attached. As far as I was concerned, a boyfriend was a direct route to drama and I wouldn't travel down that road unless all the others roads were closed for repair and I couldn't get a flight out. Generally, I found it much more to my liking to date boys who were unattainable by virtue of their girlfriends. On those extremely rare occasions when I did decide to date in a more socially acceptable manner, my *modus operandi* was the same: meet him, let him take me out a few times, sleep with him if he wasn't too stupid or too irritating, wait for him to mess up, and leave when he eventually did. And if he didn't mess up, leave anyway. Life was too short to sit around and wait for the inevitable. The entire process usually took about two months. Perhaps a couple of weeks longer if the penis-holder was brighter than, nicer than, cuter than, or more sensitive than expected.

Early in our freshman year, Nicki and I began hanging out with her cousin, Shelby, Shelby's roommate, Krista, and another one of Shelby's friends, Deidra. Shelby Vincent was a junior, majoring in business management. She was Nicki's twenty-one year old cousin by marriage. Nicki's Uncle George on her mother's side had made Shelby's mother, Ernestine, his third wife when Shelby was only two-years-old. Although he loved Shelby as much as any stepfather could and proved so by adopting her, George Vincent wanted a child whose genetic makeup matched his own. Consequently, a year later, Shelby's little brother, James, was born. Ten years later, when Shelby was an awkward 13-year-old with braces on her teeth and Coke-bottle glasses, and James was a 10-year-old Nintendo junkie, their home had turned into a house and her loving parents had turned into bitter enemies. Shelby was actually quite happy when they decided to divorce because their arguments had become endless and they had long since stopped trying to lower their voices so their children couldn't hear. Even when they weren't at war with one another, the tension was generally so thick in the house that a chainsaw couldn't cut through it. The love they once openly displayed seemed to have been sucked from them like lemonade through a straw on a hot summer day. Her parents were miserable and everyone was paying for it.

When her parents gathered Shelby and James together to announce that they were ending their marriage, void of expression, Shelby said, "It's about time," then left the room. Unprepared for her immediate approval, her parents were dumbfounded as they watched her walk away. They had expected her to become overly emotional or beg them to try to work things out or at least ask what went wrong. Their eyes literally glazed over when James followed his sister's lead and made his own telling exit. Shelby's reaction and James' instant replay were the jolts they needed to make them realize they had hurt more than each other. That night, Shelby's parents grew up. Their children had made them realize that though they no longer loved each other, they would always love them.

The adjustment to joint custody was difficult at first. Shelby never seemed to know which week she and James would be with her stepfather and his new girlfriend, and which week they would be with her mother and her new boyfriend. No matter where they were, inevitably, the blouse she wanted or the specific pair of jeans she just had to have or she would die, were at the other parent's house.

James adapted much more easily because at ten, he wasn't bogged down with the backlash inherent in making not-so-cool fashion choices.

By the time Shelby entered Roosevelt High School, straight teeth had replaced crooked ones and contact lenses had replaced Coke-bottle glasses. Even so, she was disappointed that the development of her breasts seemed to be on strike while the development of her buttocks had surprised normal growth expectations. Had she known when school began that in a matter of weeks, her black girl's bottom would become the envy of all girls and the reason most of the boys even came to school at all, she wouldn't have despised it so much. When word got back to her that boys, even juniors and seniors, used her derriere as the standard of perfection, Shelby laughed out loud. *"Man, So-And-So sho' is fine! She got a Shelby bootie!"* the boys were heard to say. In later years, Shelby would find herself utterly disgusted that her worth as a female seemed to be in direct proportion to the circumference of her rear end, but at fourteen, it was, in her mind, one of the best things Mother Nature had ever done for her.

Perfect butt aside, Shelby garnered recognition in a number of more meaningful ways during high school. She was captain of the debate team, president of the National Honor Society, and vice-president of *Mu Alpha Theta*, the national math club. Her outgoing personality made her a favorite with her peers and her intellectual prowess made her a favorite with teachers. It came as no surprise that she was voted Ms. Roosevelt High in her senior year and was co-valedictorian of her graduating class of five-hundred, eighty-six students. When the University of Oklahoma offered her a four-year scholarship, the picture was complete. Life had given her lemons—but she had made lemonade.

* * *

Krista Harrison was Shelby's roommate. They had met in a statistics class in the spring semester of their freshman year and developed an instant attachment to one another. Finding out that they shared the same birthday, they decided that in their sophomore year they would share the same apartment as well. It wasn't quite that simple, of course, but that's the way they liked to tell the story.

Below the neck, Krista was nothing particularly special. She was average in every way possible. Average breasts. Average hips. Average butt. Above the neck, however, she was an undeniable knockout. Penetrating eyes, supple cheekbones, a button nose, and positively perfect teeth. Next to her flawless face, her hair was her most outstanding attribute. It was long, luxurious, and silky, kind of like custom-made drapes. Black people regularly fawned over her *good hair*, but their comments made her feel more nauseous than anything else. She despised black self-hatred and sometimes secretly wished her mother had not been white so she would have had a better chance of having normal hair.

Krista was an only child, making it that much easier for her to become a *daddy's girl*. Her father loved her with the might of a hundred fathers and she knew it. They played together, read books together, watched television together, and did her homework together. Krista loved all the times she shared with her father, but the times she cherished most were their father-daughter talks. Since she could remember, he had made time in his busy life to talk to her and listen to her and offer advice only a father could. He taught her about life and love and God and the importance of beauty that comes from within. Best of all, he never treated her like a child, even though that's what she was. Her father was her hero and she placed him on a pedestal even higher than the one on which he had so carefully placed her. Krista had no idea that he would become the standard by which she would judge all men as she grew into a young woman.

There wasn't a person walking the earth who could deny that Krista had all six feet, five inches of her father wrapped around her little pinky finger. If her mind could fathom it, her father made it happen. Her mother regularly scolded him for spoiling her, but her father always had his patented reply ready. *Boys can take care of themselves,* he would say, *but little girls, well, little girls need their daddies.* Krista knew that regardless of what happened at school or on the playground that day, when her daddy got home from work, no matter what time it was, everything would be okay. It always was—until that heartless day in January when he didn't come home at all.

The day had begun as countless others had before. Her mother had made a hot breakfast of pan sausage and waffles which Krista and her father almost inhaled. No matter how lavish or how simple, mealtimes were always special at the Harrison home because those were the times when the family was in the same place, at the same time, sharing the same love. As Mr. Harrison popped his last bite of waffle into his mouth, he asked, "Hey sunshine, you want daddy to drop you off at school today?" Krista's eyes lit up. She didn't mind riding the bus across town to school because she was always with her friends, but nothing could make her turn down a ride in her father's squad car. Plus, it gave her twenty-two extra minutes to be with him and ask questions she hadn't thought of yet.

Krista ran to her room for her backpack and coat, returning just as her father was kissing her homemaker mother goodbye. "Bye, Mom," she said, tugging at her father's coat. "Come on, Daddy, I can't be late for school."

"Well, don't I at least get a goodbye hug, little girl?" her mother said, leaning forward to have her request granted.

"Mo-om," Krista sang in two syllables, all the while throwing her arms around her mother's neck.

"I love you."

"I love you, too, Mom. Now, we've really got to hurry. Come on, Dad, let's go." Mr. Harrison gave his wife one last peck on the cheek, told her he loved her, and promised to be home in time for dinner.

As they pulled out of the driveway, Krista said, "I'm gonna get in trouble if I'm late to school, Daddy. Can you turn on the sirens so we won't have to stop for any lights?" She knew she wouldn't be late for school if they had to stop for all the lights twice, but it was a whole lot more exciting to ride in a police car with the sirens blaring.

"Little girl, you know you're not going to be late for school. Besides, how much trouble can a fifth grader get into for being ten minutes *early?* You're just spoiled rotten, aren't you?" As he turned the knob to activate the sirens, both father and daughter laughed, partly because

Mr. Harrison had caught his daughter trying to be slick, but mostly because both of them knew it was his fault that she was spoiled rotten in the first place. When the car pulled up in front of the school, Krista hopped out, ran around to the driver's side where her father had already let the window down, and leaned in to kiss him goodbye. "I love you, honey," he yelled, as she hurried into the building. "And don't forget to catch the bus home."

"I love you, too, Daddy," she yelled back. "I won't forget." He didn't even think about driving off because when his little girl got to the entrance, she turned back and waved goodbye, just like he knew she would.

Krista came home from school that day to find her mother washing a head of iceberg lettuce and several cherry tomatoes in preparation for dinner. She could smell lasagna baking in the oven. "How was school, today?" her mother asked.

"It was okay," Krista replied. "Can I help you with dinner, Mom?"

Her mother laughed. "I can see right through you, Krista Lynn Harrison. You don't want to help me with dinner nearly as much as you want to put off doing your homework, now do you?"

Krista laughed with her mother then grabbed an apple from the fruit bowl on the countertop and headed for her room. She did have a lot of math problems to do and if she finished them before dinner, she would have more time to hang out with her father afterwards. She was fervently working on the last problem when she heard the doorbell ring. Several minutes later, she heard her mother scream, "Oh my God! No! No!"

Krista rushed into the living room to find her mother drowning in a pool of tears. Two uniformed policemen were supporting her small frame on both sides. Krista recognized one of the policemen as Daniel Drake, her father's partner of four years. Though she was only ten years old, she knew the worst had come to pass. Her parents had talked to her many times about the dangers inherent in police work, but never in a million years did she think anything would really happen. Not to *her* daddy.

Four days later, wearing her father's favorite dress, Krista attended his funeral. She sat quietly listening as one by one, her father's commanding officers, partner, and fellow police men and women praised him, not only citing his multiple commendations, but also recognizing his contributions to his family, his church, and his community. At the cemetery, her father received a twenty-one gun salute and the chief of police presented her mother with the perfectly folded United States flag that only minutes before had draped her father's casket.

The months following her father's death were a blur. Her mother felt it would be better to be safe than sorry, so she decided to find a job before the insurance money had a chance to run out. The insurance policies her father had purchased and the income from his police pension were substantial, but so were the financial responsibilities the family had accumulated over the years. Krista's mother quickly found a job doing clerical work at Riley Construction Company. It was there that she met Lance Riley, owner and operator of the small company.

Lance was the complete antithesis of Krista's father. He was short, chunky, Catholic, and white. Krista was more than a little annoyed when he started calling her mother at times that couldn't possibly be work-related, but she was downright angry when her mother responded favorably to his advances. Regardless of the fact that the dirt covering her father's grave had barely had time to harden, she had always thought her mother preferred black men. Although she didn't necessarily have any evidence one way or the other, she just thought that's the way it was.

Feeling lonely, afraid, broke, and broken, Krista's mother married Lance Riley eleven months after she began working for him. While he seemed to be in love with her mother, Lance only tolerated Krista. He knew mother and daughter were a package deal, but it didn't keep him from seeing his white wife's black daughter as an unfortunate nuisance, at best. He quickly decided he had to take the good with the bad and simply hope Krista graduated from high school early.

Krista's mother had become so depressed that she never noticed her new husband's thinly veiled attempts to hide his true feelings about his stepdaughter. Krista, on the other hand, knew exactly what father-love actually felt like, so she immediately recognized the cruelty of his contempt. By the time she was thirteen, Lance no longer tried to conceal his disgust, at least not from Krista. For some inexplicable reason, he kept up the charade in front of her mother, though he didn't really need to because she had long since been lost in the depths of the private hell that losing your one true love can catapult you into if you're not careful.

Being in her stepfather's presence felt more than creepy to Krista so she avoided him like the plague. If he was watching television in the living room, she moved to the family room. If he came into the kitchen while she was having a snack, she hurriedly gobbled down the remaining food, cleaned up her mess, and made a quick exit. She didn't like the way he talked to her or treated her and she especially didn't like the way he looked at her, as though he loved her and hated her at the same time. She habitually wished he would disappear. Or that she could.

When Krista was fifteen, she caught Lance massaging his crotch while peering at her naked body through a bathroom door she was certain she had closed before she stepped into the shower. When she saw his image through the mirror, she gasped and covered herself with herself. Embarrassed less by what he had done than by the fact that he had gotten caught, Lance quickly scurried down the hallway like a rat who had just narrowly escaped the clutches of a trap. When he was gone, Krista rushed to the door, pushed it shut, and locked herself inside. She felt as though she couldn't breathe, like she might actually suffocate right then and there. She felt violated. Used. Humiliated. All by the man who took in her and her mother just before the mortgage company was about to begin foreclosure proceedings on the dream home her parents had bought the year before.

Krista turned on the water in the shower as high as it would go then stepped back in to cleanse herself of her stepfather's presence. Lost in her anguish, she didn't notice that much of the moisture running down her skin was coming from her own eyes. She missed her father every minute of every hour of every day. Standing in the steamy hot water, Krista realized her father had been right—little girls do need their daddies.

* * *

Rounding out our college posse was Deidra Delaney. Deidra, a native Oklahoman, was twenty-one years old on her last birthday. She was a third generation black yuppie whose ancestors were as influential as they were wealthy. A coffee-with-cream complexion, elbow-length hair, and a sparkling smile made life's necessary burdens easier for Deidra to bear. Describing her as merely *beautiful* wouldn't do her justice, unless of course, justice really is blind. Truth be told, she looked like she had been airbrushed. If a physical imperfection just had to be pointed out, it would have to be that Deidra was a mere five feet, three inches tall if she had on her highest pair of pumps. Nevertheless, everyone who knew her agreed that what she lacked in stature, she more than made up for in energy, exuberance, and mystique.

Family lineage and physical characteristics aside, Deidra was one of a kind. She was a delicately balanced concoction of snobbish prude, hopeless romantic, and number one ho' (not the garden tool variety). Generally, she had no difficulty managing her various personalities in a mutually exclusive, highly manipulative, unbelievably masterful manner. Nicki, Shelby, Krista, and I routinely mocked the personalities we affectionately called *Ms. Thing, Love-Child,* and *DeeDee.*

The prude—*Ms. Thing*—was more beautiful than Lena Horne and Dorothy Dandridge all rolled into one and every guy on campus (and a few questionable girls) would have testified under oath that *fine* was her middle name. She wore the latest fashions by the hottest designers and when she cruised the campus in her candy apple red sports car with the custom paint job, all eyes were on her, just the way she liked it.

Ms. Thing always got invited to the best parties, on and off campus—and she always took her girls with her. That was the *up* side. The *down* side was that Ms. Thing was as complicated as they come. If she deemed you sufficient, she would welcome you into the fold like a greeter at church on Sunday morning. But if she decided you were a nothing, you were unceremoniously dismissed without reconsideration. The challenge was trying to figure out what made someone a *something* and what made him or her a *nothing*. There seemed to be no hard and fast rule as to who Ms. Thing embraced and who she exiled because she had just as many poor friends as wealthy ones, partied with just as many average-looking girls as beautiful ones, and hung out with just as many dark-skinned sisters as light ones. A little method to her madness would have been welcomed, but then again, that would have made her somebody else altogether, so generally everybody just accepted what they got.

One particularly entertaining quality about Ms. Thing was watching otherwise intelligent, *got it goin' on* brothers turn into bumbling idiots if she so much as smiled in their general direction. She didn't even have to be smiling at *them* for their imagination to go into overdrive. Irrespective of her being hoity-toity and self-absorbed, they all wanted to be one of *the chosen*. Unarguably, she was the one girl each of them wanted to take to bed, take home to meet his mother, and take to the hospital to bear his children, preferably in that order. Her assumed ignorance—albeit *incorrectly* assumed—added to her appeal.

Sisters who preferred more substance to their men appreciated Ms. Thing's ability to attract shallow brothers because she unknowingly helped them to weed out the riff-raff. Any man who didn't know his own name when in the presence of Ms. Thing was officially stamped *undesirable* by discerning sisters. Unfortunately, that didn't leave a whole lot of brothers from which to choose, so more often than not, those same *discerning* sisters would give a brother a second, third, or even fourth chance to act right before giving up on him completely.

Love-Child was Deidra's hopelessly romantic persona. More than food and water, Love-Child *had* to have love in her life and would travel to the far corners of the earth to find it. She was happiest when she was in love and most pathetic when she wasn't. But merely being in love was insufficient. As passionately as she loved her man, she had to be loved back—tenfold. Any man involved with Love-Child had to want, need, and desire her in ways few men could learn how to do in less than one lifetime. Like so many sisters looking for a man who would love them like their daddy's wouldn't or couldn't, Love-Child needed a man to complete her. She never even toyed with the notion that everything she needed to complete herself was inside herself.

Dysfunctional wouldn't come close to describing the nature of Love-Child's short-lived relationships. But just like all codependents, she had a heart of gold. There was no friend she wouldn't help, no stranger she would turn away, and no problem she wouldn't try to fix. Helping others seemed to be her calling and she accepted the call proudly, taking it very seriously. Occasionally, her trusting nature led others to take advantage of her dysfunction, but she never stopped giving and never disparaged those who did the taking. Because of her warm, gentle spirit, Love-Child received just as much attention as Ms. Thing, just not for as long. Without question, dating her was no easy job and more often than not, the position was vacant.

DeeDee represented the ho' in Deidra's personality. Normally, a girl's internal ho' remains dormant, coming out only behind closed doors with the man she loves or when she's in the company of her closest girlfriends. It might sound crass, but the reality was that DeeDee loved to fuck. *Making love* wasn't in her vocabulary, but *fucking* was. She rated each of her lovers according to style, technique, stamina, creativity, and size. If a boy fell short in two or more areas, his first liaison with DeeDee was his last liaison with DeeDee. She didn't mind discovering undiscovered talent, but she made it perfectly clear that she was far too busy to teach some amateur how to lay pipe like a professional.

Unlike Love-Child, the amount of value DeeDee found in commitment was less than zero. Committed sex, she said, was destined to be mundane. Kind of like watching a plant grow. For her, another girl's boyfriend was much more appealing than one of her own. In her mind, guys in committed relationships were lazy in bed, but guys in physical relationships were electrifying in bed. Just as she had grown accustomed to running water, DeeDee had grown accustomed to electricity.

Although DeeDee was streetwise to a fault, she was also intellectually brilliant. The combination generally led to her becoming her victims' lover, therapist, confidante, and sometimes, even their mother. Making sure they didn't break up with their girlfriends in hopes of being with her often proved to be a daunting task, as she found it extremely difficult to convince arrogant, self-absorbed boys that they were all of *nothing* that she wanted and the rock she was looking for was not the one they could put on her finger, but the one they could put between her legs. Their sexual and psychological manipulation left them simultaneously feeling screwed and screwed over, as DeeDee faithfully told each one of them that it was the *best sex ever* but she really needed to get home because she had an early morning chemistry exam, even though she was a liberal arts major.

DeeDee felt sorry for girls with boyfriends, especially if she happened to be sleeping with one of them. It wasn't her betrayal that bothered her, though. She had decided long ago that she was simply providing a public service for wayward boys. The thing that actually bothered her was the games the poor girlfriends and their boyfriends felt they had to play with one another. The girlfriends had to pretend they weren't bonafide freaks in the bedroom when most of them really were and the boyfriends had to pretend they didn't want a bonafide freak in the bedroom when most of them really did. Their behavior was ridiculous to DeeDee because she was of the very strong opinion that the only time people should play games is when they absolutely have to.

Although we all openly teased Deidra about her conflicting selves, each of us secretly wished we had an ounce of the secret formula that drew both men and women to her in record numbers. None of us really knew who the real Deidra Delaney was...but we suspected she was somewhere between heaven and heartache.

CHAPTER 14

Like it was our destiny, Nicki and I became fast friends with Shelby, Krista, and all three Deidras. At a bare minimum, we traveled in pairs, so if you saw one of us out in public, chances were there was at least one more somewhere in the vicinity. It was as though we had become life-sized extensions of each other and more often than not, we were routinely referred to as the quadruplets, the triplets, or the twins, regardless of which ones of us happened to be present. Naturally, when all five of us were on an outing, someone inevitably announced, *"There go the quints!"* Through no deliberate effort of our own, we became the latest clique on campus.

The Girls—as we generally referred to ourselves— loved each other like sisters. Though individually quite different, each of us brought something unique and necessary to our friendship. There was no question that all of us were scholars. The University of Oklahoma accepted nothing less than the best, except perhaps, in the cases of Heisman trophy-potential athletes or the near brain dead offspring of wealthy alumni. None of us were athletically inclined and only Deidra's family had enough money to fund a new building or endow a department chair, so we had to count on brains and ambition to gain admission into the prestigious university.

While being intelligent is certainly not a bad thing, there was a whole lot more to our repertoire than mere brain power. I came equipped with spunkiness and dependability. Nicki brought strength and understanding. Shelby was the expert in logic and practicality. Krista epitomized goodness and compassion. And almost instinctively, Deidra brought humor and excitement. All of our parts fit together perfectly to make one complete circle of friends.

By the spring semester, *The Girls* had fallen into a regular routine of meeting at Deidra's apartment every Friday night for hours of nail polishing, beauty makeovers, man bashing, man adoration, and a thousand other things we had yet to think of. Neither Deidra, nor the rest of us objected to her being the permanent hostess of our Friday night pow-wows. It just made good sense, Shelby had pointed out, because Deidra had the largest apartment, the latest music, and a maid that came in every Saturday morning to clean.

Nicki and I were always the first to arrive, partly because we lived closer to Deidre, but mostly because Shelby and Krista—especially Shelby—were perpetually late. We frequently teased Shelby that she was going to be late to her own funeral, to which she would promptly respond, *"Well, if I have to be dead, I should at least get to make an entrance!"* When she heard the banging on the front door, Deidra yelled from the kitchen, "Hey, somebody get the door, would you? I'm taking my cake out of the oven."

Deidra and Shelby loved to cook and every Friday night, they competed to see who could prepare the tastiest treat. No matter whose offering was actually better, each contestant claimed victory for herself, much like presidential candidates do after a televised debate. I opened the door to find Shelby and Krista each holding a grocery bag in one arm and a shoulder purse on the other. "Hello, ladies!" I said cheerfully, as they rushed through the door, exchanging one-armed hugs. "What's in the bags?"

"We're having a healthy snack tonight, my friend," Shelby announced. "Assorted fresh fruit!" She said *assorted fresh fruit* with such over-the-top enthusiasm that it was clear that she had already convinced herself that those were the three most exciting words in the English language.

"Deidra," I yelled into the kitchen, "You win tonight, girl!"

"Forget you, Chelsey George," Shelby said, while all of us made a beeline to the kitchen.

Shelby and Krista set about taking all kinds of fruit out of bags—strawberries, cherries, plums, peaches, kiwi—you name it, they had it. I rolled up my sleeves and began washing the fruit they tossed into the sink, while Nicki opened cabinet doors looking for a serving tray.

"If you're looking for something to put this delicious fruit on, here it is," Shelby said, removing a palatial glass platter from her grocery bag.

"Wow! That's beautiful!" Nicki exclaimed, when she turned around and saw it. "Where'd you get that?"

"Girl, my mother has been putting stuff in a hope chest for me since I started my period. I've got just about everything any good little wife needs to make a house a home." Krista took the tray from Shelby's hands and began decoratively arranging clean fruit on it.

"That prissy little tray won't make your tired fruit taste any better, my sister," Deidra said, as she spread the last of her homemade icing on a chocolate cake made from scratch, just like her nanny had taught her. "In fact, it's going to make my cake taste even better!"

"Nobody's scared of that nasty little cake you made, Ms. Thing," Shelby retorted with a laugh. "Besides, instead of eating that lard, you might as well cut out the middle man and spread the fat right on your thighs!"

"Shelby's got a point, Deidra," Nicki chimed in, as she placed her hands on her hips and strutted down an imaginary catwalk. "If you eat that cake, you won't *be* the finest girl at the party tomorrow night—you'll be *with* the finest girl at the party!" We all laughed heartily as we continued to prepare half-healthy, half-fattening treats. Within half an hour, five sister-friends were sitting on the living room floor munching on fruit and cake, discussing events of the past week and the week to come.

"Think there'll be any new talent at the Omega's party?" Deidra asked, just before biting into a juicy strawberry. "I'm so tired of seeing the same ol' lame ass brothers at those frat parties."

"Ain't that the truth," I confirmed, as I sliced a piece of chocolate cake, placed it on a saucer, and licked the residual icing from my thumb and index finger. "And they're so full of shit, too. I think brothers should be required by law to wear warning labels attached to their foreheads so a girl will know what's *really* up with them."

"You mean warnings like *Proceed With Caution*," Krista's innocence asked, as she drew a box in the air with her fingers, then popped a seedless grape into her mouth.

"Hell no!" I said. "I mean warnings a sister can use, like *Undeniable Nutcase* or *Ain't Worth A Damn*."

Drawing her own boxes in the air, Deidra laughed, then added, "And don't forget about *Born to Lie* and *Three-Minute Man*."

"You're both just plain crazy!" Nicki said, laughing as hard as the rest of us. "But I don't care what you say, there's *one* brother I wouldn't mind seeing at the next hundred frat parties. If I had just one night with him, he wouldn't have to buy dinner or even call me the next day! It would definitely be the easiest piece he ever got because my stuff goes into spasm just looking at his fine behind!"

"Kevin Robeson," the rest of us said together. It was common knowledge how crazy Nicki was about Kevin—the campus jock with the award-winning smile, the bedroom eyes, and the *cheerleader-slash-beauty queen-slash-so friendly she makes you want to puke-slash-white* girlfriend.

"Make fun if you want to, ladies, but that man has satisfied me more nights than he knows. Some mornings, I just want to call him up and say, 'Thanks for last night, baby! Was it good for you, too?'"

Deidra couldn't resist calling her out. "Nicki, you clam up every time you see Kevin, so I'm not even trying to hear you, girl. If you think he's all of that, then act like you're Wonder Woman and go get your Superman. Hell, if I ever find a guy who satisfies me like that, I'm putting him on my income tax return because I *will* be taking care of his ass from that moment forward!"

"What am I supposed to say, 'Excuse me, Kevin, I know you have a girlfriend and all, but do you think it might be possible for you to ditch old girl so we *can, oh, I don't know, uh, go somewhere and do it?'* Is that what I'm supposed to say?"

"That sounds like a perfect opening line to me!" Deidra almost shouted. "At least it's honest. It's as good as the lines the brothers try to lay on us." Deidra nuzzled up to Krista who was nearest to her, looked straight into her eyes, and launched into her interpretation of a male pickup line: "Krista, you are the most exquisite creature I've ever seen and if I die tonight, my living would not have been in vain, for I have been blessed to have had one last chance to gaze upon your remarkable beauty and for that, I will be eternally grateful to our Lord and Savior Jesus Christ."

"Okay, let me translate that bullshit," I interjected. "Hey, baby, you fine as hell wit' yo' pretty self, an' if you let me hit that ass just one time, you won't be sorry 'cause you gon' swear to God that you died an' went to heaven!" Rambunctious laughter could be heard throughout the apartment.

"Now, that brings up another question," Shelby said, as she took a tiny bite from a California peach. Can somebody tell me why every man on the face of the earth thinks he's the world's greatest lover or at least *your* greatest lover?"

Girl, who knows and *Ain't that the truth* and *Go figure* echoed everywhere there was sound. "Now, don't get me wrong," Shelby went on to say. "Derrick rocks my world, but he isn't the *best* I've ever had. I wish he would stop asking me that shit, too."

"Brothers make you lie to them, don't they?" I asked, not really needing an answer, but anticipating confirmation, nonetheless.

"They sure do," Shelby said. "I feel bad enough lusting after those fine ass frat brothers on a regular basis and on top of that, I have to lie to Derrick about his bedroom skills."

"Hell, don't feel bad, girl," Deidra reassured her. "Men have been lying since Adam bit the apple and blamed it on Eve."

"Greg doesn't lie," Krista said, in support of her boyfriend of three years. "He's honest with me about everything."

"Correction, my sister," Deidra replied. "You haven't *caught* Greg in a lie. Men are *born* to lie. I've got a part of ten different lying men, but not one honest man to call my own, and do you know why?" she asked, not waiting for an answer. "Because they all lie."

"Wait just a minute, Deidra," I said. "You wouldn't let my girl slide a minute ago, so you know I can't let you slide on this one. You don't have a man because *you* lie. I'm sorry, but you made me go there!" All the girls—including Deidra—laughed out loud because they knew what story was coming next.

"Tell it, Chelsey!" Nicki and Krista pleaded. "Tell it!"

"Yeah, tell it, girl!" Shelby chimed in. They knew they didn't have to do much prodding since I loved to tell the story as much as they loved hearing it. They also knew that it got longer—and funnier—each time I told it.

All the girls moved in closer, as if they would be able to hear a little bit better if they were three inches nearer to my voice. "Okay," I began, "I go by Deidra's apartment to borrow that blue sweater that looks better on me than it does on her, but her ass is too stingy to let me have it and—"

"Leave my sweater out of this, Chelsey," Deidra playfully interrupted, popping a slice of kiwi into her mouth.

"ANY-way, as I was saying before I was so rudely interrupted, I get there and she's in the middle of getting ready to go to lunch with Eric—the brother DeeDee-the-Ho' just can't stop messing around with. Well, there's a knock on the door and I go over to open it, right? I opened that door, and I swear, the *finest* brother I have *EV-vah* seen is standing there with flowers in his hand and a smile on his face a mile wide—and it *wasn't* Eric!"

"Go, Marcus! Go, Marcus! Go, Marcus!" the girls chanted.

"So, Marcus—the one Love-Child is hopelessly devoted to—is standing there looking all good, but he doesn't have a clue that his ass has popped up at the wrong damned time. Deidra comes bouncing out of the bedroom, expecting to see Eric, of course, and there stands Marcus talking about, 'Hey baby, you look great! Where you going?' Deidra is completely frantic right about then because Eric is already late and could show up any minute, so she says, 'Marcus! Wh-wh-what're you doing in town?' I'm telling you, *Ms. Always Articulate* was sounding like *Rain Man*!"

"I know she was!" Shelby screamed over the laughter of the rest of us.

"So, Marcus says, 'I got off work early so I thought I'd drive an hour down the road and surprise my baby by taking her to lunch. But if you and Chelsey have plans already, I guess I picked a bad time to be romantic, huh?' Y'all, Deidra didn't know *what* to do. I'm telling you, our girl was making it up as she went." Using my best Deidra impersonation, I said, "Lunch? Yes, that's where we were going, isn't it, Chelsey? Now that you're here, baby, you can come with us. Come on, we'd better hurry before the lunch crowd gets there."

"Now, I no more had plans to go to lunch with Deidra than I had of leaving her apartment without that sweater. Hell, I wasn't even hungry! But you know I couldn't leave our girl stuck out like that, so I had no choice but to do the right thing and go along with it. Besides, I knew that after this was over, that damned sweater was mine! So, we all pile into Marcus' front seat and head for *Mama's Kitchen*. We get there, go in, get seated, order, and eat. I don't think we said two words the entire time. All the while, Deidra is looking at her watch every few minutes like she's timing labor contractions. Marcus doesn't notice, but I do and it's funny as hell to me! Somehow, I managed to get through lunch and I was so stuffed I could barely move. Marcus was full, too, and he looked sleepy as hell on top of that. Anyway, Marcus asks, 'Well, are you ladies ready to go?' Just as I'm about to say, 'Yeah, let's get on up outta' here,' Deidra checks her watch again and says, 'Let's have some dessert.' Then she looks straight at me and tells me, 'Chelsey, don't you want some dessert?' Notice I didn't say she *asked* me, although she phrased it in the form of a question like she was on *Jeopardy* or some shit. Needless to say, I didn't want any damned dessert! I

113

was already so full I was about to explode! But you know our girl would have shot me dead right on the spot if I had said I didn't want any, so I pasted a normal look on my face, refused to remind myself that I had already wasted almost two hours of my day, and said, 'Sure, dessert is exactly what I want, Dee.'

"So, we're all sitting there, eating dessert that nobody wants, when right in the middle of a bite, Deidre looks at her watch again and bursts out with, 'Okay, we can go, now!' She has this relieved look on her face that Marcus doesn't notice, but that I see as plain as day. That's when I realized she wanted to stay at *Mama's* just long enough to give Eric a chance to get to her apartment, get tired of waiting for her, then leave. Later, she would make up some kind of lie to tell him about why she wasn't home when she knew he was coming by to take her to lunch and the whole lie would end up with, *'Baby, you know I love you'*. I just knew our girl had gotten herself out of yet another jam and all I could do was wish I had pen and paper so I could take notes on how a pro handles her business!

"Anyway, we leave *Mama's*, pile back into the front seat of Marcus' car, and start the drive back to the apartment when *I'll be damned* if it doesn't start to rain! Since Marcus drives like somebody's great-granddaddy who's blind in one eye and has a cataract in the other, it was the *longest* ride in history. I tell you, I was all but homicidal! After a hundred years, we *finally* get to Deidra's apartment complex and Marcus turns into the parking lot. All of a sudden, Deidra gasps like she just saw O.J. Simpson dating a black woman then she turns to Marcus and blurts out, 'There's a space, baby, park there! I'll run in and get umbrellas for us.' Marcus thinks she's lost her mind, and I do, too, because she was literally turning the steering wheel herself to park the car in *that* particular space—which was a *long* damned way from the front door of her apartment! And on top of that, *she*—the self-proclaimed Queen of Sheba—was going to get out of the car in her designer clothes, hundred dollar sandals, and pouring rain to get umbrellas for *us!*

"So, now the car is parked in a space that's about a mile away for reasons Marcus can't figure out—and me either, for that matter. Anyway, when *he* insists on going to get the umbrellas, Deidra really panics. Our girl turned to me with *nothing* but fear in her eyes and said, 'I'm going to get the umbrellas, Chelsey! You keep him in the car!' Then, she climbs over me, gets out of the car, and before I can blink, she ain't nothing but a memory! By this time, I'd spotted Eric's car, but he was nowhere in sight. So, I'm sitting there with Marcus, hoping he doesn't say a damned thing to me, when he asks, 'Chelsey, what's going on?' I pretended that he was deaf and dumb and asked, 'Didn't you hear her say she was going to get umbrellas for us?' Marcus looked at me like, *'Bitch, you know what I mean'*, but since he's so polite, he let it go. He might not have been deaf, but I'm telling you, he lived right next door to dumb!

"Eventually, about ten minutes I guess, Deidra showed up again. She opened my door, yanked me out of the car like she didn't care if I got wet after all, threw an umbrella at me, got into the car with Marcus, and slammed the door shut. I was getting drenched right about then, but I was cracking up thinking, *Nobody will believe this shit!* Anyway, as I'm walking down the sidewalk to her apartment, who do I pass but Eric—who looks mad as hell, by the way—and he has a wire clothes hanger in his hand, looking and acting like *Daddy Dearest.* Turns out, he had locked his keys in his car and had no choice but to wait for Deidra to get home. When we passed each other, I said hello, but he was so mad that Deidra wasn't home and that his keys were locked in his car and that he was wet as hell and who knows what else, that he doesn't say a mumbling word to me.

"I go into the apartment and fall out laughing! After a few minutes, Eric manages to get his car unlocked and comes back inside. I immediately go into the kitchen and open the refrigerator door like I'm looking for something to eat!"

The girls were laughing so hard they were crying and I was laughing so hard I could barely tell the rest of the story. "Now, since Eric has gotten his keys out of the car, he decides to focus on other things, so he comes into the kitchen and asks me, 'Chelsey, what's going on?' I swear, I thought I was in the freakin' twilight zone with that *déjá vu* bullshit! Anyway, I decided to pretend Eric was stupid, too, since it had worked out so well with Marcus. 'What're you talking about? I'm just looking for something to eat.' Much—and I mean *much*—to my dismay, Eric wasn't as stupid as I needed him to be right then. He said, 'Who's that Deidra's talking to in that blue Cutlass?' He looked at me like I'd better have a damned good answer or he was going to kick *my* ass. 'What Cutlass, Eric?' I asked, like my name was Stevie Wonder and I didn't have the foggiest idea what he was talking about because I couldn't see shit. 'The one your black ass just got out of!' he shouted. 'Don't try to play me for a fool, Chelsey!' I couldn't believe that brother was shouting and cussing at *me*! I started to say, *'Look here, dumb-ass, I'm not the one who's playing you for a fool!'*, but I kind of like a guy with a little thug in him, so I didn't get mad. Hell, I think I was even turned on a little bit!

"So, now, I'm caught between a rock and a hard place and I haven't even done anything wrong! I just told him, 'Eric, that's none of my business. You need to talk to Deidra about that.' I knew I needed to carry my ass home right then, but I went into the living room, propped my feet up on Deidra's expensive-ass coffee table like I'd paid for it my damned self, turned on the television, and watched it like it was the most interesting show I'd ever seen. I think it was even on a Spanish channel, but I didn't care! I wouldn't have left that live soap opera to save my life! It was definitely better than anything I could pretend to watch on TV! And, I didn't give—as my mother would say—*a fat rat's ass* about that damned sweater anymore!

"So, Eric and I are in the house about ten more minutes when Deidra comes in. Eric immediately says, 'Who the hell was that, Deidra?' He was pissed and Deidra knew she had to pull out the big guns. That's when she started crying like a black woman at a funeral! 'Eric, baby, please calm down and let me explain! *Please, baby, please!* That was my ex-boyfriend, Marcus. I told you about him, remember, baby?' I looked at Eric and he actually looked like he was trying to remember that bullshit, so I turned my head back to the TV to keep from laughing out loud at his stupid ass. Then Deidra says, 'Marcus just showed up out of the blue, Eric. He knows I love you, baby, but he's still trying to get back with me. I don't think he really wants me, baby, I think he's just jealous because I'm with you now and you look so good and all. Apparently, he's trying to stir up some trouble between us. He's trying to tear us apart, baby, but I'll be damned if I'm going to let him do that! *I love you, baby!*'

"Y'all, I'm telling you, Eric was looking into Deidra's puppy dog eyes and actually buying her story! Can you believe that shit? Our girl knew she almost had him hooked, so she started to lay it on really thick then. 'Baby, he was crying and everything, so I agreed to go have coffee with him. I even made Chelsey go with us because I didn't want to be alone with him and have him get the wrong idea. I had no intention of taking this long to get back. I'm sorry, baby. *I love you.* That's what I've been out there telling Marcus, baby. I would never do anything to hurt you, don't you know that?' Y'all, Deidra talked to that fool for what felt like three days, then barely pausing, she said, 'Let's go get something to eat, baby. I'm starving.'

"That scene was so unbelievable I couldn't even pretend to watch TV anymore! Eric looked over at me and I was looking at him like, *Damn, you're stupid,* but he must have interpreted my look as, *Yes, Eric, that's exactly what happened. She loves you, man.* Anyway, he looked back at Deidra's pathetic face and the next thing I knew, *he* was apologizing for not trusting *her*! Then they left to go get something to eat! She told me later that she had given Marcus that same old *ex-boyfriend-showed-up-out-of-the-blue* story—and Marcus had bought it, too!"

By this time, all five of us were laughing too hard to stop. "I'm telling you, ladies, our girl is the *master* of deceit! There ain't a man alive who can hold a candle to her when it comes to lying!"

"And you know that's right!" Deidra proudly proclaimed, all of us in complete and utter agreement.

CHAPTER 15

"You win this time, Shelby!" Krista said. "This peach cobbler is all that and a bag of chips!"

"Don't play favorites just because she's your roommate, Krista," Deidra chided lightheartedly. Even though she knew it was the best peach cobbler she had ever tasted, it would have been easier for the sun to rise in the west than to get Deidra to admit defeat in the friendly Friday night cooking challenge.

"I'm not playing favorites, Dee. I'm just calling it like I taste it."

"Yeah, Deidra," Nicki said, as she licked her spoon clean. "You better take a cooking class next semester if you want to keep up with Shelby. My cousin's got it goin' on!"

Turning to me, Deidra asked, "What do *you* think, my beautiful Nubian sister?"

"Flattery will get you everywhere, girl! You know this nasty old cobbler can't hold a candle to your infamous pecan chocolate chip cookies! Just because this is my third helping doesn't mean it's good. Hell, I'm only eating it because I don't want to hurt Shelby's feelings!"

"Thank you, Ms. George!"

"My pleasure, Ms. Delaney!"

"Ugh!" Nicki, Shelby, and Krista said in unison.

The five of us ate peach cobbler and chocolate chip cookies until we thought we would pop. While each of us looked forward to our Friday night get-togethers, Deidra loved them the most. As an only child, she had never experienced the bond of sisterhood. Her parents had been so busy running companies and communities that they barely had time to conceive her, let alone notice her after she had arrived. Deidra had grown into a young woman under the protective eye of Ms. Anna, her round-the-clock nanny since she was six minutes old. Ms. Anna was the first to know when she kissed a boy, the first to know when she lost her virginity, the first to know how lonely she was. Growing up, Deidra had most of her *firsts* with Ms. Anna.

The Friday nights Deidra spent communing with us were constant reminders of the special connection she had with Ms. Anna. Countless hours of sharing and caring and laughing and crying with people who loved her unconditionally comforted her just like her private talks with Ms. Anna used to do. For her, our nights together were healing, almost spiritual, even. They were like the cleansing a long, hot shower brings, only it wasn't her body being cleansed, it was her soul. Except for the times with Ms. Anna, the times with us were the closest Deidra came to being, experiencing, and loving her true self. Her three alter egos might pop in and out during the course of our evening, but it was on those Friday nights when the essence of Deidra showed up—and usually stayed until the party was over.

* * *

"Does anybody know when those Omega pledges are going over?" Deidra asked, while scooping peach cobbler onto her spoon. "That damned pledge line is messing with my quality time with a couple of their big brothers."

"Is that all you think about Deidra?" Shelby asked.

"Is *what* all I think about?"

"Men?"

"Of course not. I also think about what men can do to me and on me and in—"

Shelby cut Deidra off in mid-sentence. "You're just nasty, Dee. One of these days, you're gonna mess around and get some stuff you can't get rid of."

"Don't you think I have enough sense to protect myself, Shelby? Doesn't everybody in this room have sense enough to use rubbers?" Deidra sucked the last bit of cobbler from her spoon. "Well, those of us who *are* getting it, that is."

"Girl," I quickly intervened, "I use rubbers, birth control pills, and *Saran Wrap* all at the same time! My stuff is wrapped so tight a brother has to have a chainsaw just to get a whiff of it!"

While I was giving Deidra a high five, a smiling Nicki looked at Shelby and Krista and said, "Our best friends are hoes, aren't they?"

"Yeah, but only on the outside. You know we could never be friends with anybody who was a ho' through and through!" Shelby said, bursting into laughter.

Krista was unusually quiet, even for her. In a sincere effort to mask what she was really feeling and thinking at that moment, she smiled. She hadn't told any of us the real reason she chose not to have sex. Not even Shelby. Instead, she had told us that she saw her body as a temple and that she wanted to save herself for marriage and that she wanted to be able to give her husband a very special gift on their wedding night and that she knew it would be worth the wait. Greg had understood her request and loved her even more for it. He knew he would be the lucky man to receive that gift some day and assured her he was willing to wait.

Nicki and Shelby found a way to understand Krista's choice, but Deidra had teased her about being frigid or possibly even gay on multiple occasions, and more often than not, in matters of sex, I took Deidra's side. *Maybe I am,* Krista remembered thinking. Even when she and Greg were playing advanced romper room, she wasn't the least bit turned on. She often wondered what all the fuss was about.

Krista snapped back into the present when she heard Nicki say her name. "You hoes are making fun of Krista for choosing *not* to have sex, but you seem to be forgetting an important detail—Krista *has* a man! You two don't have a clue about real relationships or real love. That's why both of you are alone."

"Alone but not lonely, my sister! I've got more men than the law legally allows," Deidra boasted. "They're on me like white on rice."

"I've got a man, too," I said. "He just ain't mine!" Deidra and I exchanged high fives again.

"I give up," Shelby said, throwing her hands in the air.

"Me, too," Nicki added.

Krista sat in silence and within moments, Shelby and Nicki joined her.

"Okay, *damn!*" Deidra said, in an exasperated tone. "Why don't the three of you tell the two of us what's so damned fantastic about love? Come on, help us out here."

"Well, for one thing," Shelby began with the seriousness of a surgeon about to make the first cut, "you two have to understand that love is *not* the same thing as sex."

"It isn't?" I asked, cocking my head to one side and looking at Shelby with a quizzical expression on my face, while at the same time trying not to laugh. Deidra wanted to laugh, too, but she had heard the seriousness in Shelby's voice, so she bit her lower lip, instead.

"No, it *isn't* the same thing," Shelby continued. "Love is so much more than sex, so much better than sex."

"Then you're not having sex with the right people," Deidra couldn't resist saying.

"Since you don't have the slightest idea about what love is, maybe *you're* not having sex with the right people," Shelby lashed back.

"Shelby's right," Krista firmly chimed in, somehow feeling more confident. "Love is much better than sex could ever be." She didn't really know for sure, but that's what she was banking on.

Deidra and I looked at each other as though Krista had two heads and had just begun to sprout a third. "Now what would *you* know about sex, Krista?" Deidra asked. "Your legs are locked so tight it would take a truckload of kryptonite to blast them apart!"

Since Kristi wasn't planning on responding to Deidra's comment, she didn't mind that I spoke, instead. "I don't see why any of this really matters, anyway. I don't want any part of that ridiculous notion called love."

"Me, either," Deidra quickly agreed, not caring that Krista had ignored her question.

"Why not?" Shelby said, challenging both of us. "What's so bad about love?"

"You want to take this one, Deidra, or do you want me to?"

"You take it, girl. I'm way too tired to go there."

"It's really quite simple," I began, as I pushed an empty bowl of peach cobbler to the side. "The price of love is just too high."

"Love is free," Shelby said. "All you have to do is embrace it."

"That's bullshit. Love is like sex—it's never free. One way or another, you end up paying for it."

"Why do you say that?"

"Think about it, Shelby," I continued. "Very few little girls grow up knowing what love really is. Just look at the five of us. Only two of us had our father's love when we were little girls and only one of us still has it now. Life is messed up, especially for women. When we're little girls, our fathers choose not to love us or they don't know how to love us and we pay the price. Then we grow up and our boyfriends don't know how to love us or tell us they would if we would just give 'em some and we pay the price. Then a few more years go by and we get married and our husbands don't love us or tell us they would if we would just be quiet or just lose weight or just look like some unbelievable standard of beauty when they look like hell, and we pay the price. Well, I refuse to keep on paying the price for loving men who won't or can't or don't know how to love me back! My emotional bank account is overdrawn. *Of course* I know love and sex aren't the same thing. But if I had to choose between them, I'd choose sex every time. Love has always hurt me. Sex never has."

"Yeah. That love stuff hurts too much," Deidra said, almost to herself. Her body was still in the room, but her heart was somewhere else, hurting.

"The right kind of love doesn't hurt," Shelby said, compassionately.

"Then I've never had the right kind of love," I said, trying to hold in my woundedness.

Shelby was fully aware of the pain her sister-friends were simultaneously reliving at that very moment. "You'll have it some day, Chelsey. You, too, Deidra. But first, we, as young women, have to learn to love ourselves. If we don't love ourselves, we can't expect anyone else to be able to love us. We've got to stop telling ourselves that we don't deserve to be loved because we're too heavy or too thin or too smart or not smart enough. We've got to stop telling ourselves that we're not worthy of being loved because our fathers weren't there or our mothers weren't there or maybe they were both there, but still didn't teach us how to love and be loved. When we begin to love ourselves, I mean *really* love ourselves, we'll be able to love a man and he'll be able to love us back—the *right* way. We've just got to get our house in order, that's all. We've got to pick up all the broken pieces of ourselves and get our house in order."

"But what if we get our house in order and some man still comes along wanting to tear it down?" I asked, as the tears of my inner child made their way from my heart to my eyes, finally falling down my cheeks onto the brown silk blouse Mama had given to me last Christmas.

"Then that's not a man, Chelsey," Nicki interrupted, not really understanding my pain, but feeling it just the same. "That's a *boy* who needs to get *his* house in order. A real man knows how to love a woman. My father has loved my mother for more than twenty-three years. I'm not going to settle for anything less than what he gives her. None of us should settle for anything less."

"But not everybody had a father like yours or Krista's, Nicki," I said, as tears continued to flow from my eyes like water flows over rocks in a quiet brook. "If you've never seen that kind of love before, you don't know what it looks like. And if you don't know what it looks like, you won't know when you have it and you sure as hell won't know how to embrace it."

"You don't see love with your eyes, Chelsey. When it's really there, you can feel it with your heart." Nicki wrapped her arms around me just as Shelby and Krista enclosed Deidra in a circle of love right next to us. The entire world stood still as five young women shared the pain of the past…and the presence of true sister-love.

CHAPTER 16

The weather in Brighton had turned cold and gloomy as fall had slowly transformed itself into winter in my junior year. If you asked one of the locals, winters in Brighton were just shy of brutal. In their minds, the enemy—rain, sleet, and snow—showed no mercy as they descended on the city with such an uncompromising vengeance that most Brightonians wondered what they had done during the summer to warrant such a dreadful backlash during the winter. Streets were all but deserted because no one dared venture outdoors unless it was an absolute necessity. In actuality, the temperature never dipped below freezing for more than a day or two at a time throughout the entire season, but the way townsfolk stocked up on non-perishables and firewood, you would have thought Armageddon was coming.

Emotionally, the semester had been a challenging one for me. I was certainly no stranger to racism, but at the University of Oklahoma, there seemed to be no limits imposed on the perpetrators and no rules to protect the victims. The vast majority of my professors were white males who effortlessly bought into the notion of their superiority by virtue of race and gender. Two of my worst nightmares became Dr. Randolph Moran and Dr. Theodore Oakley. I was sentenced—by the requirements of the social work department—to take Dr. Randolph Moran's class. Dr. Moran was a short, stubby character who was the spitting image of Alfred Hitchcock. I swear, every time I saw the man, my mind replayed reels from the shower scene in *Psycho*. In spite of being both funny looking *and* scary looking, every undergraduate social work major had to take *Ethics in Social Work,* whether they wanted to or not. It didn't seem quite fair, especially with Dr. Moran being so *un*ethical and all, but like the words on the Lincoln Memorial, taking his class was etched in stone.

Dr. Moran's strategy was to convince his students that he had a deep concern for the intellectual development of each and every one of us, regardless of race, creed, color, or gender. Because he lulled us into a sense of security, we were blindsided when he behaved in ways that were not only unethical, but borderline illegal as well. Case in point, our midterm exam. Until then, I thought he actually meant it when on the first day of class, he announced that he didn't mind if we disagreed with his point of view as long as we used logic and fact to back up our position. When I heard that, I thought to myself, *Well, it's about damned time I got a professor who found it more important that a student be able to think for herself rather than think he was omniscient.* Although I'd be hard-pressed to remember a time when I'd been more wrong, the point is that I thought it was *finally* safe to have an opinion. And I had a lot of them stored up. If Dr. Moran said something I disagreed with, I fiercely debated it with him in class. If he told a joke that wasn't funny,

I refused to laugh along with the rest of the buffoons. If he planned a social event at his house, I was inevitably a no-show.

Needless to say, when I saw the 'C' on my midterm, I was furious. I wasn't angry because it was the only 'C' in the entire class, although that fact alone would have been reason enough, given that I was the only student of color in his class. I was angry because it was an essay question and if I didn't know anything else, I knew three things: I knew the course material, I knew I could write, and I knew I could think—and those are the only elements required to ace an essay exam. After class, I tried to talk to Dr. Moran about my grade, but he summarily dismissed me with, "If you'd like to discuss your performance, Ms. George, you know my office hours." The next day, I was at his office before he was. Our meeting lasted exactly twenty-four minutes. The first four minutes were spent with me telling him how unfair I thought his evaluation of my midterm had been. As he required, I used logic and fact to back up my position. The last twenty minutes were spent with him telling me how wrong I was, how right he was, and how he was being quite lenient with me because he really thought my essay deserved a 'D'. Because he didn't require it of himself, he used neither logic nor fact to back up his position.

That day, Dr. Moran taught me that in order to survive, I'd better learn how to play the game. So, that's exactly what I did. I lived and breathed every word he spoke. If he said it, I agreed wholeheartedly, no matter how much I actually disagreed. If he made a joke, I laughed the longest, no matter how unfunny it actually was. If he had a social event at his house, I was the first to arrive and the last to leave, no matter how much I wanted to throw up while I was there.

Several weeks after our first meeting, he asked me to come by his office for another meeting to discuss my progress. *"Certainly, Sir,"* came out of my mouth like a reflex. When I knocked on his half-opened office door, he looked up from his bifocals, smiled the widest smile I had ever seen on a white man, and said, "Ms. George, good to see you! Come in, come in!"

"Hello, Dr. Moran, I hope I'm not interrupting anything important, Sir," I said, not really caring if I had.

"No, no, this is actually a good time for me to take a break. My brain was getting a little fuzzy, anyway."

Your brain is perpetually fuzzy, isn't it? I asked, but apparently, he didn't hear me because the words didn't actually come out of my mouth. "You said you wanted to see me?" I said, as I sat down in one of his two guest chairs.

"Yes, Ms. George, I wanted to talk to you about two things. First, I want to commend you on the tremendous progress you've made in my class. Your comments demonstrate an obvious knowledge of the course material, they're backed up by logic and fact, and your ideas are innovative and interesting. I'm very proud of the improvement in your performance."

My comments demonstrate an obvious knowledge of your thought process, you idiot, and my ideas are innovative and interesting because they're mere regurgitations of your own, you dipstick! "Why, thank you, Sir. I feel like I've grown immeasurably under your tutelage." *Grown immeasurably under your tutelage?* I couldn't believe I actually said that shit. How I managed to keep a straight face and how he managed to believe everything I said, I'll never know.

"You're welcome," he said, then hesitated as though he wanted to add something else but didn't know quite how to say it. "You know, Ms. George, I have a confession to make. That's the second thing I wanted to talk to you about."

A confession? What in the world does this fool want to confess? My curiosity piqued, almost to the max.

"Yes, you see, I think you may have been on to something when you said I graded your midterm unfairly. I've since realized that I *was* harder on you than I was on the other students."

"Oh? Why do you think you were harder on me, Sir?"

"Well, it's really quite funny when you hear the story," he said, with a boisterous laugh all the way from his Alfred Hitchcock belly. "You see, when I was in graduate school, there was this black girl in one of my classes. Betty Jean Johnson, her name was. I had a tremendous crush on Betty Jean, I sure did. One day, after gathering up all my courage, I asked her out on a date. Unfortunately, Betty Jean didn't have a crush on me. I'm not even sure if she knew my name!" he said, leaning back in his swivel chair so far that I thought his roly-poly ass was going to tip over. "Well, when I asked her out and she flatly refused, I was devastated. She hurt me deeply. I didn't know how deeply it still hurt until I saw you." He leaned forward in his chair as though he needed to see me better before he began his next sentence. "Ms. George, believe it or not, you're Betty Jean Johnson's mirror image."

My curiosity vanished the moment I realized he was just another white man who thought all black people looked alike. "I am?" I asked, with feigned intrigue.

"Yes, you are," he said, as he got up from his chair, waddled over to his bookshelf, and retrieved a thin book. "Her picture is in our yearbook," he said, while flipping through the pages. When he found it, he returned to his chair and pushed the open book across his desk to me. "See, there she is. Doesn't she look *just* like you?"

When I looked at the picture, I saw that Betty Jean Johnson was, indeed, a black woman. But other than two eyes, two ears, a nose, and a mouth, that's where the similarity stopped. With all the enthusiasm I could muster, I said, "Oh my goodness, she looks *exactly* like me, Dr. Moran! We could be twins!"

"I know, I know!" he said, thankful that I saw things just as he did. "I suppose I judged your midterm more harshly because your face took me back to a painful period in my life. You reminded me of a time when I was rejected by someone I cared for deeply."

"I completely understand, Sir. Anybody would have reacted the same way you did."

"Yes, you're right. It was a perfectly human response," he said, extremely satisfied with himself.

"I know how busy you are, Sir, so I don't want to take up any more of your time," I said, using the most docile voice I had. "Is there anything else, Sir?"

"No. No, that's all. Thank you for stopping by, Ms. George. I'm glad we had this little talk."

"So am I, Sir, so am I." Dr. Moran's final exam came and went. I made an 'A' on the exam and an 'A' in his class. I had learned to play the game—and I had learned it well.

Although I played the game in Dr. Oakley's class exactly the way Dr. Moran had taught me, nothing seemed to work. Notwithstanding the fact that he knew nothing about how to conduct a class in which a student's knowledge base could be broadened rather than stunted, his course was the most frustrating experience of my undergraduate career.

Dr. Oakley was a twenty-seven-year veteran of the university who had a wife who left him and no children to speak of. He had risen from the ranks of part-time assistant professor to assistant dean in the psychology department. He had authored several books and journal articles on human intelligence, none of which garnered him any appreciable notoriety, but all of which fulfilled the 'publish or perish' requirement of all university professors. The requirement to publish within a certain timeframe or be terminated was not written anywhere specifically, but both professors and students knew the rule existed. It was, perhaps, the one area in which professors didn't have the upper hand. They were as afraid of being fired as students were of voicing their own opinions.

<u>The Truth About Human Intelligence</u> was Dr. Oakley's first book. It was a shameless narrative directly linking human intelligence to genetics. His research postulated that an individual's environment, socioeconomic status, opportunity, and determination had nothing to do with his or her degree of intelligence, rather he believed genetics predetermined one's intellectual capacity. He used research studies—designed and carried out by a carefully misguided staff of starry-eyed psychology students hoping

to gain his favor—to support his ridiculous theory. Somehow, I managed to make it to my junior year without a clue about Dr. Oakley's race-based inferiority theory—which is exactly how it happened that I signed up for his psychometrics class as an elective. Being the sadistic manipulator that he was, he carefully chose not to reveal his position to his unsuspecting crop of new students until after the drop deadline had passed. By the time I and a few of the more progressive white students enrolled in his class figured him out, it was too late to drop the course without academic penalty.

Dr. Oakley was just as convinced that it was nature's intent to place whites at the very top of the intellectual hierarchy and blacks at the very bottom as he was that the earth was round and not flat. No matter how well-prepared I was for class discussions or how expertly my papers were written or how masterful my class presentations were executed, he refused to acknowledge that there might be at least one exception to his theory. Even though I more than lived up to his unjust standard, it wasn't enough to pacify him. He was rigid, ignorant, and powerful—a frightening combination for a student of any color. My stomach religiously turned into knots every Tuesday and Thursday morning from nine to ten-thirty. I had no idea how right my mother would turn out to be when she had warned me that I would have to work twice as hard as white students to be considered half as good as they were.

I should have gotten an 'A' in Dr. Oakley's class, too, if only because that's what I actually earned. But when I looked at the semester grades posted on the wall just outside his office door, I was momentarily grateful for the 'C' I saw next to my name because since he had been gracious enough to give me a passing grade, those three hours would still count towards the 120 I needed for graduation. *Sorry bastard,* I said to myself, as I looked at the grade like it would change if I stared at it long enough. I hadn't expected an 'A' because that would prove that I was as bright as the white students and Dr. Oakley had decided that I wasn't long before he ever met me. But the asshole could have at least given me a 'B' for *black*. I suppose the 'C' was for *colored*, so in his demented mind, he must have thought he was doing the right thing. My third grade teacher, Mrs. Franks, may have been dead and gone, but her legacy was alive and well. "Sorry bastard," I said, this time out loud, then walked away with my head held high.

CHAPTER 17

The college years flew by for Nicki and me as we blossomed into spirited young women who became leaders on campus, in the community, and in our romantic relationships. With the exception of the racism we randomly encountered in the classroom, our lives were relatively unencumbered. That is until the fall semester of our senior year when I did the unfathomable and fell head over heels in love.

Christopher Lee O'Neal took me by complete surprise. He was a caseworker at Child Protective Services where I had received an internship placement in my senior year. At twenty-nine, he was seven years older than I was, a quality that appealed to both of us. He was also a twice-divorced father of three young daughters, six, four, and one and a half. It was common knowledge that he had almost seventeen more years of child support payments, was broke as hell, and had an insatiable appetite for women, but minus those few glitches, he was attractive, tall, educated, churchgoing, and employed. And unlike the other attractive, tall, educated, churchgoing, employed men in the building, he wasn't married.

His charm was inescapable and like so many before me, I was drawn to him like metal to a magnet. Lame pickup lines that failed for the average man, made hearts flutter when Christopher used them. Mine was no exception. The nonchalant demeanor I typically kept in place for brothers was nowhere to be found when it came to him. Almost immediately I fell under Christopher's spell, but in my defense, it was hard not to because he had *mind-boggling* game. When he asked if he could pray for us the very first time we talked on the telephone, he had me—hook, line, and sinker! When he told me he loved me only a week later, I believed him. Although I lied and told him I loved him, too, no real harm was done because at that particular moment in time, he didn't really love me, either. He didn't know how to love anyone except himself. Not his ex-wives. Not his daughters. Not me. Not anyone. He had the worst case of *Lester Payne Disease* ever recorded. And there was still no known cure.

Eventually, I fell hopelessly, helplessly in love with him. At some point, I think he began to love me, too, at least in the only way he knew how. The way I felt about Christopher was a different kind of feeling. A *good* different. Without question, I had loved Eddie Malone and even in his perpetual absence, I had loved my father, but I had never been *in love* with anyone. All I knew was that it was a wonderfully strange and strangely wonderful feeling that I wanted to last forever or until I died, whichever came first. When Christopher proposed, I'm pretty sure I said 'yes' somewhere between 'will you' and 'marry me'. One month after Nicki and I received our bachelor's degrees, Christopher and I exchanged marriage vows in our pastor's study in the presence of Mama, Katie,

Christopher's daughters, his best friend, Mark, and of course, Nicki.

For the first five months or so, we were as happy as any other young, infinitely clueless couple. I managed to secure a permanent position as a social worker with Child Protective Services, Christopher was promoted to supervisor, we were both actively involved in our church, and it looked like the loan was going to be approved on the brand new house we wanted so badly. Because it was the closest my life had ever come to feeling right, when it started to fall apart, I did everything I could to save us. I ignored hang-up calls, makeup stained collars, unexplained and poorly explained disappearances, and phone calls from Christopher's scorned lovers as soon as they realized he wasn't going to leave his wife for all the opened legs in the world. I ignored it all because I loved my man, my man loved me, and we were about to close on a house that didn't have a single rat or roach in it.

Sometime after our four-month anniversary, the *loving-churchgoing-praying-twice-a-day-glory-hallelujah* brother I had fallen in love with completely vanished. In actuality, *that* particular brother never existed in the first place. I should have known something was up when he thought Paul was one of the twelve disciples, but who knew a guy would be bold enough to use God and some carefully scripted prayers to seduce women? When he could no longer keep up the façade, Christopher began to frequent the local nightspot. He told me he just wanted to hang out with the boys. Oddly enough, hanging out with the boys always fell on ladies' night at Club Max. Other excuses he used to account for his whereabouts were playing basketball with the boys, working out, going to the all-men's Bible study at church, and the over-used, *Baby, I was with Mark.* In spite of his less than airtight alibis, I desperately wanted to believe my husband. So I did.

I don't really know exactly when I fell in love with Christopher. It was gradual, almost imperceptible over time, until one day, I just knew. Hating him was much different. I knew the day, the hour, the second, *the very moment* that I began to despise him. Like love, hate is an intense emotion. The power of its force can destroy you with one, single, calculated phone call.

The call that destroyed me came two days before our second anniversary, waking me up in the middle of a dream that didn't make sense. I looked at the clock on the nightstand. It was midnight. Realizing Christopher had not yet gotten home from Bible study, I immediately got nervous. Automatic anxiety was just my way. I had gotten that from my mother.

"Hello," I said. The caller said nothing. "Hello," I repeated, more nervously than before.

"Is this Chelsey O'Neal?" the voice finally asked.

"Yes. This is Mrs. O'Neal." My mind began running away with me. *Oh my God, something's happened to Christopher!* He wasn't a perfect husband, but he was the only one I had.

The caller's voice brought me back into the present. "I just wanted to let you know that your husband's been out fucking tonight." I heard a click then the phone went dead. Seconds later, a pre-recorded message was saying, *If you'd like to make a call...*

In the loneliness of our bedroom, I cried tears I didn't know I had left. Had it not been for the fact that I had already loved and lost my father and Eddie, the pain of that moment would have been inconceivable. My lifelong working hypothesis had rung true once again: If a woman allows herself to love a man—*any* man—in time, he'll shit on her. It was either a guarantee or a self-fulfilling prophecy, I wasn't sure which. Either way, it didn't really matter anymore. My marriage was over.

Twenty minutes later, Christopher quietly opened the front door. Instead of crawling into bed next to me like he usually did when he came home from his outings, he went into the extra bedroom we had transformed into a den, turned the television on, and flopped down on the black leather sofa we still had from his bachelor days. I waited for a few minutes before confronting him. I wanted to make sure he couldn't tell I had been crying. When I was certain there were no visible signs of distress, I went into the makeshift den, turned the television off manually, and stared at my disinterested husband.

"Why did you do that?"

I ignored his question because I had a few of my own. "Where've you been, Christopher?"

"Where do I go every Wednesday, Chelsey? Men's Bible study."

"I don't think so, Christopher. You see, I got a rather strange phone call a little while ago. I guess your whore, whoever she is, must be mad at you."

"I don't know what you're talking about, Chelsey." He turned the television back on with the remote control.

I turned it off manually, again. Though I hated women who yelled and screamed and acted like they were *straight-up-crazy*, holding my rage in had become all but impossible. "Damn it, Christopher!" I shouted. "Do you think I'm a complete idiot?"

"What the hell are you talking about?" he had the nerve to shout back.

"Your bitch called here a little while ago! She said she just wanted to let me know that my husband had been out fucking tonight!" Christopher didn't move a muscle. He simply sat on the sofa like a deaf mute, wishing I would go back to bed. "So who made that call, Christopher?"

Much calmer, he said, "I don't know what you're talking about, baby. I've been at church all night." Infidelity aside, he hated hurting me and he couldn't look me in the face. He decided to look at the television screen instead, all the while secretly hoping that if he looked long enough, the blank screen would help him figure out just how he was going to deal with the bitch he had just fucked.

He may have been calm, but I was still mad as hell. "Oh, so now I'm supposed to believe that Bible study went past midnight tonight, is that it, Christopher?"

"Yeah, the spirit was really in that place, baby." *Stick to your story, son, no matter how stupid it sounds.* That's what his father had taught him and that's what he decided he needed to do.

"Who is she, Christopher? Who made that call?"

"I don't know anybody who would call you with some mess like that."

"Are you sleeping with so many women that you can't even narrow it down to the one crazy enough to call your wife?"

"I'm not sleeping with anyone except you. I love you, baby. Now, go back to bed. I'll be there in a little while."

"I wish I could believe you, Christopher," I replied, this time with the same calm tone he had been using. "But I'm sick of your lies, I'm sick of this marriage, and I'm sick of you." I turned the television back on and left the room. Christopher looked at the screen for hours and saw nothing. He knew the camel's back had finally broken...and I was as good as gone.

Everyday, he pleaded with me not to leave. He said he wanted us to go to marriage counseling. He promised to spend more time with me. He even admitted to cheating and lying because in the most sincere voice I had, I told his cheating, lying ass that if he just admitted it, I would stay and we could work things out. As big of a con artist as *he* was, I couldn't believe he actually bought that bullshit. When did game stop recognizing game? Believe it when I tell you, testosterone mixed with desperation is one of the funniest things you'll ever see, though you won't realize it until much later.

"You slept with nine different women in two years, Christopher?" It was the actual confession, not the actual number that shocked me.

"Yes, baby, but I didn't care about any of them," Christopher said, as if that bit of information would make me feel better. *He's a complete idiot,* I thought. *There really should be a law against fucking the retarded.*

"What happened to them? Did they leave once they found out what a lousy lay you turned out to be?" I was lashing out, but Christopher refused to lash back. He wagered that I would give him another chance if he let me feel all my anger right then.

"They didn't leave me, baby," he finally said. "I left them." His angst was evident as he became more passionate in his defense. "Every single one of them wanted me to leave you, Chelsey, but I told all of them that I loved you and would never, *ever* leave you. When they became too impatient, I always left them."

"Why, Christopher? If you love me so much, why did you do it? And why did you *keep* doing it?" Like every other woman with an unfaithful husband, I had to know why. Knowing the *why* doesn't make it hurt any less, but sometimes it can make the acceptance kick in a little faster so you can get on with your day.

"Because they made me feel like a man. They made me feel needed. You never make me feel like that, Chelsey. You treat me like a child who needs to be told what to do and when to do it. Rather than talk to you about how I was feeling, I turned to them. I'm sorry, baby. I was wrong. Please don't do this to us. I love you, Chelsey. You've got to believe that. No one will ever love you like I do, baby."

I heard the torment in his voice. I should be ashamed to say it, but I got an enormous amount of comfort from knowing he was hurting, too. Apparently, misery *does* love company. "Well, you know what, Christopher? I don't want anyone to love me like you do. The way you love hurts too much."

I thought about having my own affair to get revenge, but decided I wanted to do the one thing I knew would hurt him the most. I would divorce him. I sold the house as quickly as I had arranged for its purchase and filed for divorce as quickly as I had applied for a marriage license. *This pain won't go away by divorcing the man I love*, I thought, *but the minute he's out of my life, it's going to hurt a whole lot less.* I was wrong again.

The composed picture I revealed to Christopher, my family, my co-workers, and a few nosey church members was easily washed away each night by plentiful tears that sometimes wouldn't stop for hours. I was frequently forced to call in sick to work because after finally falling asleep with the help of a few over-the-counter sleeping pills, I would awaken with eyes so swollen that I could barely open them wide enough to see the numbers on the telephone. The depth of my depression ran deep. Every night I prayed I wouldn't wake up the next morning. I never admitted to anyone, not even to Nicki, that I thought about dying more often than I thought about living.

Trying to make sense of Christopher's bad choices, I began to blame myself for the collapse of our marriage. *He would never have cheated if I had been the wife I was supposed to be,* I told myself. I wished a thousand times that I had been less controlling, allowing him a chance to make a few decisions. I wished I had given birth to the son he so desperately wanted, instead of swallowing *The Pill* like clockwork every night. I wished I could have pretended to be weak, so that he could have pretended to be strong.

Two months after our divorce was final, I hurt as deeply as if I had received the fateful phone call only the day before. Christopher had his faults, but he had meant the world to me. Now, he was gone. The more I blamed myself, the worse I felt. The worse I felt, the more

I isolated myself. Only Nicki had *carte blanche* to drop by whenever she felt like it and have any chance at all of getting in. At six o'clock one Saturday evening, she did just that. I was still in my pajamas from the night before. I didn't care that I hadn't washed my face, brushed my teeth, combed my hair, or eaten in two days.

"Chelsey, look at yourself! You look like hell!" Nicki said as she stormed through the door. "Have you lost your damned mind? You've got to snap out of this! That jerk isn't worth it!" After watching me feel sorry for myself for so long, she was more than a little irritated, so tough love wasn't difficult for her to find.

I was still fragile, naïve, and more hurt than a woman in love deserved to be. "Nicki, I couldn't keep the only man who ever really loved me." I looked at her through eyes that were literally begging her to understand. "Christopher was right. Nobody will ever love me as much as he did."

"You only *thought* Christopher loved you, sweetheart," Nicki said, trying to be less abrasive but killing me, nonetheless. "I know you're hurting right now, but you've got to remember that he conned you, Chelsey. He conned *all* of us with that holier-than-thou crap. We all thought he was a good guy because that's what he pretended to be for so long. I suspect that for a while, *he* even thought he had changed into the kind of man who knows how to love a woman in a way that's real and honest and true." Nicki hesitated, took a deep breath I didn't quite understand, then continued. "There's something I need to tell you, Chelsey, and it's not going to be something you'll want to hear. Christopher's engaged to one of the women he cheated on you with."

"*Engaged?* We've only been divorced two months. How can he be engaged?"

"Because he used the same Jesus-scam on her, that's how. The only difference is that he struck fool's gold this time—she's rich. Her first husband died and left her with nothing but a whole lot of money and a whole lot of time. She's already bought Christopher everything a true player needs. Custom suits. Expensive jewelry. A new car. Just like you, she thinks she has a man of God who genuinely loves her. But just like you, she's getting played like a fiddle, too." I couldn't believe what I was hearing, but Nicki kept going. "Don't be sad that he's not in your life anymore, Chelsey. Be thankful that you don't have to spend the rest of your life with a liar, a user, a completely useless waste of space."

Although every bit of what Nicki was saying made sense, I couldn't stop crying or feeling sorry for myself. "I know you're right, Nicki, but even if it was all one big lie, he made me believe his love was real. And it felt good to finally know what love was supposed to feel like. That's all I've ever wanted—somebody to love me. *Really* love me. Can't you see that, Nicki?"

"Can't *you* see, Chelsey? That's exactly what you're afraid of. You think you won't ever have that kind of love. But you're wrong about that, sweetheart," she said, as she smoothed down my nappy hair with her fingers. You'll have that and more because you're one of the most loving people on the planet. It's *easy* to love you. Taking candy from a baby is harder to do than *not* loving you," she said, smiling warmly. "Listen to me, Chelsey, and listen to me good. You deserve more than Christopher was willing to give. You deserve to be loved like that princess you pretended to be when you were a little girl. No woman should be lied to or cheated on or disrespected by the man who says he loves her. Christopher never appreciated the jewel he had in you. He never realized just how priceless you are."

"I don't feel priceless."

Smoothing down the last bit of my wayward hair with her fingers, Nicki smiled and said, "Well, Chelsey Christina George, you need to stop listening to those stupid feelings because I've got news for you—you *are* priceless."

I tried to smile back. "Why should I listen to you? Clearly, your judgment is questionable because you're best friends with someone who hasn't had a bath in two days."

"I know God made you and my grandma says God don't make no junk. And if you try to call my grandma a liar, best friend or not, I'm going to have to kick your ass!" Nicki smiled the smile that always said everything's going to be alright.

"What would I do without you?" I asked, as I hugged my guardian angel.

"Good thing you'll never get a chance to find out!" Nicki popped up from the sofa that had been my bed for the last two days, pulling me up with her. "Now, get in there and wash your stinking behind and put on some of that natural beauty you keep in that makeup bag! We're going out and have some fun!"

We hit the town and partied like we used to in the good old college days when the biggest problem we had to solve was on a math test. We danced all night long, sometimes with brave guys who got up the nerve to ask us, but mostly with each other. We behaved like the world was ours and we were just nice enough to let everyone else enjoy it for a while. At 2:00 a.m., we found ourselves in an all-night diner on Fairfax Avenue.

"Thanks, Nicki," I told my best friend from across the table. "I love you."

"You're welcome," she said. "And I love you back. It's like taking candy from a baby."

CHAPTER 18

It felt good to be able to breathe again. It felt good to *want* to breathe again. I vowed to Nicki and myself, but mostly to Nicki, that I would never allow myself to be consumed by another man. I would let them love me as much as they desired, but I would never love them back. I would, however, accept their dinner invitations, shiny trinkets, and meaningless adoration because, after all, it would be rude not to. Mama always said self-preservation is the first law of nature. This time, I wouldn't forget.

With Christopher pushed into proper perspective and reduced to merely a bad taste in my mouth, I was able to continue the life I had unconsciously put on hold. While Nicki had gone straight to graduate school, I had opted for marriage and a two-car garage. As much as I wanted to, Christopher had been vehemently opposed to me returning to school for a graduate degree. His contention was that the money we would spend on tuition and books could be used to plan for our family, instead. He wanted a son more than anything in the world and he reminded me, *ad nauseam*, that I was selfish for denying him the opportunity to carry on the O'Neal family name. Funny how what used to sound so logical sounded utterly ridiculous to me now. One Saturday afternoon, I happily mailed my application to pursue study in the Graduate School of Social Work at the University of Oklahoma and six weeks later, they happily accepted me for the Fall semester.

I absolutely loved learning. Education was a wonderfully productive distraction from my less than exciting existence in Brighton. Mama was ecstatic that I had actually learned the lesson she had pounded into our heads about it. *Get your education, girls, 'cause that's somethin' the white man cain't nevah take away from you.*

In the years since I left Georgia my mother and I had grown a whole lot closer. Being on my own made me realize how hard life had been for her and how many sacrifices she had made for me and Katie. This discovery transformed me into a reluctant, but accepting recipient of the guilt trips she didn't always realize she was laying on me. I accepted them because in my youthful adulthood, I found it completely unpalatable to stand up to someone who had made so many sacrifices for me. Regardless of how wrong she might be in any given situation, how could I fight with someone who had loved me all my life, even if she didn't always know how to express it?

Though I certainly never pointed it out to her, Mama didn't think she had ever made any decision that adversely affected her baby girls. She consistently said she wanted her children to have more than she had. And she meant it. If we achieved more, were more successful, were happier, it meant she had done her mother job well. Her daughters' accomplishments—especially those of the emotional, angry, hard-to-understand one—became her *good-mother* validation. Once I realized that every dream Mama had deferred could come to life in me, I sought to make them happen. I wanted nothing more than to make her feel that her sacrifices had been worthwhile. Doing more and being more was the only way I knew to repay the debt I had convinced myself I owed. In my distorted mind, it was the method of payment Mama preferred, too.

With each of my accomplishments, she was more proud. With each of my accomplishments, I was more stressed, wondering what I could do next to persuade her that her sacrifices had not been in vain and that an unwed mother could raise good stock all by herself if she stood on the right principles. It was a hard way to live but I decided I had to do it. When I was done living life for her, there would be plenty of time to live it for myself. It would be years before Mama knew I felt an obligation to repay her for something that seemed so natural for a mother to do. It would be years before I knew a mother's love and devotion can never be repaid—and that mine never expected me to try.

CHAPTER 19

To say my graduate school journey was challenging would be a gross understatement, but despite it all, I made it, and graduation day was nothing short of amazing. The sun was shining, birds were singing, and my family and friends had come from near and far to watch me walk across the stage to receive my second degree from, as I always called it—that white racist institution. When my name was called, I rose from my seat and approached the platform. I could hardly breathe. I had been praying for weeks that I wouldn't stumble up the three steps to the stage. A gold rope indicating my honors status was draped across my robe and on the top of my graduation cap, proudly spelled out in masking tape, were the words, *By His Grace.* Although stern admonitions to hold all applause until the last graduate's name had been called, as I received my diploma with one hand and shook hands with the dean of the Graduate School of Social Work with the other, my small, but nonetheless enthusiastic delegation uproariously shouted, "Way to go, Chelsey George!"

While I didn't remember any of the actual ceremony, as my entourage sat in *Mama's Kitchen* munching on oxtails, white rice, sweet potatoes, black-eyed peas, and cornbread, Nicki swore that after receiving the blank piece of rolled up paper, I glided across the stage with a Colgate smile, continuously waving my right hand back and forth, as though I had just won the *Ms. America* crown. Everybody, especially me, knew that Nicki was infamous for not letting the truth stand in the way of a good story, so after listening to her recant the event, adding her own entertaining twist, my knee-jerk response was, "Stop lying, Nicki! I would never have done that!" Turning to my mother for confirmation, I asked, "Would I, Mama?"

"Well, honey, I hate to be the one to tell you, but Nicki's tellin' the God's hones' truth this time. You got up there an' you waved an' waved an' waved!" Mama's eyes were beaming with pride. My second college graduation served as overwhelming evidence that against all odds, she had been a damned good mother.

My celebratory dinner lasted well into the evening. Various *Chelsey* stories were told by everybody, each one funnier than the one before. Noticing the graduation cap I refused to remove, many patrons of *Mama's* came over to our table to congratulate me. Black people are just like that. They don't have to know you. They're just proud to see one of their own get that piece of paper.

The whole world seemed to be smiling down on me when an unassuming stranger appeared out of nowhere. He had a shy smile, piercing brown eyes, and a somewhat mystical quality about him. Although his appearance was neat and clean, his shirt was straight out of *Cooley High*, his pants were boring and ill-fitted, and his shoes looked like little, brown rescue boats. He was no more than five-feet-nine on a good day and his skin was so black that it shined like midnight blue. Moments later, I discovered that his New York accent was undeniable proof that if by some chance he had been born in the South, he left the minute his mother checked out of the hospital.

"Ex-excuse me. H-h-hello." The stranger spoke in a hesitant, almost inaudible tone. Without question, social interaction was not an activity with which he felt very comfortable and it was more than clear that he had summoned up every ounce of his courage just to be able to approach the table. It didn't help his nervousness when the miscellaneous table chatter suddenly stopped and fourteen pairs of eyes focused on him. "Ex-ex-excuse me," he said again. "I, I, I hope you don't mind, but I, I, I, just wanted to, to, to come over and con-con-congratulate you. I, I, I graduated from the U-u-university, too, and that's an ex-ex-extraordinary accomplishment, especially with all th-th-the racism and p-p-politics in-in-inherent in that system."

It was no secret that graduating from the University of Oklahoma was no small feat for a person of *any* color. In spite of the fact that it took him damned near all afternoon to finish one sentence, I was impressed by his intellect. The sadistic part of me wanted to say, *Brother, try getting hooked on phonics before you step to a sister,* but glancing down at the small boats on his feet again, I couldn't help but wonder what talents he might have that I just couldn't appreciate at that particular moment. Instead of kicking a man when he was already down, I smiled the Colgate smile Nicki was talking about and said, "Thank you. But how did you know I went to UO?"

"I, I, I'm sorry. But, I, I overheard you talking about a white racist in-in-institution, so I, I, I suspected that's where you, you went to school. Besides, th-th-that 'U-O' hanging from your tassel is a dead gi-gi-giveaway." He smiled nervously, as he pointed to the two gold letters dangling from the tassel on my graduation cap.

For reasons I still don't understand, I was inexplicably drawn to the stranger. It didn't matter that he had no taste whatsoever in clothing and stuttered a little—okay, stuttered a *lot*—when he talked. "So, should I call you Sherlock Holmes or do you go by some other name in the daytime?" I said, jokingly.

"Oh, I'm s-s-sorry," he apologized again. "My name is Terrence. Terrence Jackson. My friends call me T. J." Apparently, he had practiced those lines more than once since he didn't stutter at all when he said them. I couldn't help but chuckle to myself a little bit, especially since Nicki had been kicking my leg under the table since the moment he released his first stutter.

"Stop apologizing, Terrence," I gently scolded, as I stood up and extended my right hand. "I'm Chelsey George—M.S.W.!" He smiled back as we shook hands. "And this is my devoted cheering squad," I said, as my left arm acknowledged their presence in a wavelike motion, much like that of the girls on *The Price Is Right* whenever they presented a new showcase of fabulous prizes.

"Hiiiiii, Terrence," the table sang in unison.

"Don't mind them," I said. "They're silly, but they're harmless. Would you like to join us?"

"No, no thanks. I-I-I'd better be g-g-going. It's g-g-getting pretty late."

"Oh, okay. Well, it was a pleasure meeting you, Terrence. And thanks for the kind words."

"You're w-w-welcome. G-g-goodbye."

"Goodbye, Terrence," the table sang, again. Terrence and I shook hands again and he disappeared as quickly as he had come.

"He's a li-li-little weird, d-d-don't you think?" Nicki teased, as we watched him shuffle away.

"Yeah. A little," I responded, not really listening to her.

In the next hour, I finished off dessert, two cups of coffee, and multiple conversations I wouldn't remember later. As I lay in bed that night, I couldn't stop thinking about the inarticulate stranger with the big feet. I closed my eyes and allowed my fantasies to take me to heaven multiple times before I fell into a deep, deep sleep.

CHAPTER 20

One week to the day after meeting Terrence, the telephone rang. "C-c-could I, I, I speak to Chelsey George, please?"

"Speaking," I said. I immediately recognized the voice and the speech impediment but still asked, "Who's calling, please?"

"Th-th-this is T. J. You might remember me by Terrence. Anyway, w-w-we met at *Mama's* th-th-the other night."

Although I was more than glad he had tracked me down, I wondered how he had gotten my telephone number. I didn't give it to him that night at *Mama's* (only because he didn't ask for it) and since that fateful call from Christopher's ho', I had maintained a non-published telephone number. "Hello, Terrence. It's nice to hear from you, but how did you get this number? It's unlisted."

"Yeah, I, I know. I, I have a friend who works at the phone c-c-company. He hooked me up. I, I, I hope I'm not being t-t-t-too forward."

"No, you're not being too forward, but you are being a little suspect. Watching me at *Mama's*, eavesdropping on our conversation before coming to the table, illegally obtaining my phone number. If I wasn't intrigued by you already, I'd have to call the police."

With a nervous laugh that I assumed was just his way, he said, "Well, I, I, I'm sure glad you're not going to do that."

"So what can I do for you, Mr. Jackson?"

"W-w-well, I, I, I was wondering if you w-w-would like t-t-to have dinner with me, sometime?"

"I'd love to!" I immediately regretted sounding so enthusiastic. That simply wasn't the way the game was supposed to be played. "When would you like to go?" I asked in a more matter-of-fact tone.

"Wh-wh-whenever you're a-a-available."

Even though my date book had consistently been open for longer than I cared to admit, I said, "Well, my schedule is really busy." I paused for effect, then as if just discovering an opening that surprised even me, I said, "Hey, what about Friday night, say around seven o'clock?"

"Fr-Fr-Friday at seven it is. I, I, I'll see you then."

"Wait a minute!" I yelled into the phone, trying to catch him before he hung up. "Don't you want to know where I live?"

It hadn't occurred to me that he had likely gotten my address from his hookup, too, and he preferred to leave it that way. Laughing again, this time not nervously at all, he said, "Oh, yes. I s-s-suppose I will need that, won't I?"

"Forty-one hundred Bartholomew Drive. Number 12. It's that small condominium complex right across from George Washington Carver High School."

"I, I know exactly where that is. I'll s-s-see you Friday at seven." He hung up the telephone and smiled. *Book-smart, but dumb as hell when it comes to being street-smart,* he thought. *What a perfect woman.*

* * *

"You're doing what?" Nicki asked, as if I had finally lost my entire mind.

"I'm going out with Terrence Friday night. What's the big deal?"

"What's the big deal? Chelsey, that brother is *way* past weird! I got nothing but bad vibes from him. That stupid shy-boy act, those sneaky little eyes, hunting you down like an animal—that's just plain spooky! I'd bet money that he's made some collect calls before."

"Nicki, you're being ridiculous. Just because he's timid doesn't mean he's a criminal. Besides, I like his shy-boy act, if it is one. It's a nice change of pace." I launched into player mode. *"Baby, ooh, baby, you're wrong! I wasn't gonna sleep with her! Sure, I had my thang out and it might've even been hard, but I wasn't gonna do nothin' with it! I love you, girl! I ain't lyin', baby, I swear! That's my lil' baby cousin!"* Nicki found herself laughing against her will. "At least Terrence won't cheat," I added. "Hell, who would give his st-st-stuttering ass a chance!"

"Y-y-y-you got that right," Nicki mocked. We high-fived each other and rolled on the floor, laughing so hard we cried. "But really, Chelsey," Nicki asked, as she wiped moisture from her eyes, "doesn't it feel scary that he was watching you while we were at *Mama's* then got your number and address from his shady friend at the phone company?"

"Girl, *puh-leeze!* You know brothers always have at least one friend who does some sneaky, back-alley kind of shit. I don't care if he got my information from one of his hook-ups. Hell, that just shows he's resourceful! And, as for him watching me at *Mama's*, I kind of liked his technique. He sort of worshipped me from afar then made his move. If a brother wants to worship me, who am I to complain? *Chelsey-worship* sounds like a pretty good way for a man to spend his day."

"Well, you know what they say, my sister."

"What?"

"Be careful what you ask for because you just might get it."

CHAPTER 21

There was a knock on the front door at six-fifty-five. As I hurriedly put the top back on my lipstick and closed the vanity drawer, I found myself laughing because even his knock had a kind of stutter to it. *Everything about this brother is devoid of cadence,* I thought as I opened the door. Much to my dismay, Terrence's fashion sense had only slightly improved in that his pants didn't pucker at the front anymore. Much to my delight, however, he held a dozen yellow roses and a box of assorted chocolates. He wasn't the most stylish brother on the block, but he definitely knew how to treat a lady. I accepted the gifts, thanked him for his thoughtfulness, and retrieved a vase from the kitchen for the flowers. My heart was doing flip-flops because I could now add *romantic* to his repertoire, making him a little less imperfect.

Over a quasi reunion dinner at *Mama's*, I learned that Terrence was a thirty-two year old chemical engineer who grew up in the Bronx. He was a child prodigy, graduating from high school at sixteen then coming to the University of Oklahoma on an academic scholarship. He had turned down offers to Harvard, Princeton, and Stanford because the University of Oklahoma's School of Engineering was one of the best in the country and although still as white as snow, seemed to have a more welcoming atmosphere for a young black man who wasn't accustomed to being around ivy leaguers. Six months prior to his graduation, he had already been offered several positions with multimillion dollar engineering firms across the country but remained in Brighton because his college sweetheart, Doretha, had gotten accidentally pregnant on purpose and refused to move away from her family. Almost instantly, Terrence decided they should get married because he didn't want to shirk his paternal responsibility like his own father had. He had hoped he would eventually fall in love with her.

He landed a job with the City of Brighton and Doretha, who didn't complete college because, according to Terrence, she never really had any ambition, settled into her new career as a secretary. Her meager income was barely enough to pay for daycare and diapers for Teresa Lynn but every dime helped their overburdened budget. As tight as things already were, Doretha got pregnant again and eleven months later, another daughter, Tracey Louise, was born. A year after that, when Doretha came up pregnant a third time, Terrence left. Since he had gotten a vasectomy after the birth of his second daughter, he knew the son Doretha had proudly named Terrence Anthony Jackson, Jr. didn't have an ounce of Jackson blood in him. Though he had never actually fallen in love with his wife, he had grown to love her as the mother of his children and it broke his heart to learn she had not been faithful. Family and fidelity meant everything to Terrence and he was devastated that Doretha didn't have the same core values.

Without realizing it, Terrence and I spent hours discussing topics ranging from the vast economic and social struggles of black people to the pitfalls of growing up without a father to the merits of living in a town with a good soul food restaurant. Mama would say he was one of those people who knew a little bit about everything and not much about anything, but I was intrigued, nonetheless. Sex was the topic with which he appeared to be most at ease, which was good not only because it made for some pretty interesting dialogue, but because when he became more relaxed, his stuttering all but disappeared.

"So, do you think it's okay for a girl to sleep with a guy on the first date?" I boldly asked, over my first bite of chocolate cheesecake.

"Is that a trick question?"

"No. It's a real question. So, what do you think about that?"

"Personally, I don't think there's anything wrong with it, but I'm probably more open-minded about sexual expression than the average guy. If two consenting adults want to have sex ten minutes after meeting, why can't they express themselves in the way that feels natural for them? I hate the games men and women play. Why can't everybody just be who they are?" *Is he for real or is this just some bullshit he thinks I want to hear?* Although that was the soundtrack playing in my head, I didn't really care either way because real or bullshit, it made sense in my world.

"I agree," I said. "If a woman wants to make love or fuck—and let's face it, there *is* a difference—why does she have to wait for a time when society or some man deems it appropriate? If a man has sex on the first date, everybody in the known world thinks he's a stud. But if a woman has sex on a first date, those same people think she's a slut—including the man she just accommodated! How stupid is it to judge *her* for having sex on a first date when *he* just had sex on a first date, too? And on top of that, how stupid is it for him to brag to his boys that he screwed some slut on a first date when *he* may have been the slut who got screwed on a first date? Women enjoy sex, too, so if somebody got used, it could just as easily have been him. Men are generally so arrogant that they never bother to consider that possibility."

Terrence laughed an agreeable laugh. "I know what you mean, Chelsey. There's always been a double standard when it comes to sex between the sexes. It's not fair, but it definitely exists. Personally, I'm convinced that women want sex even more than men do. There's no question that they're more mature about it. But they get dogged out if they just talk about it, let alone do it."

"Sad, but true," I said, emptying another packet of artificial sweetener into my iced tea.

Terrence could tell I felt strongly about the topic so he decided to stay with it. "So, which do you prefer?"

"What are you talking about?" Even though I knew exactly what he was talking about, I wanted to hear him say it out loud. It was like foreplay to me.

"Making love or fucking? Which do you prefer?"

"Making love," I politely said. I can tell you right now I didn't mean that shit but a girl has to play the game until she's sure it's safe to stop. "And you? Which do you prefer?"

"Fucking," he said, with a penetrating look in his eyes. "Fucking someone I'm madly in love with."

Although I'd never been to Vegas, it felt like I had just hit the jackpot. "I ain't mad at you, my brother. I ain't mad at all." As I picked up my glass for another sip of tea, I thought to myself, *Somebody is getting fucked tonight.*

* * *

We pulled up to my condo at half past midnight. Terrence walked me to the door, thanked me for a wonderful evening, and like any perfect gentleman would, asked if he could kiss me goodnight. I was already feeling warm all over and my *Victoria's Secret* panties had been annoyingly damp since dessert. "I'd like that," I said, almost shyly. He took my face in the palm of his hands and gently pressed his baby-soft lips first to my forehead, then to the tip of my nose, then to my quivering lips. His kisses were purposeful and seductive and *just plain good!* As our bodies touched, I could feel the beginning of his erection. *To hell with protocol,* I thought. He wanted me as much as I wanted him and from my perspective, that was all that mattered. "Would you like to come in?" I said, as he enveloped my waist with two man-sized hands.

"Yes," he whispered softly in my ear. We both knew what was on the other side of the door.

Once inside, our desire exploded. He kissed me again and again, each time more passionately than before. With the skill of a surgeon, he unbuttoned my blouse to reveal two small breasts that had appeared much larger in the black lace push-up bra I wore. He unfastened my bra like he had been performing the task his entire life, then tenderly kissed each nipple slowly and assuredly. I slid my hand into my panties and began massaging my crevice.

Touching myself was nothing unusual. I had long since discovered that doing so in front of an audience was a turn-on for everybody, even if there were just two people in the room. Terrence fell to his knees, taking the time to love each part of my body on the way down. He maneuvered my spandex skirt down my hips, allowing it to fall to the floor with him. Slowly and methodically, he removed my panties, taking time to admire each curvaceous leg in the process. When he gently pushed my hand away from my clit and approached it with his tongue, my suspicion that he was a full service lover was confirmed. With the rounded tip of his tongue, he licked me slowly first, then faster and faster. He forced one finger inside me, moving it in and out while rotating his tongue on my hardened clit. Within minutes, he heard me scream out in ecstasy, calling on my god. As I made myself comfortable on the floor with him by propping my head on a wayward sofa pillow, his tongue and finger serviced me again.

When I couldn't wait a second longer, I told him exactly what I wanted. *"Fuck me, Terrence! Fuck, me now, baby!"* Just before I thought I would have to commit homicide if he didn't give me the real thing, he stood up and released his throbbing cock from his pants. My eyes became twice their normal size, mainly because that's what his penis was. It was the biggest dick I had ever seen! Big and round and hard and black. No curve to the left, no curve to the right. It just jutted straight out and stood there like a private in the army eagerly awaiting his next assignment. I was in absolute awe of its perfection. I had seen all kinds of dicks before—big ones, little ones, fat ones, skinny ones—but I had never seen a perfect one. *Wait until I tell Nicki about this shit!* I thought to myself.

I wanted him inside of me badly, but I couldn't resist first exploring his manhood with my mouth. I rose to my knees, took the distal half in my hands and rubbed its hardness back and forth as I circled my tongue around the head. Although I generally love the masculine smell of men's cologne, Terrence didn't wear any. That didn't matter, though, because I found myself absolutely intoxicated by his natural odor. Looking up at him, I saw his eyes were closed and his head was leaning back. He moaned when my lips covered the tip of his penis and I began to suck him with the same skill he had demonstrated while licking me. Well, *close* to the same skill, anyway. I was good at oral sex by most standards, but Terrence performed oral sex so well I thought he had invented it. And if he didn't actually invent it, he sure as hell perfected it.

When neither of us could stand it any longer, he removed a rubber from his pants pocket, tore open the wrapper with his teeth, and carefully rolled the protection down his shaft, which after almost forty-five minutes of foreplay, was still as hard as cement. I moaned louder as he entered my wet crevice. We had sex in every imaginable position and some you can't quite imagine without tilting your head sideways and going over it two or three times in your mind to see if it's anatomically possible. When we climaxed, it was together and we collapsed into each other's arms. With labored breaths, I told him it was the best sex I had ever had. Although I had made that statement countless times before, this was the first time I actually meant it.

"So what was that?" I asked.

"Fucking," he replied, as he pulled me closer.

CHAPTER 22

"I'm in love with him."

"Don't be ridiculous," Nicki said, still hiding her head in the pages of _Ebony_. "You're not in love with _Mr. Ought-To-Get-Hooked-On-Phonics._"

"Yes, I am, so get used to it, girl. This is the exact same way I felt about Christopher and you _know_ I loved that fool."

Still holding her place in the magazine, Nicki let it drop to her lap. "You're not in love with _the man_, Chelsey—you're in love with _the sex_. Every girl on the planet has gotten the two confused a time or two."

"I know what I feel and I'm not confused. I love him, Nicki. End of story." Smiling mischievously, I added. "Earth-shattering sex is merely a bonus."

"Have you told him you love him?"

"We both said it last night."

"Please, _please_ tell me you didn't say it first."

"Of course not! I'm in love, not stupid!"

"Well, at least you haven't gone completely insane." Nicki tossed _Ebony_ on the coffee table, folded her legs under herself, leaned back on the sofa cushion and asked, "Okay, so what makes you think you love him?"

My eyes glazed over as I began to talk. "He's intelligent, interesting, romantic, funny. When I'm not with him, I can't wait to be with him again and when I'm with him, he makes me feel like nothing else in the whole world matters except me. I feel it when he touches me and I definitely feel it when he looks at me with those dark, lonely, frightened eyes." For several seconds, I retreated into my own little world where love reigned supreme, then took a deep, satisfying breath and continued. "Terrence makes me feel special, Nicki. It may sound corny to you, but he makes me feel alive. *Really* alive! I feel like I just want to run up and down the street butt-naked, screaming to the world about how happy I am!"

"Oh my god, you *are* insane."

"Nope," I said, with a smile. "I'm as sane as they come! But, Nicki, let me tell you what the *best* part is! We can talk to each other for hours and hours and hours and never get bored." I perked up even more, as if having an epiphany. "Now that I think about it, the love I have with him is *better* than the love I had with Christopher. Christopher and I never talked about anything of substance. He was never interested in what I was thinking and I thought he was a certifiable moron. But Terrence loves to talk to me. He wants to know what I'm thinking and feeling all the time.

"We have similar backgrounds, too," I continued. "His father abandoned him just like Lester abandoned me, but instead of becoming an extrovert like me, he withdrew. That's why he's so shy and stutters when he's in unfamiliar social situations." My voice was almost a whisper. "He's scared, Nicki. Just like me. He has a wounded spirit, just like me. We understand that about each other. We understand what it's like to have walked in our shoes." Looking at my best friend in search of some sign of approval, I concluded, "We're soulmates, Nicki. It was meant for us to find each other."

Nicki was torn. She wanted to be the voice of reason, yet still maintain some semblance of compassion. "But Chelsey, you've only known this man for three months. Three *short* months."

"I know, Nicki. And I've loved him for at least two and a half."

* * *

A week and three days after expressing our undying love for each other, Terrence moved in with me. He was at my place most of the time anyway, so it just made practical sense to make it official. There were just enough bedrooms for each of us to have a room of our own and one together. He didn't have any assets to bring with him because to keep his children from being uprooted, he had given everything to Doretha in the divorce—the house, the car, the furniture. *Everything.* All he had kept for himself were the bills, a few clothes, and his self-respect. He told me that when he left the marriage, he moved in with his co-worker, Kathy, herself a recent divorcee, and her three children. It was a mutually beneficial friendship—he helped her with her mortgage and she gave him a place to stay. I was amazed that he held no animosity toward the wife who had betrayed him. Hearing him tell the story of his forgiving spirit only made me fall more deeply in love with him.

* * *

"I love you, Chelsey George. Will you marry me?"

"Of course I will, Terrence Jackson. I love you more than anything."

"And I love you more than that," he said.

* * *

I never once questioned the court dates Terrence said were for additional child support or the intermittent bouts of rage he said were stress-related or the absence of regular visitation with his children he said were a byproduct of Doretha's revenge on him for leaving the marriage. Even when it was unbelievable, I believed every word, accepted every explanation. I pretty much had to. We were soulmates—and I was lucky just to have found him.

CHAPTER 23

It only took one postage stamp to turn my world upside down. I had just sealed the envelope containing my application to pursue my third degree from the University of Oklahoma. I smiled as I fantasized about someday being *Dr. Chelsey C. George.* Christopher would have cried like a little bitch if I hadn't taken his name when we got married, but Terrence wasn't insecure like that. When I told him I wanted to keep my last name because I was proud of the strong black woman who bore me and wanted to honor her strength by remaining a George, not only did he support my decision a hundred and ten percent, he even said that our son, if we ever had one, could wear my last name instead of his to carry on the proud legacy of my family. I appreciated the thoughtfulness of his suggestion, but I wasn't *that* damned proud. Any son we had was going to be a Jackson, just like his daddy.

My acceptance into the program was all but guaranteed. I had a 3.8 grade point average in the master's program, impeccable references, work experience, life experience, and perhaps my strongest asset of all, unbridled determination. All I needed now was one little postage stamp. I looked in every drawer in my desk, but came up empty each time. *Maybe Terrence has one,* I thought as I walked down the hallway to the third bedroom. When Terrence moved in, he had transformed the room into his own private sanctuary and except for those few times we were messing around and ended up doing it right there on the floor, I hadn't set foot in his personal space for longer than the time it took to give him a quick kiss. It wasn't that the room was off limits to me. I had simply made a conscious decision to respect the privacy of my husband-to-be, irrespective of the fact that my name was the only one on the mortgage. I had to rummage through Christopher's personal space regularly just to stay a step behind his lying ass, but I trusted Terrence. It was a breath of fresh air to be with someone who didn't have anything to hide.

When I opened the door, my eyes immediately fell upon the framed 8X10 portrait of me that sat so lovingly on the corner of his oversized oak desk. I smiled. One thing was for sure—Terrence Jackson loved him some Chelsey George. As I sat in his big executive chair, his familiar smell found its way to my nose and I smiled again. I wished he was home so we could christen the floor again, instead of working late at the office for the fourth time in as many days.

"Now, where would he keep stamps?" I asked myself out loud, as I began opening the drawers to his desk. It was in the bottom, left-hand drawer that I found them: four empty bottles of vodka. "Oh my God!" were the next words I heard myself say. My heart started to race just as my hands started to tremble. Suddenly, I found myself looking around the room for other evidence that might explain Terrence's mood swings, forgetfulness, and declined life insurance policy. In four drawers of the six-drawer file cabinet, I found a total of twenty-eight bottles of alcohol of various shapes, sizes, and brands. It would have been a full-fledged liquor store if the bottles actually had liquor in them. The fifth drawer contained seven unopened containers of alcohol, including a gallon of rum. I speculated that since there were only twenty-four hours in a day, he just hadn't gotten around to drinking any of those yet.

I opened the last drawer fully expecting to find more of his stash, but except for a cigar box and a computer printout of names, addresses, telephone numbers, and social security numbers of people I didn't know, it was empty. When I opened the cigar box, I saw something that made my heart race even faster—a .38 caliber handgun. I was frozen with fear. People think that *frozen with fear* shit can't really happen, but I'm serious, I literally couldn't move a muscle. My head was bombarded with a million questions. *Who was this man I had allowed into my life? Had Nicki's intuition been right all along? Was I in love with an alcoholic? A thief? Or worse?* The sound of Terrence's voice interrupted my thoughts.

"Now you know," he said, as he began slowly walking towards me.

"Who are you?" I managed to whisper. I hadn't planned on whispering, but that's all that came out.

For the next three hours, Terrence told me everything. "I do love you, Chelsey, but other than that, I'm not who you think I am. For starters, I don't really have a stuttering problem. I just do that to make people feel sorry for me. You see, when people feel sorry for you, they trust you and when they trust you, you can get them to do almost anything. I'm not really a bad person, baby. It's just that I do bad things sometimes and even after I met you, I didn't know how to stop. But thank God, now you know. Now I can get some help." Tears began to fall from the loneliness of the eyes I had trusted so implicitly. "I've been drinking since I was eight years old, Chelsey. Both of my parents were alcoholics, just like the aunt I was sent to live with when I was eleven, so it was easy to get my hands on something to drink. If there was no beer or wine in the house, I'd have my friends who were old enough buy it for me. By the time I was thirteen, I had my own fake I.D. Alcohol numbed the pain. I needed it to survive the hell that had become as familiar to me as my own name.

"I conned my way through elementary, junior high, and high school. I'm the world's best at creating my own reality and selling it as truth to everyone around me. After high school, I joined the army. That's where I met Doretha. We got married and before I knew it, we had three kids. I hated her and I hated my kids because I felt like they were holding me back from some wonderful life I was supposed to be living. I felt trapped, Chelsey. Eventually, I got myself kicked out of the army for gambling, disorderly conduct, and public intoxication. Doretha had received an honorable discharge six months before that. We moved from place to place trying to start over and somehow we landed in Brighton. A forged college transcript and three letters of recommendation I wrote myself helped me to land a job with the City, but I'm not a chemical engineer. I work in that department as an administrative technician. I do low-level paperwork and make coffee, mostly. You've got to understand that

I would have done anything to keep food in my kids' mouths and a roof over their heads, Chelsey. Even though I saw them as a burden rather than a blessing, I didn't want to be the deadbeat dad my father had been.

"With the fake documents, I managed to get a job, but I was still addicted to alcohol and gambling. I began hanging out with the wrong crowd and found myself involved in a scam where we would buy credit cards and checkbooks from people who were desperate for quick cash. We would pay them small amounts of money, say, no more than $250, for their credit cards and checks. Then we would use them to buy whatever we wanted, which we later sold for a profit. We would even pay petty criminals to go right into the bank and get cash advances for us. You wouldn't believe how easy it is to find somebody desperate and convince them to commit a crime. It's incredible what people will do for money, Chelsey. After a few days, the people we bought the stuff from would be instructed to call everything in as stolen. They were liable for the first $50 and the banks absorbed the rest.

"I was satisfied for a while, but as time passed, I got more and more greedy. Eventually, I got careless and got caught. I spent eighteen months in jail because of it. When I got out, my former boss gave me another chance. Doretha didn't. The day I got out of jail, she served me with divorce papers. Because she still loved me, though, she let me live with her and the kids until I could find a place to stay. Two weeks later, I met you. I made up the story about living with a co-worker because I knew you would never give me the time of day if you knew I was still married and living with my wife. Our divorce was final only two months ago. Baby, when I proposed to you, I knew I had to stop the illegal stuff if I wanted to begin an honest life with you. I love you, Chelsey, so I stopped. I stopped everything just for you. This is old stuff I just haven't gotten rid of yet."

Terrence's tears increased as his pleading voice said, "Please don't leave me, baby. I'll do anything you want me to! *Anything!* I need you, Chelsey. I need you more than ever, now. I don't do anything illegal anymore, but I've still got a big drinking problem. Please stand by me, baby. I know I can beat this thing but I need your help. I know I can be the man you want me to be, the man you *need* me to be. Please, Chelsey, please give me a second chance! I love you! I loved you even before I met you because you were the kind of woman I had always dreamed of having someday. Please, help me, baby! *Please!*"

I would have needed a heart of stone to remain unmoved by Terrence's cry for help. Although I wanted to believe everything he said, I still had one burning question in my head. "What's the gun for, Terrence?"

"It was for my own safety, that's all. I did a lot of shady deals at night in bad areas of town. I needed a gun for protection. I'm not a monster. I'm an alcoholic. You've just got to believe me!"

I believed Terrence was telling the truth because I wanted to believe him. I believed he wanted to change because I wanted to believe that, too. More importantly, every part of me believed that every part of him loved me through and through. My need to be loved was as strong—if not stronger—as his need for alcohol. Holding each other, we cried together well into the night. At eight o'clock the next morning, I sat beside him as he dialed the number to the Fresh Start Drug and Alcohol Rehabilitation Center.

Terrence began the rehab program with twenty-three other men and women who were either alcoholics, drug addicts, or both. On graduation night, he was one of only seven who had made it through fourteen weeks of three-hour meetings four nights a week, random urine checks, and *AA* meetings every Friday, Saturday, and Sunday. At the start of the program, the facilitator had announced that most of the addicts there in the beginning wouldn't be there in the end because one by one, week by week, they would be sucked back into the lifestyle that brought them there in the first place. I was more than proud that Terrence had made it through the fire. Lies and alcohol were no longer a part of his repertoire and he had a peace about him that I had never seen before.

All of the graduates and their families had become like a family to every other graduate and every other family, so when I presented him with his graduation gift, there wasn't a dry eye in the room. "Will you marry me?" I asked, as I pulled a small box out of my purse.

"Yes, baby" he replied, as he held on to me tightly. "Yes, I'll marry you."

Three weeks before we were to have a small ceremony at my home church in Wade, the letter came. Terrence read it out loud: *Dear Ms. George: We are pleased to inform you that you have been accepted to the University of Oklahoma to pursue a doctor of philosophy degree in the School of Psychology..."* Everything had finally fallen into place. As I watched Terrence dance around the room, waving the letter in the air, my mind said, *Thank you, God*...then the three of us danced together.

CHAPTER 24

I wasn't at all anxious about my second stint in graduate school because I had become an expert at playing the games so necessary for black students in white academia. Like a master thespian, I used childlike submissiveness, feigned inferiority, and disingenuous smiles to win the hearts of all but the most hardcore establishment professors in the department and though they were completely unaware of it, even some of them had fallen for my act a time or two. But even though I was playing the game exactly as it was supposed to be played, it felt like I was leading a double life because I had to write what the white professors wanted to read, rather than stand up for what I truly believed. I had to hold my tongue, rather than speak out against the racist ideology taught in their classrooms. I had to smile on the outside, while consumed by anger and helplessness on the inside. The feeling was akin to what W. E. B. Dubois called *double consciousness*. Because I was nowhere near the intellectual genius he was, I just called it *fucked up*.

In their historically arrogant stupor, most of the professors had convinced themselves that my accomplishments were a result of *their* positive influence. It was automatically assumed that I had no father and they wouldn't even allow themselves to entertain the possibility that my mother had played a major role in my intellectual development because their extensive research had confirmed, after all, that families like mine found no value in education. Administrators, deans, professors, and sometimes even my peers, systematically judged me as inferior, foolishly using my race and gender as concrete evidence. Had they not heard that it was *my* people who performed the first open heart surgery and developed the life-saving concept of blood banks? Had they not heard that it was *my* people who invented the gas mask that saved their lives in World War I, the air conditioner that keeps them cool, the ironing board used by their underpaid black maids, and their precious little golf tee? Had they not heard that it was on the backs of *my* people that this great country was built and that Mother Africa was the original birthplace for all humanity? I regularly wondered when the miseducation of America's children would stop. There was no question that somebody definitely needed to wake the hell up.

Since I had become so incredibly proficient at convincing my professors that they were responsible for every thought in my head, none of them had any idea I could actually think for myself. The power they wielded, however, had long ago convinced me that changing their attitudes and demanding their respect had to be put on a back burner in deference to my primary goal—graduating. After graduation, with doctorate in hand, I would change the world, beginning with the University of Oklahoma. For now, though, I had to suck it up.

As did so many other graduate students, I worked during the day and attended classes four nights a week.

My lunch hours and weekends were spent studying and making preparations for the small wedding ceremony Terrence and I had decided would take place over the Christmas break. Like every other Monday and Wednesday since the semester had begun, I arrived fifteen minutes early for my *Theories of Psychology* class. Dr. Jeremiah Bradley's infinite wisdom and dry humor assured that the classes he taught were filled to capacity every semester. Although Dr. B—as his students affectionately called him—had taught at the University for nearly forty years, it was common knowledge that he wasn't a proponent of the racist ideology openly supported by too many of his peers and quietly supported by too many administrators. Being the progressive academician that he was, however, came with a price and he was kept in subjugated professor status year after year. But Dr. B didn't seem to mind. The privilege of challenging the minds of tomorrow's leaders was, apparently, reward enough for him.

When addressing his students, Dr. Bradley preferred the formality of using our surnames, although most of us chose the informality of Dr. B when addressing him. "Ms. George," he began, "How do you think your compatriots would feel about discontinuing our dialogue prematurely this evening?" Although he spoke like a member of the British Parliament, he was born and bred in Oklahoma. The entire class knew that I was Dr. B's favorite. While most of the students didn't seem to mind my elevated status, they didn't understand how I had become the chosen one. I didn't quite know how the usually nondescript teacher/student relationship had blossomed into a meaningful, mutually respectful friendship, either. I only knew that, unlike with the other white professors in the department, I felt safe with Dr. B. I chuckled whenever I thought about the two or three blond-haired Heathers in the class who despised both me and Dr. B for his clear choice in teacher's pet.

In the most formal voice I could muster, accompanied by a big smile already invading my face, I replied, "Well, Sir, I am certain I speak for the entire group assembled here today when I say, "Long live Dr. B!" All but the Heathers burst into hearty laughter while all, including the Heathers, simultaneously slammed shut their textbooks and notebooks in preparation for an early departure. Few things were more precious to working graduate students than a cancelled class.

"Very well, then. Class is dismissed." With a playful warning, he added, "And, anyone not fully prepared to discuss Jungian psychology at our next meeting will be required to bathe Mr. Whiskers for the remainder of the semester—and Mr. Whiskers hates baths!" Laughter and miscellaneous chatter continued as we gathered our belongings and headed out into a world in which we now had the rarest commodity known to working graduate students—an unanticipated *extra* hour and fifteen minutes.

"Goodnight, Dr. B," I shouted with enthusiasm, as I waved goodbye from the doorway of the classroom. The first thought in my state of newfound freedom was to call Terrence to let him know I'd be home early. Maybe we could even make it to the tuxedo shop before it closed. My second thought was to surprise him with an early arrival and seduce him right on the kitchen table as he was preparing dinner. Almost immediately, I chose the surprise homecoming because the tuxedo shop was open late on Wednesdays and we could go, then. Besides, for some reason, Terrence had been in a blue funk lately and a little freaky-deaky sex might do a lot of good.

On the short drive home, I couldn't help but smile as I thought about the life changes Terrence had made simply because he loved me and didn't want to lose me. Since that fateful day when I discovered I was in love with an alcoholic, the *new and improved* Terrence had not had one drop of alcohol, had faithfully attended *AA* meetings, had washed his hands of all illegal activity, and had even managed to obtain a small promotion at work. His actions not only solidified my belief that he loved me with every fiber of his being, they successfully shielded me from the wounded little girl within because I finally had somebody who loved me more than anything. In spite of pursuing a doctorate in psychology, it never occurred to me that if Terrence had loved himself enough to make those same life changes, we both would have been better off.

I bounced through the front door, shouting, "Baby, I'm home!" Hearing Marvin Gaye crooning about getting it on from the stereo in Terrence's study, I ran up the stairs, two at a time. As I entered the doorway, the sweet homecoming I had envisioned abruptly vanished. My heart dropped when I saw Terrence sitting on the floor, reunited with a fifth of vodka. Sprawled across the floor beside him were credit cards and checkbooks, all of which were indisputable evidence that the *new and improved* Terrence was just as much a liar and a con as the old one had been. Staring blankly at me, he seemed to be unable to form intelligible speech, but it wasn't readily apparent if it was because he was shocked to see me or because he was as drunk as a skunk.

"Get out, Terrence," I heard myself say. The calmness with which I spoke was bone chilling, even to me.

As if suddenly rediscovering language, Terrence's panic stricken voice cried out, "Baby, I can explain! I can explain!"

"I don't want to hear any more of your lies, Terrence. I want you out of my house and out of my life right now." I knew it was my mother's strength that kept my knees from buckling right under me.

"You don't mean that, baby! You can't throw away everything we have just like that! Remember, the facilitator at Fresh Start said relapses are common! I promise I'll get help! I'll go back to rehab!" Tears began to roll down the uneven texture of his face. "I'll quit the scams, too, baby! I only kept doing them to make sure we had enough money to pay for the kind of wedding you want, the kind of wedding you deserve. But, no more, baby. I'm done with them, now! I swear! I'll do whatever it takes, baby! Please don't do this to us! Please don't do this to me! I love you, Chelsey. Can't you see that? I love you!"

This time Terrence's pleas were falling on deaf ears. "It's over, Terrence," I said, as I turned to walk away. "It's over."

Still crying, he ran after me, grabbing me by the arm. "Baby, please don't do this! It'll destroy me! You've got to give me another chance, Chelsey! If you leave me, I'll die! I don't have anywhere to go. Please don't do this!"

Pulling away from his grip, I looked directly into a face that looked twenty years older than it actually was. "You'll be fine, Terrence," I said. "There are plenty of hotels and liquor stores in this town. Now, get out of my house."

In the next instant, Terrence lost his mind. I don't mean *lost his mind* like that fake-ass brother in <u>Waiting to Exhale</u> must have when he decided to leave a together sister like Angela Bassett for that stringy-haired white woman. I mean *lost his mind* like Charles Manson when he decided it was okay to cut a baby out of a pregnant woman or that fool near Waco who thought he was Jesus but didn't have one miracle to show for it. Terrence grabbed me by the arm again then threw me against the wall in the hallway, rendering me immovable with the strength of his upper body. Rage had replaced the tears in his eyes. "I'm not going anywhere," he said, with anger spewing from every pore in his body. "I pay half this goddamned mortgage which makes this just as much my house as it is yours. I'll leave it when I get good and damned ready!"

Seeing his lack of control and remembering the gun, I got scared. *Really* scared. Did he still have it? Would he use it on me? "Terrence, you're hurting me," I said, trying to free myself.

"Shut up, bitch! You think you're better than me, that's your problem. That's always been your problem! I do everything I can to make you happy and it's never enough! Now, after all I've done for you, you're trying to ruin me! Well, I'm sick of the way you treat me and I'll be damned before I'll let another man move into my house and sleep with my woman in my goddamned bed!" Then, in the most frightening calm I had ever seen, he made one final threat. "I'll see you dead before I'll see you with another man, bitch. And you can take that to the bank."

My trembling body remained against the wall as Terrence released me from his grip. I watched him as he stumbled back to his study. Seconds later, in between thirsty gulps of vodka, I heard him pick up the telephone and dial a number. "Yeah, man, it's Terrence," I heard him say. "Listen, I need a job done. This bitch knows too much and she's giving me trouble. I need somebody to take care of her." I couldn't believe what I was hearing. "How much will it cost? Well, do you think it'll be five figures? When can you get it done?"

"Oh my god! He's going to kill me!" my voice whispered out loud without any direction from me or my vocal chords. I ran into the bedroom we shared and picked up the telephone extension. "The police are listening to this call!" I screamed into the receiver.

"Hang up the phone, Chelsey," Terrence demanded.

"The police are listening to this call and they know who you are!" I screamed again.

"Don't say anything, man," Terrence said to his partner in crime. "Just be cool. I told you she was crazy."

The anonymous person hung up. Almost immediately, Terrence appeared in the doorway of our bedroom with his arms folded. He peered at me with eyes that betrayed him by revealing the depth of his very real, albeit very sick, love for me. Plunging myself into survival mode, I attempted to appeal to the love I was certain I saw. "Why are you doing this to me, Terrence? I thought you loved me? I don't even know who you are anymore."

Terrence's voice sounded sad and despondent. "Who am I, Chelsey? A man who tried to love you. A man who would have killed for you. A man who would have died for you." The momentary sadness turned back into rage as he continued. "But you never gave me a chance! I was never good enough for you! Now, you're going to pay for everything you've done to me! You're going to pay for trying to destroy me!"

Clearly, Terrence's mind had moved to a place specifically reserved for the innately insane. "What are you talking about, Terrence?" I said. "What do you think I've done to you?"

"Shut up, you selfish cunt! Nothing is ever your fault is it? You think you're perfect!"

"But, Terrence—"

"I said shut up! You're so lost in your own little perfect world that you can't even see what you've done to me! You can't see how you've messed up my life! Well, it's all over now! But not because *you* said so. It's over because *I* said so. Terrence Jackson is calling the shots, now."

CHAPTER 25

As outrageous as it sounded, I took Terrence's phone call about murder quite seriously—especially since it was mine—and called the police. I was absolutely mortified when they told me there was nothing they could do. *No*, I had not taped the conversation, I told them. And, *no*, there were no witnesses. And, *no*, he had not physically harmed me. And, *yes*, he did have personal effects in my house. *Then there's nothing we can do at this point, ma'am*, they told me without an ounce of empathy. It was with that slap in the face that I became a prisoner in my own home.

Although I had started out as just another mark from the moment he spotted me at *Mama's*, somewhere along the way, Terrence found himself just like me—hopelessly in love. That old saying that true love knows no limits is definitely true because there was no limit to how low Terrence would stoop in order to win back my affection. He quickly decided that for his plan to work, he would have to take complete responsibility for everything. He concluded that if he took the blame for the drinking, the lying, the scams—*everything*—my heart would soften and I would give him another chance. Whether his new scheme would be best classified as reverse psychology or a good, old-fashioned mind fuck is up for debate.

Eight days after he had plotted my murder, Terrence apologized. His tears came quickly as he apologized profusely for insecurities, addictions, character flaws, deceptions, threats, and emotional abuse. And he was especially *oh-so-sorry* for scaring me with a phone call that wasn't even real. How could I have possibly believed he would so much as hit me, let alone have me killed, he had asked. He would never hurt me because he loved me more than anything. As long as he was alive, I was safe, he said, and I could take that to the bank.

He wanted me to know, too, that he was not coming clean in order to get me to take him back. No, that wasn't it at all. In fact, he *couldn't* be with me, he said. He had too many problems that he needed to work out for himself. There was no way he could be in a relationship right now. Besides, he didn't deserve me. He didn't deserve anybody, at least not until he worked his problems out. It would be hard to do alone, but he was determined to become a better man. A man he could be proud of. A man who could be what a woman like me needed. What a woman like me deserved. He knew he had lied. Lied so many times that he often forgot what the truth actually was. But he had learned a very valuable lesson and *now*, he was telling the truth. The god's honest truth. *Really.* All he wanted from me was friendship. That was all. Friendship. He would do the rest by himself. He *had* to do the rest by himself.

Terrence then remembered one more thing. He needed me to allow him to live in my house just a little longer. Just until he could find a place of his own. He promised it wouldn't take long. He had looked at several apartments just yesterday. Hadn't I seen the brochures on the kitchen table, he had asked. Couldn't I see that he was doing everything in his power to move out as quickly as possible? Certainly he would understand, he said, if I didn't want him to stay. After all, he had treated me horribly, scaring me and all. But he really needed my help just one more time. Just this once, if I could find it in my heart to help him, he would be forever grateful.

I'm sure Terrence thought his little speech was brilliant but I couldn't have been less moved. I decided that to get him out of my house and my life, I needed to try a little reverse psychology of my own—or mind fuck, depending on how you see it. I quickly accepted his apology with a few concocted tears of my own. I told him I believed that he was *oh-so-sorry* and that he meant it when he said he would get help. I never really believed he would hurt me, I said. Not really. After all, I knew how much he loved me and I loved him just the same. Besides, I should have been more supportive of him, more patient with him. I knew he had problems and I should have been there to help him work through them instead of focusing on my own needs. I had truly been selfish and that was the god's honest truth. *Really.* And, I had no intention of putting him out on the street. I cared about him too much to do that. Sure, he could stay with me until he found another place. It would only take a week or two. I knew he would look as hard as he could. After all, I had seen the apartment brochures on the kitchen table.

As I hugged him tightly and we both cried fake tears together, I thought to myself, *This alcoholic bastard is crazy. Truly crazy.*

* * *

Certain that he had regained my trust, Terrence decided the time was ripe for Phase II of his plan. When I got home from class that evening, I would find it—the suicide note. Sipping on the bottle of vodka he substituted for courage, he chose his words very carefully as he began to write: *Dear Chelsey, I've decided that the time has come for me to stop causing you so much pain. You deserve so much better than I have given you and I want your life to be as happy and fulfilled as you have made mine. By the time you read this note, I'll be dead. I've taken enough pills to make sure I never cause you pain again. But, don't blame yourself, baby. You have done nothing but try to love me. I just didn't know how to accept that love because I've never known how to love myself. I've left $12,000 in the bottom drawer of my file cabinet. It's not very much, but it's legit and I want you to have it. I wish I had more to give. Thank you, Chelsey, for your kindness and your love. I love you.*

When he finished, he placed the note on the small end table next to the answering machine where I would see it as soon as I walked through the door. He knew it would take more than a few aspirin to do any real damage, so he fearlessly swallowed a handful with the last of the vodka, poured the remainder of the pills into the commode, and flushed. The doctors had to find something in his stomach in case they decided to pump it. He placed the empty pill bottle on its side, next to the note, then poured water into a glass and carefully positioned the overturned glass on the floor next to the end table. When he was done, he looked around to make sure all of the pieces were in place. He couldn't afford any careless mistakes. If his plan to garner my sympathy was to work, every detail had to look completely authentic. When he was satisfied that it did, he hid the empty bottle of vodka in the bottom of the trash can in the garage, practiced looking lifeless on the sofa....and waited for me to come home to save him.

CHAPTER 26

As I drove home from class, I prayed that Terrence had found an apartment. Three weeks had already come and gone and I was tired of playing the part of a cover story from *Psychology Today*. While a body fuck can wear you down, a mind fuck can wear you out. When I opened the front door, I immediately saw his muscular body sprawled across the sofa. His right arm hung limply over the side with the palm of his hand facing upward. It looked like he had been drinking but he was so good at hiding it that I could never be for sure. As I moved closer to the sofa, I saw the overturned glass on the floor. Within seconds, I saw the note and the pill bottle. Total lunacy aside, I never thought he would take things this far. My heart raced as I read the note. Everything after that was a blur. I must have called 9-1-1 because EMS, a fire truck, two police cars, and several nosey neighbors showed up almost immediately. Terrence was taken to the County Hospital where over the course of the next twelve hours, his stomach was pumped and a psychiatric evaluation was performed. Three days later, he was released into my care with instructions to seek outpatient mental health treatment at the MHMR clinic on Traylor Avenue. His discharge diagnosis was *major depression, single episode.* The last line of the discharge summary read: *Patient no longer a danger to self or others.*

Exactly four weeks to the day of his discharge, Terrence moved out. Call me stupid, but the truth is I didn't want him to go. Since he had gotten out of the hospital, he had become the loving, caring, thoughtful man with whom I had fallen in love. And, apparently, his ordeal had made him rethink the whole dying thing. Looking death squarely in the face tends to have that effect on a person. No one knew that better than I did.

His gratitude to me for saving his life was endless. After he moved out, he began to romance me like he had in the early days of our courtship. Desperate for the love we had once shared, I willingly accepted all the affection he willingly gave. Besides, he seemed to be the only one I could depend on when I began to have flat tires on my brand new car, leaky water heaters, computer crashes, and malfunctioning washing machines. These problems set me back financially, but I could always count on Terrence to ease my burdens by replacing every irresponsible tire, faulty water heater, defective computer, and unreliable washing machine. No amount of money was too much to spend, he said, if it would lighten my financial load. He loved me and did not want to see me struggle. Not after everything I had done for him.

To add to my worries, I began to receive excessive hang-up calls, sometimes as many as twenty in a single day. Terrence pointed out that it was obvious that someone must be watching my house because whenever he was there, not one scary phone call was received. Although money could fix my other problems, there was nothing he could do about the phone calls except offer to spend the night on my couch so I wouldn't be alone, and assure me that the person making the phone calls probably didn't pose any *real* danger. He said he didn't mind coming over at a moment's notice because he would do anything to make me feel safe and it was the least he could do for all I had done for him. Amidst the endless display of love and affection Terrence had shown since his discharge from the hospital, I had neglected to remember one crucial element: I had fallen in love with the devil.

It wasn't until mid-October that his madness spiraled out of control again. My classmate, Carter, and I were busily putting the finishing touches on our class presentation when the doorbell rang. Although I didn't know it, Terrence had been watching my house even before Carter's arrival almost two hours earlier. Although it was forty-five degrees and raining, there he stood in shorts, a T-shirt, and untied tennis shoes. Apparently, he had decided that a coat, long pants, and socks weren't necessary to act a complete fool.

"Terrence, what are you doing here? And where's your coat? It's freezing outside."

"What's *he* doing here?" Terrence asked, while coming through the door, uninvited.

"Carter?" I asked, somehow still incredibly dumb as hell. "He's in my class. We're working on a project together." As soon as the explanation came out of my mouth, the light bulb in my head came on. "Terrence, I think you need to leave. We can talk about this later."

"No, *he's* the one who's leaving!" Terrence shouted, simultaneously pointing to Carter.

"Terrence, leave or I'll call the police," I said, trying to remain calm.

Carter didn't know what kind of relationship I had with Terrence, but he quickly decided that whatever it was, he wanted no part of it. "It's okay, Chelsey," he said. "I'll leave." Before I could beg him not to, he grabbed his coat and briefcase and rushed past Terrence out the front door, leaving me defenseless against a madman.

Terrence was standing in front of me looking crazy as hell and I wondered who had hit the goddamned rewind button on my life. "Get out of my house, now," I said. I prayed that he hadn't heard the trembling in my voice.

"Why are you doing this, Chelsey? I love you. That guy was just using you, baby."

"Terrence, you're crazy! Carter isn't interested in me. He's married with a baby on the way for Christ's sake!" I ran to the telephone and picked up the receiver. "Get out now, Terrence, or I swear I'll call the police! I mean it!"

"Baby, you don't mean that. Put the phone down," he said calmly, as he walked slowly toward me. "Put the phone down and let's talk."

"There's nothing to talk about, Terrence. Please leave." I was so frightened I could barely hear my own voice and the tears pouring from my eyes were real this time.

Terrence sensed my fear and moved closer. Before I could react, he leapt toward me, grabbed the phone, and wrestled me to the floor. "You're gonna call the cops on *me*, bitch? After everything I've done for you? You lie and cheat and then you want to put *me* in jail? Have you lost your fucking mind?" Each painful accusation was followed by a more painful blow to my head with his fist.

"Don't you know I love you? Huh? Don't you know that?" he asked, as he beat me, unrelentingly.

In my mind, I heard myself repeatedly say, *Stop, Terrence, please stop!* In reality, unconsciousness had rendered me silent.

The trial was short. My tearful testimony, bloody clothing found in Terrence's home, pictures of my battered face and body, and his history of domestic violence all served as overwhelming evidence of his guilt. Terrence stood before the judge in jailhouse clothing and mandatory chains, awaiting the decision.

"Terrence Jackson," the judge began, "I find you guilty on one count of stalking and one count of assault and battery. Therefore, according to the laws of the State of Oklahoma, I hereby sentence you to one year in the State penitentiary and a twenty-five-hundred-dollar fine. Court is adjourned."

The last sounds I heard were the bang of the judge's gavel, the clanging of prisoner's chains as they led Terrence away, and the unmistakable hatred spewing from his mouth as he said, "You'll pay for fucking with me, Chelsey George…and you can take that to the bank."

CHAPTER 27

Of all the places on the face of the earth, Dr. Sandra Hollander's office was the very last place I wanted to be. Freud had intended therapy to be for those who were rich, white, and male, and none of those criteria defined me. As I approached her office door, I was overcome by a sudden urge to turn around and run all the way back to Georgia, straight into the comfort of Mama's bosom. But I knew I couldn't. That would be the first place Terrence would come looking for me when he got out of jail and discovered I had disappeared. I was also acutely aware that my penalty-free academic withdrawal from the university for a semester would be rescinded faster than Sybil could change personalities if I didn't at least *begin* mental health treatment for what psychologists called *post-traumatic stress disorder.* Personally, I would have called it *scared-like-a-motherfucker disorder,* but I'm guessing that particular diagnosis wasn't in any of their manuals.

The reminder of my reality was just the persuasion I needed to turn the knob to suite 750. When the door opened, the smell of burning incense greeted my unsuspecting nose. Looking around, I found myself in a waiting room that time seemed to have forgotten. In spite of being situated in a rather modern office building, complete with indoor waterfalls and museum-quality art, Dr. Hollander's office space seemed to have been decorated by none other than Rip Van Winkle himself only minutes after waking up from his forty-year nap. As my eyeballs continued to survey the room, the urge to run like a thief came back. I couldn't believe what I was seeing and had it not been for the fact that I was wide awake, I would have thought I was in the middle of some weird-ass dream.

Sitting unashamed on brown and gold shag carpeting—which *had* to have been a special order—was an extraordinarily unappealing, multicolored sofa and an equally unappealing, matching loveseat. On each side of the sofa sat identical wooden end tables with storage compartments below. On a coordinating wooden coffee table placed in the center of the room were various publications focusing on women's issues. As if to mock the furnishings, the magazines were current and crisp, just waiting for an opportunity to free some distressed woman of her emotional baggage. Momentarily forgetting my resistance to therapy, I found myself wondering if rolling papers and roach clips were hidden in the compartment doors of the end tables.

"May I help you?" a voice from a now-opened glass window called out.

Still holding onto the door handle, I turned my head toward the voice. "Uh, yes. Yes, I have a three o'clock appointment with Dr. Hollander," I said, as my feet moved me from the doorway to the window.

"Your name, please?"

"Chelsey George."

"Oh yes, here you are Ms. George," the woman said, as she placed a checkmark on a piece of paper. *God forbid they have a computer system up in here,* I thought to myself.

The receptionist presented me with a sunflower-covered clipboard that had a pen dangling from it by a string. "Since this is your first visit, you'll need to complete this paperwork, Ms. George. I'll let Dr. Hollander know you're here."

"Thank you." I took the clipboard and proceeded to the loveseat. When I sat down, the billowy cushions immediately swallowed my body. I was busily completing the last form when the door to the inner office opened. I looked up into the face of a tall, Amazon-like woman. She was wearing a long, tan skirt and a beige blouse with lapels that were only slightly smaller than the state of Rhode Island. On her size ten feet, she wore dark brown, leather clogs with thick, wooden heels. Bangle bracelets adorned each wrist and daisy-shaped earrings hung proudly from each earlobe. Although she, too, seemed to have gotten stuck in a time warp, the sheer power of her presence reminded me of my mother. As she walked toward me, she extended her hand.

"Hello, Ms. George. I'm Sandra Hollander." Her welcoming smile was accompanied by an even more welcoming voice.

"Pleased to meet you, Dr. Hollander," I said, finding myself comforted by the gentleness of her handshake. "And, please, call me Chelsey."

"Okay, Chelsey," she said with a smile, as she reopened the door leading to the inner office, motioning for me to follow her, "but only if you call me Sandra."

"Sandra, it is." I smiled inside. Something told me things might just be alright.

I followed Dr. Hollander to a rather large office that, to my surprise, wasn't decorated with post-Woodstock era furnishings. In spite of the tasteful, rather contemporary nature of her private office, the doctor offered no explanation for the aesthetic mistakes that were so apparent in her waiting room and in her appearance.

"Please have a seat," she said, as she took the clipboard from my hand and sat in a swivel chair to review my paperwork.

"I didn't quite finish the last page."

"That's alright. You can finish it when the session is over." After reviewing the forms for several minutes, Dr. Hollander put the clipboard aside, removed her glasses, and said, "So, tell me, Chelsey, what brings you to therapy?"

Although there was no real reason to do so, I cleared my throat before speaking. "I can't sleep and I'm scared all the time." I spent the next thirty minutes retelling the story of my victimization. Not expecting it, I also found myself talking about Mama, Lester, and even Captain Eddie Malone.

CHAPTER 28

I began to look forward to my weekly sessions with Dr. Hollander. I marveled at how in such a short period of time, I had come to learn so much about myself and life and love. But the fifty-minute sessions were rarely easy. Dr. Hollander made me work hard, regularly pushing me to the outer limits. She demanded that I confront the demons of my past and my present and she made no apologies for it. As difficult as the sessions were, however, I always found myself in a better, freer place on the drive back home. I can't say that I always understood the madness in her methods, though, and I absolutely despised it when she fell into true therapeutic mode, making me find my own answers, discover my own truth. Wasn't *she* the one with the Ph.D.? Why did I have to figure out my own shit? But despite it all, week after week, like clockwork, I came back for more. It was a cleansing the longest shower couldn't provide. It was nothing less than magical.

I was in the middle of reading an article about women and depression in _Redbook_ when Dr. Hollander opened the door to the waiting room, announcing the beginning of our weekly session. Like a duckling following its mother to the tranquility of the water, I followed her to the four walls that had become my sanctuary for healing. For some reason, I was anxious to get started and began talking before she had even closed the door or picked up her pad.

"You know, Sandra, I just can't figure out why I always end up with the wrong kind of man."

"What kind of man is that?"

"The kind who cheats on me or lies to me or drinks like a fish or uses God to make me believe I'm falling for a Christian man, instead of just another lying cheater. The kind who puts me on a pedestal and tells me I'm the woman of his dreams so I'll believe anything he says, no matter how crazy it sounds. Maybe I'm just too gullible. Terrence once told me that he loved me even before he met me. When I asked him how that could be, he said, 'Because you're the kind of woman I've always dreamed about, baby.' Isn't that just the most beautiful thing to say to someone? It was definitely a beautiful thing to hear, so as usual, I believed it. Now, I realize it was all a part of his manipulation but back then, you couldn't tell me his love wasn't for real. Obviously, he told me what he thought I wanted to hear so he could get what he wanted from me. I was probably the easiest target he'd ever had." Dr. Hollander had picked up her pad and pen, but apparently didn't have anything to add, so I kept going, not quite sure where I would end up this time.

"I don't know why I always meet the no-good, trifling men." Although I was smiling on the outside, it didn't feel all that funny on the inside. "And I stay with their sorry asses long after I know I should leave. I make excuses for their conniving behavior and convince myself that if I love them enough, they'll change. I tell myself I'm good for them and they're good for me because I love them and they love me. Damn! How stupid am I?" I asked, peering into Dr. Hollander's eyes for a definitive answer.

"What evidence do you have that you're stupid, Chelsey?"

"Are you listening to me?" I asked, feeling more than a little frustrated. "I just told you! I attract and *stay* with the wrong kind of man for too damn long!"

"Why do you think you stay?"

"I don't know." I paused, looked into the air for an answer then finding it, continued. "I suppose it's because I believe in my heart that they love me and having their love gives me hope."

"How does being loved feel?"

"Great! Fantastic! There's no better feeling in the world than to love and be loved back."

"What's love to you, Chelsey?"

I hated the endless barrage of questions the good doctor regularly threw at me, but they always seemed to take me somewhere I needed to be, so I indulged her a little longer. "It's a feeling that you matter and that someone matters to you. When someone loves you, it means you're good enough just the way you are. It's the most incredible feeling in the world."

"Who was the first man to ever love you?"

"Eddie. When I was twelve, I wanted my mother to marry him." Because I could no longer look at Dr. Hollander, I immediately shifted my gaze to the floor. "He met me. Then loved me. Then left me." The room was quiet and contemplative until she spoke again.

"Who was the first man you ever loved?"

"My father. He conceived me. Then ignored me. Then left me." I continued to stare at the floor. After several minutes, I focused my gaze back on Dr. Hollander as though I had just discovered the cure for cancer. "Maybe that's why I stay."

"Why?" she asked, knowing I was headed in the right direction even if I didn't know it myself.

"Because I want a man to love me. My own father never did. All my life, I've searched for men to love me to prove that I was worth loving. To prove that my father was wrong. The search was so consuming that in high school and my first few years of college, I didn't give anyone a chance to *not* love me. I left before they even knew I was gone. I left so they wouldn't leave me first. But somehow, all that changed the minute Christopher told me he loved me. Since then, whenever I find someone who truly loves me, I hang on for dear life. I stay in bad relationships just because they say they love me. Having their love makes me feel special and needed and worthwhile. It makes me feel good enough. I stay because I'm afraid that if I leave, I won't be able to find another man who'll love me. I'm afraid I won't find another man who'll believe I'm good enough just the way I am. My father's absence taught me everything I know about loving a man and loving myself...so I never learned how to do either."

Tears began to roll slowly down the sadness of my soul. On the drive home, I had another revelation—Dr. Hollander had worked her magic again.

CHAPTER 29

"I hate him," I said, as I plopped down on the brown leather sofa for the eighth time in as many weeks.

"Who?"

"My father."

"Okay. Let's begin there, today," Dr. Hollander said.

"What do you want to know?"

"What do you want to tell?"

"Damn you, Sandra! Can't you give me a straight answer to just *one* lousy question?"

"You have all the answers, Chelsey."

I sprang from the sofa on which I usually sat so calmly and stomped to the far left corner of the room. "*You're* the one with the goddamn Ph.D.! Can't you help me out just a little bit, here?" I said what I had been thinking for weeks. "I'm so goddamned tired of this psychological mumbo-jumbo I could scream!" I didn't realize I was already screaming.

While I was carrying on like a spoiled brat, Dr. Hollander remained seated in her usual position in the chair across from the now unoccupied sofa. As if she had done it a million times before, she swiveled the chair around to face me. When she came to a stop, she placed an elbow on each arm of the chair then clasped her hands together allowing them to rest comfortably in her lap. After several minutes of silence, she said, "If that's what you want to do, do it."

"What?" I asked, without a clue as to what she was talking about.

"Scream."

"Scream?" *What in the hell is this woman talking about now?*

"Yes, scream," she said, with complete indifference. "That's what you said you felt like doing."

From the bottom of my gut, I released a straight from the soul, ain't holdin' nothin' back, good ole' Georgian scream. I screamed until nothing else would come out. Then I cried. I cried until my head hurt. *"I hate him! I hate him! I hate him!"* I repeated through hot, angry tears.

"Tears cleanse the soul, Chelsey," Dr. Hollander whispered. "Tears cleanse the soul."

When I finally stopped crying, an hour and a half had come and gone.

CHAPTER 30

"I want to talk about my father, today."

"Okay. Let's talk about him."

"I don't know where to begin."

"Begin where it hurts the most."

"That's an easy place to find." I showed no emotion whatsoever. I had no intention of wasting another session mourning someone I hated.

"Tell me more," Dr. Hollander said, as she removed her black-rimmed glasses, put her pad down, and leaned forward in her chair.

I looked around the office. My eyes stopped when they came to the small painting hanging on the wall by the window. I walked over to it and focused on the smiling little girl walking hand-in-hand through a field of burgeoning wildflowers. She was holding the hand of a man who was also smiling. At the bottom of the painting in cursive lettering, I read the title of the work: *Daddy's Girl*. Looking at the little girl, her father, and their smiles, I slowly began to speak.

"He thought loving me was a choice. Isn't that the craziest thing you've ever heard?" I didn't expect—or need—an answer because although Dr. Hollander was there, I wasn't really talking to anyone. "My father thought loving his daughter was a goddamn choice." I bit my bottom lip until I was aware of the pain.

"Don't fathers know that loving their daughters is never a *choice*? It's not some stupid option like cheese on a hamburger or leather seats in a car or 'Should I wear the blue suit or the black one?' Loving a daughter is an obligation! Mess that up once and you mess her up forever!" Looking *through* the painting, I continued. "I was never a daddy's girl. I was only my father's daughter." Pointing to the little girl in the painting with my forefinger, I said, "Now that little girl's life was different. Just look at how happy she is! I bet she had a father who loved her very much."

"Tell me about that little girl's father, Chelsey."

"That little girl's father?" I inquired, pointing to the picture again, this time with my thumb as I walked away. "Her father loved her from the moment she was conceived. When she was still in her mother's belly, he began to call her his little African princess. Although he didn't think it was possible, he loved her even more when he first saw her. The day she was born was the happiest day of his life.

"When she was a baby, he held her and comforted her and rocked her to sleep. She was a sickly baby, too. Almost died, in fact. But when she heard the sound of her daddy's voice or felt the touch of his soothing hand, that was all it took to calm her down and make her a little less fussy.

"When she got older, he took her to her first day of kindergarten and stayed with her until she forgot he was there. He loved her so much that he didn't want to leave. But he knew he had to. Just as he was about to walk out the door, something made her look up. She saw him standing very still by the door. She stopped playing with the other children and waved goodbye to her daddy, but just as she was about to look away, she thought she saw a tear in his eye. She didn't want him to be sad, so she ran over to hug him. Just in case. He hugged her back, too, tighter than he ever had before.

"Oh, and you won't believe what they did on Saturdays! Every Saturday, after he mowed the yard and trimmed the hedges, he would take his little girl to the corner store and let her buy anything she wanted! She especially loved lemon drops! He did, too!" I wasn't aware that I had begun to smile just like the little girl in the painting.

"When she left for college, she thought she saw him cry like on her first day in kindergarten, but she wasn't sure. So, she hugged him again. Just in case. Without fail, he called her once a week while she was away at school. Guess which day it was? Saturday. He called her every Saturday because that had always been their special day.

"Just as with every other major event in her life, when she graduated from college, her daddy was right there with his camera, camcorder, and unconditional love tucked neatly away in his back pocket.

"When she got married, there he was again to proudly walk his little girl down the aisle. Her daddy had shown her how to love and be loved and as a result, she had chosen a wonderful man to share her life with, so he wasn't worried. He knew she would accept nothing less from life than what she had gotten. But even though she knew her daddy was happy that she'd found someone to love, she thought she saw him cry then, too. So she hugged him real tight. Just in case.

"When he died, for a while, she thought she would, too. She loved her daddy with all of her might and she couldn't imagine a world without him in it. From the very day she was born, until the very day he died, he had told her he loved her in one way or another. Usually, his voice simply said it to her. But sometimes, *oh sometimes,* she would know just by how he smiled at her or how he sounded on the telephone or by the cards she got in the mail for no reason at all.

"At his funeral, she spoke. She told everyone how loving and caring and compassionate her daddy had been. When the ceremony was over, she leaned over the casket, kissed his right cheek, slid a box of lemon drops inside his jacket then kissed him again. 'I love you, daddy,' she told him one last time, 'I love you'.

"She cried softly as his body was carried down the aisle and placed in a long, black hearse. Her daddy was gone, but not forgotten. His love, his spirit, his strength—all of those things would be with her forever. She felt safe…at peace…complete. Her father had done his daddy job well and she was fully equipped to go on without him. For that little girl's father, loving his daughter was never a choice."

Dr. Hollander remained silent when I paused to allow the emotion in my throat to subside. By the time my story was finished, I found myself again seated on the brown sofa. My face was wet with the same emotion I had successfully willed away only moments earlier.

"Who was that little girl, Chelsey?" Dr. Hollander asked, ever so softly.

"Me," I answered through the quiet rain of my tears. "That's the little girl I always wanted to be."

"And was that the father you always wanted?"

"Yes," I whispered. "That was him."

CHAPTER 31

"No man has ever loved me. Not my father, not Eddie, not Christopher, not Terrence—none of them ever really loved me. I wanted them to, but they didn't."

"What about you, Chelsey? Have *you* ever loved you?"

"How can I? I don't even know who I am."

"Who do you think you are?"

"I told you—I don't know. All of my life, I feel like I've lived in a virtual fog. The windows of my world are so foggy that I've never been able to clearly see who I really am."

"Then tell me how someone who knows you well might see you? Let's take Nicki. What do you think she sees when she looks at you? What would she say about you?"

"I guess she would say I'm a nice person."

"Would she say anything else?"

"That I'm lovable and thoughtful and probably that I have a good sense of humor."

"Anything else?"

"I can't think of anything else."

"Okay, so Nicki would say that you're a nice, lovable, thoughtful person with a good sense of humor. Would you believe her?"

"No," I said, as gravity began to tug at the anguish in my eyes. I no longer tried to hold back my tears during our weekly sojourn. I had come to realize that crying somehow enabled me to breathe.

"Would you like to believe her?"

"Of course I would."

"Then why can't you?"

"I just can't."

"Can't, Chelsey, or won't?"

"Can't."

"What would it mean if you *did* believe her?"

"I don't know."

"Take a wild guess. What would it mean if you did believe that you were loving and thoughtful and nice and had lots of friends who loved you back?"

I closed my eyes and took a long, deep breath. Finally, I answered. "It would mean I couldn't hate my father, anymore." My head suddenly became too heavy for my neck to support. I doubled over and sobbed, relentlessly.

Dr. Hollander quietly rose from her chair and moved to the sofa. She sat down next to me and began gently rubbing my back in a circular motion. She spoke in a soothing tone as I released my pain.

"In the past, Chelsey, hating your father worked quite well for you. It was what you had to do simply to survive. Your very life depended on it. But that's not working for you, anymore. It's killing you, now, Chelsey. It's killing you." In a near fetal position, I cried for what seemed like hours. Dr. Hollander never once left my side. As

215

my tears grew lighter, my will to make her understand grew stronger. I sat upright, wiped away the remnants of my tears, sat on the edge of the sofa, and turned my body directly towards her. I was determined to make her understand what my life had been like because if she understood, she could hate him, too, and we could both move on with our lives.

"My life has been miserable all because of my father, Sandra. *He's* the reason I've felt abandoned and unwanted. Afraid to love. Afraid no one could ever love me. Afraid to look in the mirror because I might see what he saw—a little girl not worth loving, a little girl not worth fighting for. My life would have been so much different if he had simply been there for me like a father should. Like a *daddy* should."

"What if I tell you that I'm glad you experienced all of those things, Chelsey?"

I stared into Dr. Hollander's eyes as though a trusted loved one had once again betrayed me. "Then you'd be no different from all the other assholes who've hurt me."

"On the contrary, Chelsey. I'm glad for your experiences because those experiences have made you who you are today. That loving, caring, thoughtful person Nicki believes you are is a direct result of your experiences. *All of them.* Had you not had them, you may have turned out to be somebody not so loving or somebody who's not at all caring. Your experiences, Chelsey—*especially* the bad ones—are your blessings in disguise. All of them have created the incredible you that Nicki sees…the incredible you that I'm looking at right now."

Although I had been trying to make a breakthrough with Dr. Hollander, she had somehow made a breakthrough with me. "I never thought of it like that," I said, as I allowed myself to relax by leaning back on the sofa. "But I still don't know how to stop hating him."

"I have an idea. Would you like to hear it?"

"Not really, but I know you're going to tell me, anyway." We both smiled, but only she knew the fog was about to lift.

"Forgive him, Chelsey. Forgive your father."

"Wrong answer, Sandra. Forgiving him isn't an option. I'll never forget what he did to me. I'll never forget what any man has done to hurt me."

"Forgiving isn't a gift you give to the person who hurt you, Chelsey," Dr. Hollander said, as she took my hands into hers. "It's a gift you give to yourself because it liberates you and frees you to move forward. Forgiving doesn't mean you have to forget the past, either. In fact, forgiving is *remembering* the past. You must remember it, Chelsey—*all of it*—then you must let it go."

That night, as I sat in the darkness of my bedroom, I confronted my past. I conjured up every person and every experience that had ever hurt me. I forced myself to remember all of it...then I let go...

...I let it go...

...I let all of it go.

CHAPTER 32

When the tornado in my head finally subsided, I realized I was still sitting in a chair in the lobby of the Carlyle Hotel, there was still a dead body in a room upstairs, I still desperately needed a drink of water, and I was still in one hellacious mess. Except for Nicki and, of course, Mama (that is, if I had actually told her I was seeing a married man), I couldn't think of one person who would believe that I didn't kill Michael. After all, who would believe in the innocence of a woman—especially a poor, black, adulterous one—when the deceased was a rich white man with a white wife and four white kids? Even I found it hard to believe.

Unconsciously scanning the lobby while simultaneously pondering my fate, I devised a flawless plan. Well, it seemed flawless to me, particularly since it was the only one I had at the time. I decided that to solve my problem, I didn't need a drink of water. I needed a pay phone. I promptly negotiated a deal with myself in which I would trade all the water in the world for just one damned pay phone. I scanned the lobby again, this time consciously, but all I saw was a bunch of useless shit. A Victorian sofa. A gaudy floral arrangement. An expensive umbrella rack. Not one damned pay phone. Had the world finally gone to hell in a hand-basket like Mama had always predicted?

It was becoming more and more difficult to breathe. I had to get outside. Outside, where there was air that while polluted with smog and indifference, didn't reek of inevitable doom. Outside, where everybody was alive and well and I had absolutely no personal knowledge of those who were not. Outside, where there were phone booths.

Realizing I didn't have the motor skills required to maneuver my body through a revolving door, I made my way to the motionless door just to the left of the one that wouldn't be still. As if my world was suddenly turning right side up again, almost immediately I saw a phone booth only a few yards away. I must have willed myself to it because I don't remember my feet ever touching the ground. As I stood outside the booth, I prayed that the woman inside would drop dead right there on the spot. I really didn't care who else might die that day. I just needed to make my call, that's all. A full ninety-eight seconds passed before the demon-woman replaced the receiver and exited the booth. "Self-serving bitch," I said, as she passed by. If she heard me, she acted like she didn't. Good thing, too, because I was just about ready to start kicking ass and taking names. At that particular moment, I was definitely my mama's child.

I rushed into the booth and picked up the still warm, still sweaty receiver. Only the vision of Michael's lifeless body made me more nauseous than the humid box in which I now stood. After carefully scripting the dialogue in my head, I slowly pressed 9-1-1.

"Emergency operator," the dispatcher announced, *"how may I help you?"* I'm guessing my vocal chords refused to cooperate because they were all but paralyzed. *"Hello? Emergency operator,"* repeated the concerned dispatcher. *"May I help you, please?"*

In a tone not much louder than a whisper, I heard my voice say, "I'd like to report a murder."

"I'm sorry, I can't hear you. Please speak clearly and directly into the telephone."

I cleared my throat and began again. "A man has been shot. The Carlyle Hotel. Penthouse suite. Please hurry."

"Is the victim still alive?"

"No. I think he's dead." Who was I kidding. I *knew* he was dead.

"Do you know who shot him?"

"No."

"What's the victim's name?"

"I don't know."

"What's your name, ma'am?"

I knew the question was standard procedure, but all I wanted to do was report a murder. Who I was didn't matter. Anybody could see that. Good sense told me the better course of action would be to ignore the question and hang up. But something just below my skin and just above my soul wanted to believe that I *did* matter—at least to the voice on the other end of the phone. Before I could stop myself, I said, "N. P. My name is N. P."

"Is that 'N' as in Nancy, 'P' as in Paul?"

"Yes."

"And your last name, ma'am?"

"Smith," I said, as hot, burning tears fell down my face. In the middle of the dispatcher's next question, I hung up the phone. I decided she had enough information already, and enough has always been just that. *Enough*.

CHAPTER 33

When I stepped out of the phone booth, had it not been for the fact that the first taxi I saw was for hire, I would have sworn I had died and gone to hell without a chance to first explain to St. Peter why he should unlock the pearly gates and let me in. I climbed into the back seat of the musty taxi and closed the door. The Latin-looking driver said nothing. He merely peered at me through the rearview mirror, waiting for instructions. I turned my head away, hoping that he couldn't tell from looking at me that my boyfriend was dead. "Seventy twenty-three Paisley Avenue, please."

The drive to Nicki's apartment seemed to take hours, though in real time, it was no more than fifteen minutes. When the taxi came to a stop in front of her building, the driver turned his head and spoke for the first time since picking me up. "Fourteen dollar, twenty cent," he said, with an accent so heavy that I had to read the meter to see how much I owed. I shoved a twenty dollar bill into his opened palm then vaulted from the car like it was an Olympic event. In my haste, I never even heard his grateful, *"Muchas gracias, senorita!"*

I slipped into the pseudo-secure building behind a short, fat woman who had just been buzzed in. She pressed the elevator button and together we waited in excruciating silence. With blatant disregard for my best interest, the elevator doors took a painfully long time to open. When they did, the fat woman rushed inside, pushed the button to the 4th floor, then before I could say, *'Seven, please',* stepped aside so I could push my own button. Since it wouldn't have been right to slap the hell out of her, I rolled my eyes, promptly took a half step forward, and pushed the button to Nicki's floor myself. The button didn't light up. I pushed it again. Nothing. *Why won't the damned button light up?* I thought frantically. I was beginning to sweat. So was the fat woman. I pushed the button repeatedly, almost violently. Still nothing. The elevator came to an abrupt stop on the 4th floor. With the speed of an African cheetah, the fat woman darted out, bumping the sides of the slow-to-open doors. Completely consumed by number sevens and lights, I was oblivious to her fear.

The elevator doors closed again, imprisoning me like a caged animal. It seemed to get dark in the square box. Never mind that the back panel was made of clear glass—in my mind, darkness was everywhere. Panic, a state of being that was beginning to feel much too normal, overtook me. "Please don't do this to me!" I pleaded out loud to the mute elevator button, all the while pushing it over and over again. "Please, please don't do this!" As if hearing my plea, the doors opened on the 7th floor. I bolted from the elevator, ran down the hall to apartment 714, and began pounding on the door like my very life depended on someone answering it.

"Okay! Okay!" an annoyed voice shouted.

"It's me, Nicki!" I yelled like a madwoman. "Hurry up and open the door!"

Nicki unlocked the deadbolt and opened the door. There I stood, her best friend of fourteen years, looking as though I was having much more than a bad hair day. "What the hell happened to you?" she asked, as I rushed past her into the small, but tastefully decorated apartment. Fresh-cut flowers were perfectly arranged in a crystal vase on the small dining room table just like she liked them. Contracts were sprawled across the desk in the home-office located in the far left corner of the living room. The computer's screensaver of geometric shapes danced across the room without a care in the world. Always the risk-taker, Nicki had made the career move from social work to image consulting when she made the physical move from Oklahoma to California. I fell onto the suede sofa, tears carelessly staining the cream-colored pillows. Nicki instantly knelt down beside me. As was the case throughout the years, my sister-friend was there for me no matter what kind of fix I found myself in.

"What's the matter, Chelsey?" she asked, gently caressing my shoulder.

"Michael's dead!" I blurted out.

"What? Michael's dead?" she repeated in disbelief, only hers was a question.

"Somebody shot him!" I continued. "There was blood everywhere, Nicki!"

"Okay, Chelsey, just calm down. Now, tell me what happened. When? Where? Tell me everything."

"I woke up this morning, went to *La Perla* to pick up a few things, came back to the Carlyle to meet him for lunch, opened the door, and there he was—dead!" Hearing my own words, I began to feel out of control again. "I didn't do it, Nicki! You know how much I loved him! I didn't do it!"

"Of course you didn't, honey, of course you didn't." Her mind went into overdrive. "But who did? Who would've done something like this?"

"I don't know! I don't know!" I was crying uncontrollably and shaking worse than that. "What am I going to do, Nicki, what am I going to do?"

"It'll be okay, Chelsey. Just breathe. Just relax and breathe," she said, trying to think quickly and calm me at the same time. The authority in her voice made me feel a little better, but not much. We sat in silence for several minutes. "Did you call the police?" she asked.

"No. Yes. I mean, not at first. I had to get out of there, Nicki. All I could think about was that it looked like *I* killed him! So, I left, found a pay phone, called the police, then came straight here. I didn't know what else to do! The police will think I did it, Nicki! Everybody will think I did it!" Panic was resurfacing and normal or not, it felt like shit.

"What did you tell the police?"

"I told them Michael was dead."

"Did you tell them his name? Did you say 'Michael'?"

"I don't remember. I don't think so."

"Did you tell them your name?"

"No. I told them my name was N. P."

"Good. Now, is there anything in his room that belongs to you? Clothes? Shoes? Makeup? Think hard about anything you might've left, Chelsey."

I frequently accompanied Michael on his business trips, but just in case the unexpected happened, like the time one of his business associates came to his room unannounced, we always got separate rooms on separate floors. That was Michael's idea from the very beginning. Until now, I hadn't realized what a damned good idea it had been. "Most of my things are in my room, not his. But I think I left some earrings there last night." Hysteria surpassed panic as I remembered taking the earrings off and placing them on the nightstand just before we made love. "Oh my God, I *know* I left them there! I've got to get those earrings back, Nicki! I've got to get them back!"

"No, Chelsey," she said, again reminding me to breathe. "Forget about those earrings. They don't matter. They could belong to anybody."

"I guess you're right," I said, only slightly less hysterical.

"Do you think you left anything else? Think hard, Chelsey. Think as hard as you can."

My mind was moving at the speed of light trying to remember anything else that might implicate me. "My perfume! I was putting some on last night and I dropped the bottle on that damned marble floor! The smell of my perfume is everywhere!"

"Relax, Chelsey!" Nicki commanded with supreme authority. "That doesn't matter, either. Thousands of women wear that same cheap-ass perfume every day." Nicki knew that 'cheap-ass perfume' was two-hundred, seventy-five dollars an ounce, but hoped her attempt at humor would make me relax. It didn't. After a moment of reflection, she said, "You're right, Chelsey. The police will think whoever owns those earrings and wears that perfume knows something. Or at least that's who they'll come looking for first for some answers. If they find out you were seeing Michael, they'll think you killed him because he wouldn't divorce his wife or because of the shit he's put you through or any damned motive they can come up with to pin it on you." She didn't sound worried. She sounded angry.

I felt as though I was losing my mind. I knew there was a thin line between love and hate but had never considered how thin the line might be between sanity and insanity. "Nicki, what am I going to do? I didn't kill him. Maybe I should just go to the police and tell them that."

"You can't do that, Chelsey. They'd never believe you, not now." Nicki cradled me in her arms, moving back and forth in a slow, rocking motion. "Everything's going to be fine," she said again and again, as if repeating the statement would make it true. As she held me tightly, her reassuring voice and soothing touch became a calming force for me. Finally, she said softly, but firmly, "You have to behave as though nothing has happened, Chelsey. Do you understand me?" Holding my shoulders with both her hands, she looked straight into my eyes. "Do you understand me, Chelsey?"

"Yes," I said, only because I knew I was supposed to.

"Good. Now, what time is your flight?"

"Four-fifteen."

"Okay. That gives us three hours. We'll go back to the Carlyle, get your things, check out, and I'll drive you to the airport. You'll get on the plane, fly back to Brighton, and go on with your life as though nothing ever happened. Do you understand me?"

"Yes," I responded, mechanically. "I understand."

CHAPTER 34

Within minutes, Nicki and I were racing down the 405 in her Ford Expedition. When we reached the Carlyle, the entrance and surrounding area were swarming with police cars, ambulances, and even two fire trucks. Nicki drove into the underground parking garage, took the ticket, and parked in the first open space. A uniformed policeman stopped us as we were about to enter the hotel.

"Are you ladies guests of the hotel?" the policeman asked, in a *John Wayne* kind of voice.

"Yes, sir," Nicki said. Then, as though she had not seen or heard the drama unfolding above ground, she asked, "Is there a problem, officer?"

He ignored her. "I'll need to see some identification, please."

"Sure." Under the watchful eye of a second policeman with his hand skillfully positioned on the revolver on his right hip, she reached into her purse to retrieve her wallet. Like a robot, I did the same. "Is there a problem?" Nicki asked again, trying to act as though there wasn't.

"Just official police business," he said, as he compared the names on our licenses to the names on the printout attached to his clipboard. Looking at me, he asked, "Can you confirm your room number, Ms. George?"

"Five-thirty-six."

"Do you know a man by the name of Michael Anthony Arrington?"

Even in light of the bizarre events of the day, I was completely mortified by the question and, almost instantaneously, my heart tried to force its way out of my chest. "Excuse me?" I asked, not quite sure if the words had actually come out.

"Do you know a man by the name of Michael Anthony Arrington?" he repeated.

"No. No, I don't," I managed to say in a voice almost as normal as if I was saying, *Have a nice day.* I couldn't help but wonder if he could see the summersaults in my head.

Giving my license back to me, he said, "You're okay to enter, ma'am." Turning to Nicki, he said, "I'm sorry, Ms. Mitchell, but you're not a registered guest of the hotel so I can't allow you access to the building."

"But she's with me, Sir," I hastily added, certain that such information would be sufficient to make him see reason.

"I'm sorry, ma'am. Only registered guests are being allowed to access the premises at this time."

"It's okay, Chelsey," Nicki said, as she turned to me with an empathetic smile that was a sure *Oscar* contender. "I'll just wait for you here. Go on, now. Hurry and get your things. You don't want to miss your flight."

Somehow managing to close my mouth and move my feet, I voluntarily entered hell for the second time that day. Exactly sixteen minutes later, my small Tumi carry-on was packed. I triple-checked the bathroom then took one last glance around the rest of the room. Declaring it empty, I closed the door behind me. In my haste, I never noticed the corner of the blue envelope peering from underneath the bed. It was a card Michael had given to me the day I arrived in Los Angeles: *Please be patient, my sweet Nubian princess. Not having you in my arms every night hurts me as much as it hurts you. We'll get through this, I promise. Remember, baby, I'll love you forever—and one day. Always, Michael.*

CHAPTER 35

Three hours later, I was in seat 4-A on American Airlines flight 1940, waiting for the pilot to be given final clearance for takeoff. How many times in the last three hours had I wished Michael alive? At least a hundred. Maybe two. Before I could devise a plan to stop them, the tears came. I tried to will them away by opening my eyes real wide like Betty Davis' but doing that only made me conscious of the headache I didn't know I had. I tried to wipe them away, inconspicuously of course, but the cold, old white man seated next to me was nonetheless irritated. He demonstrated his disdain by sighing loudly and turning his rotund body toward the aisle. *Sitting next to you for the next three hours isn't going to be a picnic in the park for me, either, asshole.* That's what I thought but I didn't say it out loud. At least I don't think I did.

Right in the middle of hoping a trap door would open up, suck seat 4-B and its entire contents into oblivion, and close back up again, one thing was obvious—the depth of my pain had no limit. Somebody once said that pain is the breaking of the shell that contains your understanding. That's pure bullshit. I didn't understand any of this at all and worse yet, my particular kind of pain forced me to remember things I knew I had to forget, not the least of which was Michael Anthony Arrington.

When Michael ushered himself into my world like a quiet storm, he caught me completely off guard. How could he have known that for as long as I could remember, I had been afraid of the rain? We talked on the telephone first. I knew that our mutual friend, Randy, had given my number to him only two days before so quite naturally, I was surprised that he had called so quickly. Presidents of Fortune 500 companies didn't typically call so soon, did they?

Three days later, he decided it was time for us to meet face-to-face. His excitement was reminiscent of a teenaged boy about to have his first erotic experience that didn't involve a girlie magazine and a jar of petroleum jelly. I found it funny that he made no attempt whatsoever to hide his enthusiasm about our rendezvous. Not funny, as in *ha-ha*, but funny, as in *unusual*. Unbridled expression of emotion was something I wasn't used to in a man. His gung-ho attitude gave back to me the cockiness that his wealth, whiteness, and marital status had initially taken away so I accepted his invitation for lunch with feigned reticence. Just because he was open about his feelings certainly didn't obligate me to be open about mine. Even though I would never have admitted it, especially that early in the game, his openness was actually a complete and absolute turn-on. But that was a secret I planned to take to my grave. Of course, it was understood that I would tell Nicki long before then.

When he suggested we meet in the lobby of the Ritz Carlton on the corner of Sixth Avenue and Kingston—smack dab in the middle of downtown Brighton—my first thought was that somebody might see us in such a public place. My second thought—which was about three seconds behind my first—was, *If he doesn't care, why the hell should I?* Later I would discover that he did care and that his decisions were never uncalculated.

From the second floor landing, he saw me the moment I stepped into the all but deserted lobby. He wanted to observe me from afar to see if I would panic at not finding him immediately or if I would accept the unanticipated glitch and wait calmly for him to find me. He watched me walk the length of the lobby once, check my watch, politely dismiss a bellman's unwanted offer of assistance, then walk the length of the lobby again. When he saw me casually stroll over to a subtle corner of the lobby, sit in an unobtrusive armchair, pull out a notebook, and begin to write, he was more than pleased. As it turned out, Michael required all of his indiscretions to have brains as well as beauty. To him, at that impressionable moment, I appeared to have the perfect balance of both. He smiled to himself. I had passed a test I had no idea I was taking. He decided to reward my public display of indifference by coming downstairs. Little did he know that writing wasn't a sign of indifference so much as it was an escape route I had employed for years whenever I felt nervous, out of place, or otherwise disenfranchised.

"Chelsey George?" he asked, as if there were a hundred other black women in the lobby of the Ritz that day.

I casually looked up when I heard his voice. To say it was nerve-racking when I first saw him would be an understatement but it was even more agonizing when I saw *him* first see *me*. The blueness of his eyes refused to show any mercy toward my insecurities, which had suddenly returned with the wrath of a woman scorned. Something inside of me was radically afraid that those eyes of his would see right through to my core and he would know precisely why I had come. I wasn't in the habit of taking up company with married men or white men or even wealthy men, for that matter. Funny how money has an uncanny way of making otherwise good girls agree to things to which they would normally not give a second thought. My courage said, *I'm out of here*, and there I was, standing in front of Michael and his piercing blue eyes, wondering if I was completely naked— or just felt that way. I wanted to look down to check but instead managed to say, "Yes. And you must be Mr. Arrington?"

"Please, call me Michael," he said.

Damn! Where did he get that smile! "Michael it is," I said, as we shook hands like two world leaders at a televised summit.

At his suggestion, we retreated to the more discreet lounge on the second level. As we made the short journey, I remembered Randy's exuberance as he was telling me about Michael. They had initially met at an exclusive charity benefit in New York to which Michael had been cordially invited and Randy had weaseled his way in. The event was a huge fundraiser, meaning Randy's presence made about as much sense as a rainstorm in the desert, but he would be the first to tell you he was the master at making the impossible happen. Although he often boasted about being on this or that guest list—whether he actually was or not—Randy's philosophy was *in is in*, regardless of how you got there. The fact that he would have sold his great-great-grandmother to the highest bidder just for a chance to be under the same roof with a room full to the brim with millionaires really didn't matter too much. He swore allegiance to only three things—God, money, and women—and never in that order. The New York fundraiser promised to have at least two of his holy trinity—and all three if you counted the miniature cross he usually wore around his neck.

As fate would have it, Randy bumped into Michael again at LaGuardia Airport two days later. They discovered they were both headed back to Brighton and the rest is history. During the flight, Randy won Michael's trust and a not so small donation to his own—and I use the term loosely—*charitable* organization for at-risk minority youth. It was actually a cleverly disguised front to funnel money into Randy's personal bank account, but who am I to judge?

Randy had already told me that Michael was worth somewhere in the neighborhood of a gazillion dollars, give or take a zillion. Even if he turned out to be a lousy lay, Randy had said, he'd make an excellent benefactor for a girl who needed some quick, tax-free cash to pay for another semester of graduate school. Like diamonds, furs, and women, Randy had said, Ph.D.'s don't come cheap. As much as I despised his misogynistic attitude, the past-due tuition bill on the nightstand next to my bed seemed to prove his calloused point.

Though he would never admit it, I was well aware that Randy didn't have my best interest at heart. He could have cared less about my education or my financial struggle. Personal gain had always been his driving force. He was a street-hustler-slash-businessman and I knew that if the white mogul with the green money liked me, Randy would never let either of us forget who was responsible for our introduction. I knew he would indiscriminately call in on the favor as often as his greed dictated. It wasn't about a brother helping a sister out. It was about a brother getting a hook-up. I got angry just thinking about my asshole of a friend.

Forcing myself to redirect my thoughts, I filed away perfect notes about Michael in my mental rolodex. I knew Nicki would grill me later and I didn't want to forget anything. It was apparent that he was six feet, three, maybe four inches tall. His weight, I guessed, was between 180 and 190 pounds. His hard, toned physique left the accurate impression that he was a picture of health. I'm a stoned cold sucker for straight, pretty teeth and Michael's were both. Without question, he had never smoked a day in his life, brushed and flossed after every meal, stayed away from coffee and tea, and visited his dentist at least quarterly for cleanings. In addition to sparkling white teeth, he had naturally curly brown hair that was prematurely graying around the edges. The color of his skin was embarrassingly pale, so I made a separate mental note to find a way to darken him up at least three shades. I didn't mind dating white, but dating a ghost was completely unacceptable. Every relationship, regardless of how shallow, needed some basic ground rules.

Michael wore a dark blue Armani sport coat, black trousers, a white linen shirt, a gold wedding band, and bright, red confidence. No tie, no socks, Ferragamo loafers. He had large hands and feet and a nose to match. I knew those were generally good signs when it came to brothers and hoped the same held true for white men. The actual size of his magic wand wouldn't really matter in the long run since our interlude was only scheduled for a short run, but I found nothing wrong with hoping for the best. Between his designer clothing and shoes, his Cartiér watch, his award-winning smile, and the money I guessed he had in his wallet at that particular moment, I decided he was probably worth at least a hundred thousand dollars right there on the spot. *He could definitely get a girl through a rainy night or, perhaps, a long winter,* I thought to myself. Maybe Randy really did have my best interest at heart. Why get mad at a brother for trying to help a sister out?

I was so preoccupied with sizing up Michael that I never considered that he was tallying up a score on me as well. I knew he found me attractive. For years, I had passed mainstream society's so-called standard of beauty. People, especially white people, fawned over me. It wasn't that I was drop-dead gorgeous or anything. It's just that they're usually so shocked to see that we come in all shades of beautiful that when *they* decide we've got it going on, they go overboard with the compliments. Or they just stare at us like we just walked out of a spaceship.

When he described me to Max, his golfing buddy and fellow philanderer, he said I was a curvy, brown-skinned woman who appeared to be five eleven counting my cheap, three-inch pumps. He said I had coal black hair that stopped at the nape of my neck, high cheekbones, doe-like eyes, a tiny mole on the left side of my mouth, and an infectious smile. Max laughed out loud when Michael told him about my cubic zirconium earrings and matching necklace that looked out of place on the long, almost elegant neck I had gotten from my mother. Besides the fact that I wore no one item over fifty dollars,

Michael told Max he could find nothing wrong with me. His personal opinion was that my spirit seemed to be full of beauty and grace and I had an innocence that made me even more desirable. To him, I looked like a Nubian princess—tall, regal, and beautiful. He told Max that he couldn't wait to feel the inside of me with the outside of himself, only he didn't say it that politely. They both went home that night and fucked their wives like there was no tomorrow.

* * *

Michael knew the Ritz so well because his office was located in the business center complex in the adjacent building. When we made it to the second floor lounge, he chose a corner table in the back. Once we were seated, he broke the silence we had both preferred up to that point.

"Well, I'll have to call Randy immediately." His tone was unmistakably serious.

"Why is that?" I nervously asked. More than anything else, I wanted him to like me, if only so I wouldn't have to take out yet another tuition loan next week.

"Because he lied to me."

"About what?" My armpits began to tingle.

Michael smiled, showing most of his pearly whites. "He said you were pretty."

"And you would disagree?" I said, returning his smile with one of my own.

"Yes, very much so," he continued to tease. "The simplicity of 'pretty' doesn't do you justice. From where

I sit, 'striking' or, perhaps, 'stunning' would have been a more appropriate description."

Sincere or not, the compliment was more than welcomed. "You know, Michael, I like you already," I said, just as my armpits settled down.

A clearly annoyed waitress suddenly materialized from nowhere. Her skin was a shade or two whiter than Michael's, as if that was humanly possible. Arrogantly ignoring me, she spoke only to him. "Can I get you something to drink, Mr. Arrington?" My blood boiled, but I said nothing.

Michael leaned in close to me as though I was the most important person in the universe and asked, "What would you like to drink, Ms. George?" Now, don't misunderstand his gesture. Sure, it felt nice for him to fawn over me, especially at that moment, but it wasn't like he was defending my honor or anything. Being gentlemanly and attentive was just his way. Though the waitress' snub had slapped me in the face, I knew it had gone right over his curly little head.

"A Coke will be fine, thank you." I made another mental note to discuss the minimum wage waitress with Michael some other time. No need to talk about such heavy issues as overt disrespect, covert racism, or the dark *faces at the bottom of the well* right this minute. Hell, maybe not ever.

"The lady will have a Coke and I'll have a martini with a twist, please." The waitress shot a look of disdain, again noticed only by me, then turned on her *Payless* loafers to fetch our drinks.

"It seems they know you here," I commented when she was out of earshot.

"I suppose I've been here more than a few times. My office is right next door."

That's when I realized I wasn't his first case of infidelity and likely wouldn't be his last. Changing the subject, I said, "So, tell me, Michael, how many children do you have?"

"Four. Four hard-headed boys."

Feeling a lot less nervous and a lot more flirtatious, I said, "You need a little girl."

"And why is that? Because I have all boys?"

"It's never that simple, Michael. You need a little girl so you can spoil her. Daddies are the absolute best at spoiling little girls, you know."

"Why don't I just spoil you, instead?" he replied, with a devilish grin.

"If that'll make you happy," I responded in kind, all the while wondering exactly what 'spoiled' would turn out to mean.

As we continued to talk, I discovered Michael was a forty-one year old, self-made millionaire with another birthday only a month away. He had been married to Natasha Coldwater, the daughter of a prominent plastic surgeon and socialite homemaker, for twenty-one years. Though they had little in common, Michael had fallen for her intellect and her trust fund. Against her parents' staunch opposition, they got married five months after they met. Less than a week later, Natasha was stripped of her inheritance and the multi-million dollar trust fund she was to receive on her 25th birthday became merely an unpleasant memory of what used to be.

Everything went smoothly when they first got married, in spite of the fact that they were as poor as dirt and neither of them was in love in any of the ways that created a solid foundation on which a lifelong commitment could stand. Their only real bond was that they were both immensely driven to succeed. Michael, because he had come from a family who defined poverty, and Natasha, because she wanted to prove to her parents that she could be a success even if she didn't have a silver spoon as a head start. Creating their own family fortune became the glue that held their marriage together. Within four short years, Michael's business acumen—backed by a few wealthy investors, easily obtainable loans, and incredibly good luck—had amassed an enormous amount of wealth for their growing family.

As he sipped on his martini, Michael described Natasha as a doting mother and one of the brightest women he had ever met. She had graduated *summa cum laude* from Harvard Law School where she served as editor of the <u>Law Review</u> for two years. She had published several books and journal articles over the years and was vice-president of Administration at the University of Oklahoma at Brighton.

Shortly after the birth of their third son, Michael said he began to notice a change in Natasha. She became emotionally unavailable, verbally abusive, and sexually disinterested. The worst part for him was that she never seemed to be able to escape the shame of knowing that her husband was born into an impoverished family consisting of an alcoholic father, a chronically depressed mother, a schizophrenic brother, and two, plain, overweight sisters. Not caring how much her attitude hurt her husband, she refused to acknowledge the existence of his family or their history. She purposefully shielded her own trust fund baby boys from their unaccomplished paternal relatives. It never occurred to her that the strength and compassion of her young sons came from their father's side of the family.

Now, I know as well as anybody that there are three sides to every story. But I was only interested in Michael's side, and truth be told, I wasn't all *that* interested in his. At any rate, according to Michael, the marriage had long been over. It felt more like a business arrangement than a loving, caring relationship. Completely fed up with his unfulfilling marriage, he had decided years before he ever knew I existed that it was time for him to meet his emotional and sexual needs outside of their union. That was the sole reason he found himself with me in the second floor lounge of the Ritz Carlton at that moment. As brilliant as he was, it never occurred to him that divorce was a viable option.

By his third martini and my second Coke, Michael knew that I was a twenty-nine year old, second-year doctoral student at the University of Oklahoma. I watched his reaction to the news that I was a student on the same college campus at which his wife worked. His absolute nonchalance intrigued me. I found myself telling him that I was seven months out of an abusive relationship, and continued to be emotionally haunted by my psycho ex-fiancé who swore he would rather see me dead than with another man. Before the stalker, I was a social worker for five years, a wife for two, a working student for six, a romantic fool for ten, and a wounded little girl forever. With so much at stake, I have no idea why I told Michael my life story. Maybe it was because he was such a good listener. Maybe it was because I was such a bad liar. Maybe both. I didn't know…and for those few hours, I didn't really care.

I also made no secret of the fact that I was unapologetically black and maybe even soft-core militant. Momentarily forgetting the perks that inevitably accompany one's millionaire status, Michael asked why a woman who was so fiercely proud of her ethnicity and the tenacity of her people would agree to meet a representative of the other side for a drink. Before I could conjure up a politically correct reply, he let me off the hook by actually apologizing for the thoughtlessness of his question, saying that he knew that my interest in him had more to do with his intellect and his heart than with his tax return and his wallet. Yeah, I laughed, too. The thought couldn't have been more absurd, of course, but it seemed to be what he needed to believe so I just smiled, took another sip of Coke, and told my eyes to say, *Yes, that's it, Richie Cunningham.* Apparently, Michael's intelligence occasionally fluctuated somewhere between *absolute genius* and *dumb-as-hell.* At that particular moment, there was no question as to which direction the pendulum had swung.

I can't pretend that Michael didn't get to me eventually, though. He did. His eyes told me secrets I'd never heard before. When he looked at me, it was like an art collector looking at the *Mona Lisa* or a mother looking at her newborn baby for the very first time. Before I could prepare myself, he did the unthinkable. He reached over and caressed my hand ever so softly. A lethal injection would have been more kind because then I would have known what to expect. Even condemned prisoners were given time to prepare. He never even bothered to tell me that his touch was so magical, so comforting, *so-*

very-nice. As minutes turned into hours, I found myself more intrigued with Michael than I ever expected to be. Definitely more intrigued than I ever wanted to be. The internal struggle with my psyche was driving me insane. *Get a hold of yourself, Chelsey George!*, my subconscious scolded. *He doesn't give a damn about you and you definitely don't give a damn about his white ass!*

To protect myself, I decided to become like a snowball in winter. My smile remained frozen as I dared his presence to melt my defiance. Only once before—with Christopher—had I felt so incredibly fragile. I hated that feeling the first time and I didn't like it any better now. As he touched my hand, Michael pretended not to notice my coldness. I pretended not to care if he did. But the longer his magical, comforting, *so-very-nice* hand touched mine, the deeper it penetrated me. And the more I liked it. Just after nine, he said goodnight, making no plans for the future. I hated him for that much longer than he ever deserved.

That night, in the stillness of my bedroom, Michael and I made love. Oddly enough, he wasn't even there. In the darkness of my fantasies, his curious hands explored the newness of me. My hair. My smell. My taste. With the smoothness of silk, his experienced tongue titillated my body and found places I never knew existed. My body tried desperately to resist, but earth-shattering ecstasy forced my unwilling surrender. Before I knew it, my sheets were as wet as I was. The first time we were together, Michael had the audacity to not even be there. But even in his absence…he satisfied me completely.

CHAPTER 36

The next morning greeted me with a new resolve. Fear was no longer an issue because overnight, I had convinced myself that Michael wanted me. I dialed the number to his office. "Michael Arrington, please," I said with confidence.

"May I tell him who's calling?"

"Ms. George. Ms. Chelsey George."

"One moment, Ms. George, I'll see if he's available."

Listening to Beethoven's *Fifth Symphony* as I waited on the line, I couldn't believe what I was about to do. I had never pursued a man before. Never had to. But this one was different. I wanted power over him like a dying man in a desert wants a cool drink of water. Sure, the money was part of it. Hell, who was I kidding—it was most of it. But my motivation was more complex than that. Michael was now the hunted. In my mind, acquisition of his assets would make up for some of those times when white women made wealthy, yet nonetheless powerless, black men their prey. Black men who, without their wealth, were of no value at all to their blond hair and blue eyes. In the great tradition of those bold women, I would take one of *their* best, then toss him out like old bath water when I was done. Is intentional manipulation of another human being for personal gain or revenge or *whatever* wrong? Of course it is. Did it make it any less wrong because the target was white? In a matter of seconds, I decided that it did.

For my next encounter with Michael, I would be master over everything, including him. And I got the added bonus of getting revenge on brothers. You can take it to the bank when I tell you that brothers can't stand to see a sister with a white man. They'd rather buy a lifetime membership in the Ku Klux Klan than see a white man with a black woman. And the magnitude of their anger is in direct proportion to the fineness of the sister. Get mad if you want to, but you know I'm telling the truth. As far as I'm concerned, to hell with the black man who turns his back on the same sister who fought the hard fight *with* him, and sometimes *for* him, only to get shit on when he decides he prefers the taste of white meat, instead. Black men, white men, brown men—regardless of the shade, they *all* get on my last nerve because they're all fucked up in their own little fucked up way. I swear, if women had a little more dick and a little less drama, I'd date them instead.

"Chelsey, what a pleasant surprise!" Michael's voice finally said into the receiver.

Just what I needed to hear. "Hi, Michael. I hope I didn't catch you at a bad time."

"Not at all. It's good to hear from you, actually. I have a really good feeling about you. About us."

This is going to be easier than I expected, I thought to myself. "I was hoping you'd feel that way. I have a good feeling about us, too," I lied. I paused for effect, just like

I was supposed to do, then continued. "Listen, Michael, can I ask you a quick question?"

"Sure. Anything."

"Can you get away for a few hours?"

"It depends. What am I getting away for?"

"To make love," I boldly proclaimed.

"To whom?"

"To me." Momentarily unsure of myself, I hesitated. "Isn't that what you want, Mr. Arrington?"

"As a matter of fact, it is, Ms. George."

"Well, don't you always get what you want?"

"As a matter of fact, I do," Michael replied, not missing a beat.

Just as his enthusiasm had had a twofold effect on me during our first interaction, his arrogance simultaneously pissed me off and turned me on, too. "Then meet me at the Ritz in an hour," I said, "and I'll give you everything you want—and then some."

An hour and fifteen minutes later, Michael and I were naked in a suite overlooking a man-made lake on the 18th floor of the Ritz. I immediately noticed that the size of his hands and feet had, in fact, been misleading but I didn't care. I was quite accustomed to working around life's disappointments. What Michael lacked in size, however, he more than made up for in substance. He was a full-service lover, taking the time to explore every inch of my body with the softness of his tongue. To describe his talent as 'amazing' would be an understatement punishable by death. Just imagine the most orgasmic experience you've ever had. *Twice.* That's what it was like being with Michael. Not a minute too soon, he entered me and the tightness of my womanhood willingly expanded to give him every opportunity to please me. As he pulsated inside of me, I prayed I wasn't dreaming. Without warning, my screams of pleasure answered my prayers. We fucked three times that day. He told me he loved me the second time. Of course I didn't believe him. But I fucked him once more so he would.

CHAPTER 37

Michael thought it was too risky to rendezvous at the Ritz every time so we saw each other at the Renaissance or the Lexington or wherever I felt like making a reservation. When we couldn't see each other, we talked on the telephone like long-distance lovers. It was all a part of the game for me. Make him believe I cared about him and collect the cash and prizes behind door number three. I trained myself to view him as a fresh, new sunrise, knowing all along that I preferred dusk to dawn. I had no intention whatsoever of falling for him. He didn't plan on falling for me, either. After all, he was a married man with four kids. He had had affairs before me and he planned to have them after me. I was his toy, not unlike the Lamborghini in his six-car garage. Apparently, he was looking the other way when he stumbled and fell into the dark, starry night called me. The irony had taken him by surprise because he had always preferred the predictability of the day.

Two people could not have been more different. I loved to write. He loved to read. I was compassionate by nature. He was philanthropic by choice. I went to the office because I had to. He went because he wanted to. I was immersed in my culture. He took his for granted. I wanted to traverse the world. He had already taken the trip five times. We found out by chance that we both loved bookstores and talking and watching ourselves make love. I became even more enamored when I discovered he was concerned about children and healthcare and poverty, and that he despised racism and bigotry and injustice, and that he *knew* he was a benefactor of white privilege, and that he gave away as much as he earned, and just like me, he hadn't grown up with a trust fund, either.

Michael also discovered things about me that he had not anticipated. He learned rather quickly that I was passionate about anything I loved or anything I hated and nothing in between. My passion, he said, was infectious, rarely leaving him untouched. He once told me that my soul was deeper than a mother's love, that my laughter could light up a room, and that he was more moved by the beauty no one ever bothered to consider than by that which happened to show up on the outside. He said all the things a woman needs to hear a man say. Some of them I even began to believe.

We were fascinated by each other, to say the least, and it wasn't long before we began to wonder if our paths had crossed by chance or if fate had carefully mapped out our course long before either of us knew the other existed. Who would have guessed that vinegar and oil and loneliness and desire would mix so well when properly shaken? Somewhere along the way, we forgot how wrong we were for each other.

While still enjoying the newness of a relationship gone right, Michael shared with me one of his favorite things. The safer gesture would have been to reveal a favorite book or song or restaurant. But Michael went out on a limb and shared with me his favorite tree. A poet might say that the tree had the depth of the deepest valley, the beauty of the widest sea, the tranquility of the calmest wind, or the color of a little boy's happiness after he catches three of God's best turtles. Michael thought the tree was positively beautiful. In my opinion, *beautiful* wouldn't quite describe it. *Scary like a motherfucker* would. It looked like a mushroom on steroids. But his willingness to risk being laughed at moved my adoration of him to heights I never thought possible. Like a fingerprint and a snowflake, I knew that particular tree and that particular man were one of a kind. Michael was no longer my prey. Somewhere along the way, he had become my prince.

Nine weeks after we first made love, he told me he loved me again. We weren't in bed at the time, so I decided he meant it. When I said it back, I meant it, too. After all, he was the one who had made me feel alive and beautiful and desired and safe again.

"How long will you love me, Michael?"

"Forever."

"And one day?"

"And one day," he said, as he took my hand, kissed my palm, and held it to his heart.

I hadn't felt *real* joy, *real* passion, *real* love in a very long time—and, *damn*, did it feel good! Strangely enough, Michael's wife and children rarely crossed my mind. He took care of everything else. I suppose I just assumed he would take care of those inconveniences, too.

CHAPTER 38

The cold, old man seated in 4-B sighed and shifted his body again. It was then that I remembered where I was and realized I had never stopped crying. I wasn't sure if the tears were for Michael, for me, or for an almost perfect fairy tale gone horribly wrong. The only thing I knew for certain was that whoever was responsible for Michael's death had ended two lives that day. My fingerprints, my scent, my presence were all over that penthouse. With such irrefutable evidence, who would ever believe that when I last saw Michael that morning, we kissed goodbye, said *I love you*, and agreed to meet back in his room for lunch and an afternoon of lovemaking before I had to catch my flight back home. Besides the ones I left on his back the night before when we made love, he didn't have a scratch on his body when I left.

As I took inventory of the future in my mind, my hands went into my purse, instinctively found two valium tablets, and popped them in my mouth. I swallowed them without water or a second thought. The last thing I wanted to be on the long flight back home was awake. I could have cared less about nibbling on the mixed nuts, cleansing my hands with the hot towel, or filling my belly with filet mignon, garlic potatoes, mixed vegetables, *Cabernet Sauvignon*, and rhubarb pie. Before I could sleep through my immediate past, I heard the pilot announce, *Flight attendants, prepare for arrival.*

As I struggled to reorient myself, I noticed that the cold, old white man was no longer sitting next to me. I wondered if he had parachuted out of the plane in complete disgust over my fragility or if he was simply taking a pee in the lavatory at the nose of the plane. The rest of the first class passengers were all present and accounted for. The two businessmen in the left bulkhead seats. The tall woman and short man in the right bulkhead seats. The young, white man with the gold wedding band, perpetual smile, and unmistakably Asian baby that must have been obtained through an international adoption agency. The overgrown, obviously steroidal giant who likely used his muscular physique as a distraction from body parts that steroids couldn't alter. The former attorney general of Oklahoma and his hair-sprayed wife. And the two attractive, gay men who appeared to want to remain in the closet. My seatmate exited the bathroom just as I had accounted for the last passenger. As he sat down, pulled the seatbelt around his rotund abdomen, and returned his seat to the upright and locked position, I noticed that he was just as cold, just as old, and no less white than before I had fallen asleep.

As I visually inhaled the picture surrounding me, I wondered if normal, everyday black people like me would ever cease to be an anomaly in first class. There was certainly no evidence of things heading in that direction on any of the flights I had been on. Michael and I had taken scores of trips together and except for the one black man who was upgraded because he took a bump on his scheduled flight, I was always the sole representative of my race and, more often than not, the sole representative of my gender. While diversity was par for the course in coach, everyone seemed to be either white and male or just white when it came to the first class cabin. With each trip, I wished my people had gotten those forty acres and that damned mule we had been promised so we could live the first class experience, too.

Always feeling guilty about the privileged status my wealthy, white boyfriend afforded me—I was never sure if the guilt was because he was wealthy or because he was white—I would either lower my head to avoid making eye contact with the poor people boarding the plane to go back to coach or I would intentionally board the plan last so they wouldn't see me seated comfortably in the first class cabin. I didn't want them to think I was uppity or something just because I had an oversized leather seat, a drink before the plane ever left the ground, and a curtain. I was no better than they were. I just happened to be dating a representative of the people who owned their land and their mules. I wasn't uppity. I was just lucky, that was all.

As I watched the flight attendants dash about the plane, I remembered recent history and thought, *Well, perhaps I am a bit more than just lucky.* In three short years, Michael had shown me most of the United States and a good portion of Europe, Africa, and Asia. Each trip was first class from the moment the attentive driver picked me up from the tri-level condominium Michael had leased for me, to the moment I was safely returned by a different, but no less attentive driver.

Michael's definition of 'spoiled' turned out to be much more than I bargained for. He took me to East Africa for my birthday, Rome for spring break, and Paris just because he wanted a kick-ass cappuccino. I had experienced life among the beautiful Maasai people in Kenya and Tanzania, toured medieval castles in London, stood in indescribable awe as I gazed upon the ceiling of the Sistine Chapel, and spent hours inhaling the magnificence of exquisite treasures like the *Mona Lisa, Winged Victory,* and *Venus de Milo* in the most romantic city in the world. Michael loved being single-handedly responsible for exposing me to all the pleasures money can buy and watching childlike happiness burst out of me like candy from a piñata whenever I experienced something that without him, I'd only be able to read about in books and magazines.

Of all the amazing moments that became a part of my everyday life, spending a week among the regal men and women of a Kenyan Maasai tribe moved me the most. From a tribal guide, I learned that cattle and children, not stocks and bonds, represented one's wealth and prosperity. Ownership of a thousand head of cattle meant little if the family didn't have almost as many children. I found myself telling endless stories about the colorful Maasai people. One lazy, summer afternoon while on a conference call with Nicki and her latest *Mr. Right Now,* Gary, she asked me to recant one of my favorites.

"Girl, Gary doesn't want to hear about male circumcisions in Kenya," I weakly protested, secretly hoping differently because I loved talking about my adventures.

"Yes I do," he enthusiastically interjected, knowing that if he listened to the tale and pretended to be interested or amused or whatever it took, it would be an easy way to score brownie points with Nicki. Like most guys, there's hardly anything they won't do when trying to impress a girl. Gary was certainly no different.

"Well, Gary," I began, "in the Maasai culture, the *emorata*—which means male circumcision—is an extremely important tribal custom. It's a major life event for both male and female children because it signals a boy's entrance into adulthood and warrior status and a girl's entrance into adulthood and readiness for marriage. Now, while it's not a big deal if a girl screams and rants and raves during her circumcision, a boy is considered a coward and a disgrace if he so much as flinches during the five-minute procedure. He's just supposed to stand there and take it like a man! Anyway, if the boy was able to keep from screaming out in agony, you could count on somebody saying, 'He was definitely too ugly to be a coward!', because the Maasai believe that God would never be so cruel as to make one person both cowardly *and* ugly!"

"*Damn*, that can be hard on a brother!" Gary exclaimed, through genuine laughter. "I can tell you right now that if a dude has a knife in one hand and my meat in the other, that *'take it like a man'* bullshit is out the window! I'd just have to be one ugly coward!"

Nicki and I doubled over in laughter for the umpteenth time since the three of us had been on the telephone. Gary thought his latest quip was funny, but not *that* funny. "You two are just plain country," he said, while listening to us cackle like hyenas.

I caught my breath, then in my best *Ellie Mae* impersonation, said, "Well, I might be countree since I ain't nevah been outta' the South an' all, but since Nicki done moved to Califor-nee, she 'bout as far from countree as they come. She what they calls L.A. chic, now."

"She only says that because I like fresh-cut flowers," Nicki chimed in, still laughing.

"Yeah, she's just like my boyfriend," I added. "Only people who live in L.A. and white people like fresh-cut flowers."

With his trademark quick wit, Gary asked, "Your boyfriend lives in L.A.?"

Nicki and I laughed even louder than we had before. "No," I said, through breaks in hysteria. "He's white!"

When Nicki and I finally regained our composure, it was so quiet we could hear each other breathing from my condo in Brighton to her apartment in Beverlywood to Gary's townhouse in The Valley. Because he knew Nicki loved black men and he strongly suspected she would never disrespect her black brothers by dating white, he was struck dumb. The incredible wit he had shown only moments earlier couldn't comprehend how her best friend could sell out.

Breaking the uncomfortable silence, Nicki said, "He's not a *regular* white guy, Gary. He's a millionaire."

Gary wasn't impressed. "Of course he is! White boys *have* to be paid in order to get our women! They have to be able to provide the material bullshit most black men don't even have access to—like a goddamn private jet!" Gary had remembered Nicki talking about her friend's boyfriend's private plane soon after they met. At that time, it hadn't bothered him one iota because he had automatically assumed her friend was white.

"Wait just a minute, Gary," I interrupted, defensively. "I don't date Michael just because he's able to do nice things for me. I date him because he's the complete package." I didn't think mentioning Michaels's wife and children would add any validity to my argument, so I conveniently left that part out. "He does little things that make me feel special, like call me in the middle of the day for no reason at all and give me *I love you* cards just because it's Wednesday. He thinks of everything. And he's compassionate, too. Not one black man I knew understood what it was like for me when I had to deal with my crazy ex-fiancé. When it was time to go to court, all they said was, "Why you tryin' to bring a brother down?" But Michael—that white man you despise so much—*he* understood. He didn't victimize me all over again like the brothers did. I've always cherished black men, Gary, but it took a *white* man to cherish me back!" My anger was apparent, though I wasn't sure if I was angry with Gary, angry with black men in general, or just angry *period*.

Trying to be a good girlfriend to both of us, Nicki added, "You know, baby, dating white isn't so bad for a sister."

"Oh, so I guess you want a white boy, too, now?"

"No, that's not what I'm saying. If I did, I wouldn't be with you, now would I? I'm just saying that it's been my observation that a white man will treat a black woman like a princess."

"Yeah, Nicki, and do you know why?" Gary spat. "Because he stole her from the black prince!" Without question, he was no longer interested in racking up brownie points. "Well, guess what, my sisters? Even though the average white guy can generally shower a black woman with more material shit than the average black guy, they'll never be able to compete with us because white boys just don't have what it takes to truly connect with black women."

"What makes you think that?" Nicki asked, before I had a chance.

"Because white men don't have that spiritual component it takes to make a black woman happy. A relationship isn't real unless the two people have a true spiritual connection. And, I'm not talking strictly from a *go-to-church-with-her-on-Sunday* perspective, although that's definitely important to the average black women. I'm talking about a connection on a level so deep that each of them understands what the other is feeling without a word being spoken. It's like cooking. When you go into a white woman's house, you smell nothing coming from the kitchen. You're not moved by anything. You're just there. But when you step into a black woman's house, you smell so many enticing odors coming from the kitchen that you want to luxuriate in the aroma. You *want* to be there because it's full of flavor." It was clear that Gary knew what he was talking about. I instantly recalled the delectable smells coming from my mother's small kitchen and whenever I was there, that's exactly where I *wanted* to be. I especially liked coming home to the smell of her country-fried chicken sizzling in the deep fryer. The Colonel had no idea how 'finger licking good' *really* tasted.

Gary continued with seemingly renewed perseverance. "A *real* sister—one who's proud of who she is—might go out with a white man for a while if she's mad at some fool who did her wrong or if she's just plain bored. But she sure as hell won't stay there because they're just too bland. White boys don't have flavor and just like a black man, a black woman *needs* flavor. She needs a spiritual connection she can only get from a black man."

Without question, I was moved by Gary's conviction, if only because I was well aware of that spiritual connection of which he spoke so passionately. The connection that automatically understood why you always asked what color the accused was in a television news story and the connection that made you eternally grateful when he or she turned out to be white or Hispanic or Asian—it really didn't matter, as long as they weren't black. The connection that made you hold hands and bless your food together before eating it, even in public places. The connection that didn't interpret African clothing as un-American and urban slang as unintelligent. I felt a profound loss as I replayed Gary's words in my head. Unarguably, that spiritual connection he so eloquently pointed out was a glaring omission in my relationship with Michael. An omission I desperately, yet silently, craved. Nevertheless, I believed in my heart that I loved Michael just as much as I had loved both Christopher and Terrence. Differently maybe, but just as much. I decided to hold steadfast to my resolve, even if it was a little flimsy.

"I have to disagree with you on that one, Gary. Michael and I have an extremely strong connection. It's straight from the heart, straight from the soul. I don't edit myself when I'm talking to him, no matter how militant I might want to get and he doesn't edit himself with me, either. We feel safe with each other. We're connected on a very special, very deep level."

"That's bullshit, Chelsey!" Gary lashed back, with unmistakable disdain. "You wouldn't have given that white boy the time of day if he wasn't paid like a motherfucker! You know it, Nicki knows it, and I sure as hell know it!"

"You're right, Gary," I said, with condescension. "I would never have agreed to go out with Michael if he didn't have money. And that's pretty damned sad."

"Damn straight," he self-righteously added. "It's all about the greenbacks."

"Let me finish," I said. "It's sad, Gary, but not for the obvious reason. It's sad because if Michael hadn't been 'paid like a motherfucker' as you obviously prefer to put it, I would never have found out that he was also compassionate and sensitive and that he cares about many of the same things I care about, like poor people and women and people of color. If it wasn't for his money, I would have missed out on getting to know a truly incredible human being just because he's white. *That's* the sad part."

I felt more confident, so I intensified my defense. "Michael is white. *Period*. I can't change that and I would never want to." That was a straight up lie. More often than not, I did want to. "But he's one white man who gets it, Gary. He even understands the concept of white privilege and that's a major hurdle for any white man to get over, let alone a rich one. Sure, it was hard for him to admit that while some of the doors to his success were opened because he was a brilliant man with brilliant ideas, some of them were opened simply because he was white. My point, Gary, is that he *did* admit it. Not only does Michael understand what our struggle is about, he'll fight right along beside us to change things. Some of us have gotten so far removed from our blackness that *we* don't even stand up for us!"

Gary seemed a fraction less irritated. "Don't get me wrong, Chelsey," he said. "Of course, there're some white people who *do* get it and who *are* willing to show up on the front lines and fight for a level playing field right along with us black folk. Hell, white liberals helped to start the NAACP. But, Chelsey, those so-called liberals are few and far between. And, as my man Julius Lester wrote, they're usually more white than liberal. You happened to find one that *might* be more liberal than white. Unfortunately, you won't know for sure until your first real argument when 'nigger' slips out or, in passing, he decides to remind you that if it wasn't for him, you'd be visiting Paris, Texas instead of Paris, France and your black ass would be living in an efficiency apartment on the Eastside instead of a luxury condominium on the Westside. Remember, Chelsey, Mr. Fresh-Cut Flowers is loyal to only two colors—and black isn't one of them." Gary's words cut like a knife, especially after he paused dramatically to give them a chance to sink in. "Just a little food for thought, my sister. Just a little food for thought."

Indeed, my life *had* been a veritable bed of roses since Michael made his grand entrance. I specifically remember waking up one morning in the middle of summer in a luxurious suite in *Le Bristol*, one of the most elite hotels in Paris. As the sun was thinking about creeping over the horizon, I opened my eyes to find Michael sound asleep, holding his pillow as though he thought it was me. I smiled at the drool that made his pillow damp, kissed his cheek, and crawled out of bed. After easing my feet into soft, cozy slippers and wrapping myself in a silk robe—both compliments of our gracious landlord for the week—I quietly made my way to the bathroom. I marveled at how I had gone from the drabness of linoleum floors and vinyl countertops in a housing project in Wade to the opulence of marble floors and vanities in a suite fit for a queen in France. Believe it when I tell you that if I could imagine it, Michael made it happen. In one lifetime, I had experienced two distinctively different worlds—one real and one make-believe. As far as I was concerned at the time, *real* might do in a pinch, but *make-believe* was where I preferred to wake up every morning.

I know it sounds cliché-ish, but I don't know how else to say it—being with Michael felt like a dream come true. Most of the time it was, anyway. Far too often, I paid an exorbitant price for his excessive generosity. His manipulative, controlling behavior seemed to be an intrinsic part of him and his jealousies bordered on the insane. When he wasn't declaring his undying love for me or showering me with elaborate gifts and dreamy vacations, he could be found carelessly trouncing on layer on top of layer of my pain. Though he never made the mistake of saying 'nigger' during one of his bouts of rage, he called me 'bitch' like it was the name my mother told the nurse to write on my birth certificate. That myth that you can't call a black woman a bitch and get away with it is just that—a myth. If a woman—*any* woman—doesn't love herself, she'll accept anything, no matter how fucked up it is.

Just as with Christopher and Terrence, I regularly threatened to leave Michael if he didn't change. Just as with Christopher and Terrence, Michael's offenses were typically followed by apologies that he fully meant at the time or material tokens of love such as designer suits, expensive perfumes, or, if the most recent victimization had been particularly gruesome, cold, hard cash. In all three cases, I stayed with each of them, hoping that someday, somehow, they would change. Never once did I realize that the person who really needed to change was me.

After Terrence, I swore I would never allow empty words to cloud my overall good judgment. To keep my promise, I convinced myself that Michael's lying, jealousy, and verbal abuse were no where near the severity of Terrence's lying, jealousy, and verbal abuse. It wasn't until much later that I became aware that self-hatred and fear of never being loved by a man controlled me more than Michael or Terrence or Christopher before them. Because I had succeeded in convincing myself that all three men loved me more deeply than I (or them) had ever known, I remained with each one long after I had more than sufficient evidence that the kind of love they gave so willingly was destroying my already wounded spirit.

CHAPTER 39

"Ladies and gentlemen, welcome to Brighton. We know you have a choice when it comes to flying and we thank you for choosing American Airlines as your carrier, today." Having performed her last major task, the senior flight attendant joined the rest of the flight crew checking to make sure our seatbelts were fastened and our trays in their upright and locked position. When the plane came to a complete stop, the captain promptly turned off the "fasten seatbelt" sign and impatient passengers who had not already defiantly unfastened their seatbelts, did so and stood to wait in the aisle. Slowly, the line began to move as travelers scurried down the jetway in single, double, and triple file. With no reason to hurry back to the life I had left, I took my time gathering my purse and small carry-on, then joined the processional.

Instead of wondering what I was going to say to the driver who was scheduled to pick me up, all I could think about was, *Who hated Michael to death?* I certainly had enough reasons to justify pulling the trigger myself, but I didn't kill him. *So who did?* I began lining up possible suspects in my head. *Had Natasha found out about our affair and gladly shot her husband in the head herself? Had his business partner become so enraged at Michael's refusal to sell his share of the company that murder became the means to an end? Was it a simple act of random violence?* Almost immediately, I realized that while it was definitely violent, nothing about it pointed to random.

Just as I was in the midst of investigating the crime in my mind, a masculine voice asked, "Are you Chelsey George?" I focused my eyes on a middle-aged, Latino male in a dark suit. Out of the corner of my eye, I saw at least five more uniformed policemen, each with one hand resting on a revolver.

"Yes," I responded, with beads of perspiration already forming on my forehead and in my armpits. "Why?"

One uniformed officer removed my purse from my shoulder while another relieved me of my carry-on. Following the Latino detective's instructions, a third officer began reading my *Miranda* rights. "You are under arrest. You have the right to remain silent. Should you waive the right to remain silent, anything you say can and will be used against you in a court of law. You have the right to an attorney…"

I didn't hear any of my inalienable rights, nor did I see the scores of blinding camera flashes, overzealous reporters, and curious onlookers who didn't seem to care if they missed their departing flights. As handcuffs were clamped to my wrists behind my back and my head pushed into a waiting police car, it occurred to me that Lester, Eddie, Christopher, Terrence, and now, Michael, had all participated in my eternal damnation. For the fifth time in one lifetime, I had died and gone to hell.

CHAPTER 40

My extradition back to Los Angeles was immediate. As I sat in the dark, humid room about to be interrogated about Michael's murder, I was reminded of how I felt in the phone booth when I called 9-1-1 to report it. Neither experience seemed fathomable, then or now. Two plain-clothed detectives performing a less than dramatic rendition of *good-cop-bad-cop* paced the floor. I wondered how, in a three-hour flight, they could have decided with such certainty that I was a killer. The good cop stopped pacing and sat in the metal folding chair directly across from me. After coughing up some phlegm, then swallowing it down again, he spoke in a gentle, sincere voice.

"Can I get you a glass of water, Ms. George?"

"No, thank you," I responded with what I felt was appropriate apprehension. Black intellectuals have called it *minority paranoia*. It's a kind of apprehension that comes from centuries of being shit on by white people, even those you thought you could trust. Good white people don't understand this notion. Smart white people do. They know it's a survival mechanism, not a personal assault.

"I want to make this as simple as possible for everyone," the good cop continued. "I can probably get the District Attorney to go easy on you if you cooperate, Ms. George. But you're going to have to tell us everything. Do you understand what I'm saying?"

"Yes."

"Okay." He pushed two buttons on a tape recorder placed at the far end of the table, then began his interrogation. "Do you know Michael Anthony Arrington?"

"Yes."

"Why did you lie about knowing him before?"

"I don't know."

"Have you seen Mr. Arrington, today?"

"Yes, I saw him this morning."

"Approximately what time did you last see him?"

"About 9:45 a.m."

"Was he alive when you last saw him?"

"Of course he was."

"You last saw Mr. Arrington alive at 10:45 a.m.?"

"No. I said I saw him at 9:45." Though I didn't say it, *asshole* was implied by both the tone of my voice and the look in my eyes.

"When you saw Mr. Arrington this morning, Ms. George, did you kill him?"

"No. I did *not* kill Michael!" I said, loudly and clearly into the recorder, enunciating every syllable as though my life depended on it. In actuality, I suppose it did.

Louder than necessary even for dramatic purposes, the bad cop interrupted. "Then can you tell us how three bullets found their way into Michael Arrington's goddamned head, Ms. George?"

I glared at the bad cop who was now leaning against the wall. "I don't know," I calmly replied. "It's my understanding that L.A.P.D. doesn't mind breaking a few rules every now and then. Maybe you or one of your boys put them there."

The bad cop rushed toward me, kicking over a chair on the way. He leaned on the small, yet sturdy table, holding himself up with two hairy arms. The long-sleeved shirt he wore had been rolled up to his elbows and the knot in his sixties tie had been loosened. The staleness of his breath was within inches of my nose. "Listen!" he shouted, in a concentrated effort to intimidate me. "You can make this hard if you want to, little lady, but we have enough evidence on you to make sure that you fry like a country hen! Is that what you want?"

My anger gave way to courage and I screamed back at him with equal fervor. "You don't have a shred of evidence against me because I haven't so much as shot a dirty look at anyone except your stinking ass, let alone put three bullets into the man I love!" I was no longer angry—I was mad! "You and your pal, Barney Fife here, are just a couple of two-bit K-Mart cops trying to get your big break by forcing me to confess to a crime I could never commit! As far as I'm concerned, you can take your so-called evidence and your silly bag of tricks and shove them up your ass!" As I began to hear the words I spoke, I found myself grateful that *that* particular part of Mama lived in me eternally. And that could only mean one thing—I was *not* to be fucked with.

The bad cop turned red with a rage that paled in comparison to my own. He promptly turned off the tape recorder and performed his final scene with a chilling calmness. "Whether you cooperate or not, I'm going to make sure that you're one dead bitch." He didn't seem to be acting anymore. In the next second, he was gone.

The good cop rose from his chair. At a snail's pace, he walked toward the door. Still in character and hoping for a confession, he paused at the door with one hand on the knob. Turning slowly to face me, he said, "I'm sorry about my partner. He gets a little hotheaded, sometimes. But can't you see that *I* really want to help you? Will you let me help you?" Though his green eyes were pleading, I transformed myself into a deaf mute. He opened the door. "God rest your soul," he said, in true Academy Award fashion. And he, too, was gone. Moments later, he re-entered the room to give me one last chance to confess. I watched as he methodically picked up the tape recorder, looked longingly at me again, nodded his bowed head in sorrow, and disappeared for the second time.

Thirty-six hours later, Judge Elizabeth Watts had the audacity to ask, "Do you understand the charges against you?"

"Yes, Your Honor, I do."

"How do you plead?"

"Not guilty."

CHAPTER 41

Like St. John's Tabernacle the day of my father's funeral, Los Angeles County Courtroom Number Four was filled to capacity the day my murder trial began. Local and national television camera crews, reporters, photographers, witnesses, spectators, Michael's wife and two oldest sons, Mama, Katie, Nicki, Shelby, Krista, Deidra, a small delegation from Wade, and even Terrence, were all out in full force. Whether present by choice or by chance, it seemed no one wanted to miss the trial of the poor, single, black woman accused of murdering her wealthy, white, *married-with-children* lover. In true Perry Mason fashion, almost immediately, the news media had dubbed it *The Case of Murder in Black and White* because everything that mattered about it seemed to be either black or white. One black defendant, one white deceased. Six black jurors, six white jurors. One black alternate, one white alternate. One black defense attorney, one white prosecuting attorney. One black bailiff, one white court reporter. Ironically, even the judge was a product of one black parent and one white parent.

"Is the State's attorney ready to present his opening statement?" Judge Watts asked.

The District Attorney sprang from his seat as though he had just heard the shot signaling the beginning of a race. "Yes, Your Honor, the State is ready." With a few confident steps, he placed himself directly in front of the jury box.

"Good morning, distinguished ladies and gentlemen of the jury," he began. Except for one juror who had what appeared to be a nasty-ass piece of chewing tobacco crammed in his cheek and another who looked like her picture was already up at the Post Office, I saw nothing distinguishing about them, let alone distinguished. Nevertheless, he waited until five or six of them responded to his greeting with a barely audible, *"Morning,"* and one or two others with nervous, throat-clearing grunts.

"I would like to begin," he continued, "by saying that in spite of what the media would have you believe, this is not a case about black or white. This is a case about murder. Cold, calculated murder. The State will show that on the morning of June twenty-sixth, the defendant willfully shot three bullets into the head of Michael Anthony Arrington." Pointing to me, he added, "The State will show that *that* woman murdered Mr. Arrington in cold blood." The veteran prosecutor paused for dramatic emphasis, as he usually did after pointing a decisive finger at a murder defendant. Loud whispers scattered throughout the courtroom.

"I'll have order in this court, immediately!" the judge sternly announced.

"Ladies and gentlemen," he began, again. "You will learn that the defendant had long wanted Mr. Arrington to divorce his devoted wife of more than twenty years and that upon learning he had no intention of abandoning her and their four children, decided that if she could not have him, no one could. That's when she decided to take the law into her own hands." He paused again to allow the jurors ample time to believe him.

"The evidence in this case is overwhelming, ladies and gentlemen. The State will prove that the defendant was so full of rage on that fateful morning that she shot three bullets at point blank range into the head of Mr. Arrington, killing him instantly. The State will prove that the defendant's fingerprints, earrings, and distinct scent of perfume were found in Mr. Arrington's hotel room on the day he was murdered. The State will prove that the defendant was also a guest of the hotel and that she checked out on the day Mr. Arrington was murdered. The State will prove that Mr. Arrington frequently referred to the defendant as *Nubian princess* and that a greeting card addressed to a *Nubian princess* was found in the room occupied by the defendant. And, finally, ladies and gentlemen of the jury, the State will prove that it was the defendant who reported this insidious crime to the police, shamelessly using the initials, 'NP.'"

The buzz in the courtroom grew louder. "Order! Order!" commanded Judge Watts again. Her admonishment may as well have come from the burning bush because in an instant, an ominous silence fell over the courtroom. The District Attorney was quite pleased with himself. Smiling on the inside, but maintaining a solemn demeanor on the outside, he concluded his opening statement.

"Yes, ladies and gentlemen, it *is* shocking that this defendant would commit such a sinister act of violence. No one wants to believe that she could be a murderer.

Even I did not want to believe it was true! But the State will prove that the defendant is, indeed, a cold-blooded killer." The seasoned DA stood before the jurors as though dreadfully sorry for the news he had just broken to them. After he was assured they had felt his pain, he graciously thanked them and returned to his seat.

Looking as though he had already been defeated, my attorney rose from his seat to recite his opening statement. He approached the jury box with a face almost as grim as that of Mama, Katie, and Nicki. The only difference was that three of the four grim faces were certain of my innocence. He buttoned two of the three buttons on his new jacket, rubbed two sweaty palms together, and began to speak.

"Ladies and gentlemen of the jury, Chelsey Christina George is an innocent woman. I intend to prove to you that she could not, would not, and did not murder the deceased. Look at her." He pointed to me just as the State's attorney had done only minutes earlier. Fourteen pairs of eyes followed his raised palm to visually evaluate me again. I sat tall and straight in my chair, just as he had instructed me to do. My makeup was minimal and my shiny, black hair was pulled back into a braided ponytail to emphasize the height of my cheekbones, the fullness of my lips, and the sadness of my eyes. I wore a dark grey Italian suit that Michael had given to me on our one-month anniversary. My attorney had already warned me that the jury's finding of guilt or innocence would depend partially on the facts, but mostly on my appearance. I wished I could tell if my well-dressed librarian look was working, but I couldn't.

Still pointing to me, he continued, "She, ladies and gentlemen, is not a woman capable of hurting anyone or anything. She is a woman who serves her community, works in her church, lends support to her family and friends, and most importantly, abides by the laws of this great country. She is a woman who any of us would want for a daughter, a sister, a neighbor, a friend." Suddenly convinced of my innocence, he lowered his hand, faced the jury, and continued with the conviction of someone who believed I was innocent all along.

"Ladies and gentlemen, the State's attorney wants you to believe Ms. George committed this despicable crime. Worse than that, he insults you by presenting only circumstantial evidence. Indeed, the murder weapon hasn't even been found! The State's attorney is right about one thing, however. This is not a case about black or white. This is a case about life and love. Chelsey George, ladies and gentlemen, is guilty of only one thing—loving a man who was not free to love her back."

Just as he had learned in law school six and a half years earlier, my attorney paused. When sufficient time had passed, he questioned the jurors with anguished eyes. "Good men and women of the jury, have you ever made a mistake in matters of the heart? Have you ever fallen in love with a person with whom you shouldn't have?" His honest eyes looked straight into the eyes of each juror and spotted at least three sympathizers. That was good. He only needed one of them to establish reasonable doubt.

"I know I have certainly made mistakes in the past. I have fallen for someone I should not have, a time or two." He spoke with such incredible sadness that even the District Attorney momentarily wanted him to be right about me. "It is a fact that Ms. George loved the deceased very, very deeply. No matter how hard she tried, she could not make her heart stop loving him. But falling in love with a man—even a married man—is not a crime. A gross lapse in judgment, yes, but a crime, never." He walked over to my chair, stood squarely behind me, and placed his hands on my shoulders. "I will prove to you that Chelsey George is innocent." My Haitian-born attorney decided that pausing for effect was a good thing in an American court of law, so he did so again. The courtroom was silent. "Thank you for your time, ladies and gentlemen." He sat in the chair next to me, placed his elbows on the table, and rested his chin on two clasped hands that, in spite of his newfound belief in my innocence, were still a little sweaty.

CHAPTER 42

Five weeks of seemingly endless testimony came and went. A timid night manager confirmed my registration at the hotel. A meddling, old woman testified that on the night of June twenty-fifth, she overheard me and Michael arguing about his decision to stay with his wife until their youngest son graduated from high school. Fingerprints confirmed my presence in Michael's room and his in mine. A handwriting expert testified that it was Michael's penmanship on the card found in my room. A voice analyst confirmed that it was my voice on the 9-1-1 tape. A county coroner estimated an approximate time of death that conveniently gave me a window of opportunity to commit the crime. The jury had deliberated exactly four hours and twenty-eight minutes when they were escorted back into the courtroom.

"Has the jury reached a verdict?"

"Yes, Your Honor, we have."

The stoic bailiff retrieved a folded piece of paper from the jury foreman and delivered it to Judge Watts. Showing no emotion, she silently read the verdict. Looking directly into the eyes of the foreman, she asked, "How do you find the defendant?"

"In the matter of the State of California versus Chelsey Christina George, we the jury, find the defendant guilty."

Mama released an anguished scream. A usually unresponsive Katie fainted. Nicki and the rest of the girls began to cry uncontrollably. I simply stared into oblivion. Nothing surprised me anymore.

* * *

At my sentencing hearing one week later, representatives from both sides spoke. Natasha, Michael's wife. Brandon, his oldest son. Phillip, his business partner. Mama. Katie. Rev. Johnson from Wade and Deacon Williams from my church in Brighton. I faced a sentence ranging from forty years without parole to death by lethal injection. Neither option was particularly appealing, but given a choice, I wanted to live. Against the stern advice of my attorney, I decided to speak on my own behalf. Mama had demonstrated time after time that when the odds are stacked against you, there are only two possible outcomes. *You'll win. Or you'll lose with dignity. Either way, you should go down fighting.*

"Your Honor," I began, first acknowledging the authority of Judge Watts before turning my focus to Michael's family. "I would like to apologize to Mrs. Arrington and her sons for my unfair intrusion into their lives. My involvement with a husband and a father was inexcusable and I am very, very sorry. I would also like to express my deepest sorrow for their loss. I am especially sorry for Michael's´ sons. I lost my father in a tragedy several years ago, so I know the pain they must feel."

Turning my attention back to Judge Watts, I continued. "Your Honor, I am devastated that Michael Arrington has been killed. Besides perhaps his family, no one is more devastated than I am. But I did not kill him. In spite of what twelve people who know nothing about me decided, I am not a murderer, Your Honor. You may be able to call me many horrible things and you may even be right about some of them, but if you believe I have the capacity to kill another human being, you're wrong—dead wrong. Thank you for your time."

After all parties had spoken, my attorney and I rose from our seats, following Judge Watts' command.

"Chelsey Christina George, this court finds murder to be one of the most heinous crimes a person can commit. This court finds it even more deplorable when the defendant refuses to take responsibility for her own actions. Therefore, abiding by the laws of the State of California, I hereby sentence you to death by lethal injection."

I heard her words, but was neither sad, nor afraid. My only thought was, *Who's going to take care of Mama?*

CHAPTER 43

Four days after the State of California decided I deserved to die, Terrence visited me in jail. I had seen him sitting in the back of the courtroom every day of my trial. He had never tried to speak to me then, so I wondered what he could possibly want to say now. His face still looked at least twenty years older than it actually was and the whites of his eyes were a mixture of patchy beige and red stripes. Had the glass not separated us, I would have been able to smell the alcohol on his breath and the stench of his body.

"Hello, baby," he said, as he spoke into the telephone receiver. He put one hand up to the glass window hoping I would respond likewise. I didn't.

"What do you want?" I asked, void of emotion.

"Do you have to be so mean, Chelsey? Don't you see I'm hurting, too? Can't you see I'm dying?"

"Dying, Terrence? Is that what you came to talk to me about? Dying?"

"Yes, that's part of it." He removed his hand from the glass. "I thought I'd be happy to see you die, Chelsey. When you left me, I died a thousand deaths. That's how cowards die, you know. A thousand times." I remembered the line from his favorite movie: *A coward die a thousand deaths. A soldier dies but one.* He was still as sick as the day I met him.

"When you left me, Chelsey, I hated you," he continued. "When I went to jail, I found time to hate you even more. I wanted to punish you for what you did to me. I wanted you dead."

"Well, congratulations, Terrence. Your wish has been granted." Tears began to form in his bloodshot eyes. I almost felt sorry for him.

"But last night—," speech was becoming increasingly difficult for him. "Last night, I realized that I still love you, baby. In fact, I never stopped loving you. Even when I hated you, I loved you." Tears began to slide down his face, as he forced himself to continue. "I'm here because I want to apologize for everything I've done. I'm sorry, Chelsey. I should never have hit you. You never deserved any of the things I did to you. Will you forgive me? I need to know. With God as my witness, baby, I need to know if you will forgive me."

God? I thought. *Since when did Terrence give a damn about what God thought?* Remembering his steadfast denials during his testimony at his own trial, I sarcastically asked a question for which I could have cared less about the actual answer. "But Terrence, you testified before God and everybody that you never did anything to me, remember?"

"Stop playing games, Chelsey. We both know I lied. Will you forgive me or not?" he asked again. "I know I don't deserve your forgiveness, but I have to know."

I had never been as hard as I wanted the men in my life to believe. I was as fragile as an eggshell. Probably

281

more. At that moment, I remembered the words of Dr. Hollander. *Forgiving is remembering and letting go.* I thought I had done that already. But the words coming out of my mouth were not those of somebody who had let go of the pain of the past. I put my hand to the glass. As tears clouded my vision, I said, "Yes, I forgive you."

Terrence slowly and methodically traced the outline of my hand on the window, as he studied every crease. Finally, he covered my small hand with his own. "Thank you, baby. Thank you for forgiving me. I love you. Goodbye." He replaced the telephone receiver and stared at me through the glass, remembering, one by one, each reason he fell in love with me. After a lifetime had quietly crept by, he stood up, mouthed the words, *I'll always love you*, then buzzed for the guard to let him out. As he stood in the glow of the midday sun, he knew he had one last thing to do.

After Terrence left, the guard escorted me back to my cell. Although I had never seen myself as particularly religious, I promptly got down on my knees and had a one-on-one conversation with God. Somewhere between Wade, Georgia and the California State Penitentiary, I had forgotten the lesson my mother had taught me so long ago—*God answers prayers.* For the first time in months, sleep came easily.

CHAPTER 44

When he sat in his 1979 Monte Carlo, Terrence saw the letter he had written the night before lying on the front seat. Until his visit with me, he didn't think he would mail it. Now, he knew he had to. He drove to the Post Office and dropped it in one of the drive-through mailboxes. After returning to the small apartment he had rented in East L. A. since the beginning of my trial, he took a worn picture of me from his wallet, kissed it, and sat in a wooden chair with both feet planted firmly on the floor. Needing the courage to finish the task at hand, he drank a pint of vodka straight from the bottle. Talking to his demons out loud, he said, "A coward dies a thousand deaths, a soldier dies but one." He then placed the barrel of the gun in his mouth, closed his eyes, and pulled the trigger. At that same moment, I sat straight up in my cot. I didn't know why I had awakened—but something felt very different.

* * *

Two days before I had no more days, his letter arrived: *Dear Chelsey, when I realized you were going to die because*

I had taken things too far, I could not stand it. The truth is, without you, I have no reason to live. To save you, I know I must die. My address is at the top of this letter. By the time the police get here, I'm sure maggots will be feeding on my decaying body. I know you're going to feel sorry for me because you would never find joy in my death. But don't, Chelsey. You see, in death, I'm finally able to do the one thing I was never able to do in life—take care of someone I love. Tell the police that the gun lying next to me is the murder weapon they've been looking for. I know I might seem like a monster to you, but I'm not proud of killing a man, Chelsey. I am glad, though, that by finally telling the truth about something, I can give life back to you. It's the only good thing I've ever done. Thank you for sticking by me for as long as you did, baby. I truly did not deserve your love, but you loved me in spite of myself and I'll always be grateful to you for that. Most of all, Chelsey, thank you for forgiving me. You never had to, but you always did—especially when I needed it most. All my love, Terrence.

EPILOGUE

On a warm, sunny day, just when the bluebonnets were beginning to bloom and the sweet smell of a fast approaching summer was in the air, I returned home to Wade. It was my thirty-third birthday. I had spent more than seven months behind bars because a man I once loved had killed a man I still loved. Both those men were dead. But I felt like I had been born again. *Apparently*, I thought, *God is not through with me, yet*.

As I made my way down the jetway, I spotted Nicki. It was as though time was in slow motion as we ran toward each other. Our embrace was long, loving, and genuine, just like it was every semester when we returned to school after being separated all summer. As our cheeks touched, tears of joy and thanks ran together.

"Welcome home, Chelsey," Nicki said, as she held my face with two petite hands.

"Thanks, Nicki," I said. "Let's go home."

As we drove down the winding, dusty roads of Wade, I saw both beautiful and painful memories of years gone by. The small hospital where I was born. The dilapidated church where I was baptized. The boarded-up store Eddie and I used to walk to for candy. Mr. Jack's Chicken

Shack. Ms. Eula's beauty shop. The cemetery where my father's body slept. Everything was still there.

The sound of Nicki's voice snapped me back into the present. "So, how does it feel to be back in Wade?"

"Wonderful. *Really* wonderful. When you come that close to dying, Nicki, it makes you want to live life to the fullest. I won't ever go to bed again under the assumption that I'll wake up the next morning and everything will be the way I left it. I'm not even going to go to bed at night under the assumption that I'll wake up at all because that might not be God's will for me. You know how old people always say, '*God willing, such-and-such*'? Now, I understand what they mean. I won't ever take God's grace for granted again, Nicki. It feels like I've been given a second chance and I don't plan to waste it."

"What do you think you'll do with that second chance?"

"I don't know just yet. But the way I see it, there must be something else for me to do." I closed my eyes and breathed in the fresh, country air. I had never felt more at peace. "What do you think it is, Nicki? What do you think He wants me to do?"

"Hmmm, that's hard to say," she said. "I think He wants to hear your voice, though. Not your mother's or Terrence's or Michael's. Yours. I think He wants you to tell your story of pain and loss and courage and triumph.

"Why?"

"Why not?" Nicki smiled the same smile she used for whenever she felt passionate about something. "I think he wants the world to look at you and say, *"Wow! That Chelsey George is pretty amazing!"'*

I smiled back with the same smile I used whenever I more than halfway believed something was true. "Yeah," I said, as I pulled down the sun visor to block out the rays that had begun to beam down on my forehead. I immediately saw my reflection in the mirror. Looking into my own eyes, I said, "Yeah, I *am* pretty amazing!" It felt good to say it, but it felt even better to know that for the first time in my life, I *meant* it.

As the car pulled into Mama's carport, I smelled the unmistakable aroma of country-fried chicken. I couldn't have stopped my face from grinning from earlobe to earlobe if I had wanted to. It was my birthday, I was surrounded by people I loved, and Mama had prepared my favorite meal. When I made my way to the kitchen, I saw her removing another batch of wings and drumsticks from the deep fryer. On the table was a cake that read: *Happy Birthday, Chelsey!* I stood in the doorway, studying the back of my mother's strong frame. More memories of years gone by came flooding back. While in the midst of my thoughts, I heard an old, but still familiar voice.

"You sure have been on television a lot lately, princess." I turned around and there he was—Captain Eddie Malone. Although it had been more than 20 years, he hadn't changed a bit, save for a few distinguished wrinkles and black hair that was now a salt and pepper color.

"Eddie!" I screamed, in genuine surprise. "What are you doing here?"

"I came back to be with my three best girls. Your mother and Katie were pretty happy about that. What about you?"

"I couldn't be happier!" I said, as I wrapped my arms around his neck like I was twelve years old again.

"Hey!" Mama said, as she wiped her hands on her apron. "What about some love for your mother?" As Mama and I held each other like we would never let go, we both began to cry. "I love you, Chelsey," she whispered in my ear.

"I love you, too, Mama." As I clung to my mother tightly, I remembered what Nicki said to me on the drive home. *I think He wants you to tell your story.* Then I remembered something Eddie had told me years before: *You're one of the best daughters any father could possibly hope for. I know it and your father knew it, too.* Still wrapped in the serenity of my mother's arms, I began the manuscript in my head: *She had always wanted to be daddy's little girl—and that's exactly what she was…*

C♉ ♊Ꙩ

CARLESS A. GRAYS is available for book club meetings, book signings, speaking engagements, and other special events upon request. Please visit her online at www.carlessgrays.com to schedule.

C♉ ♊Ꙩ

Made in the USA
Middletown, DE
31 March 2018